THE KANSHOU

THE KANSHOU

Sally Miller Gearhart

Spinsters Ink Books
Denver, Colorado
USA

First edition published May 2002
10-9-8-7-6-5-4-3-2-1

Spinsters Ink Books
P. O. Box 22005
Denver, CO 80222
USA

Cover Design:
Lightsource Images
Warrior Figure Design:
Buzzworks Studio
Interior Design:
Gilsvik Book Production

Library of Congress Cataloging-in-Publication Data

Gearhart, Sally Miller, 1931–
The Kanshou / Sally Miller Gearhart. -- 1st ed.
p. cm. -- (Earthkeep; bk. 1)
ISBN 1-883523-44-3
I. Women--Fiction. I Title.

PS3557.E2 K36 2002
813'.52--dc21

Printed in Canada

The Earthkeep Series is dedicated to
Dorothy A. Haecker and Jane Gurko,
its *sine qua non.*

Contents

ACKNOWLEDGEMENTS

In the years since 1987, *The Kanshou* and other Earthkeep books have been given both substance and form within the network of my friends, enemies, lovers, colleagues, comrades, teachers, students, chance acquaintances, and animal companions. In addition to Dorothy A. Haecker and Jane Gurko, who shepherded the Earthkeep material through its most major transformations, a number of people have generously blessed the books with their special abilities and their time.

My Intrepid Editor, Vicki P. McConnell, marvelously astute and skilled, endowed the bulky manuscript with one of its first professional affirmations and then streamlined it—and my writing habits—with a devotion far beyond any duty set upon her by Spinsters Ink. Elizabeth Saria, Karla McDermid, and Carla Blumberg educated me in crucial aspects of chemistry, zoology, medicine, virology, technology, and marine biology. I called upon Vivian Power for aid in Spanish, enhancement of my understanding of science, and audacious challenges to my utopian vision. Adrian Tinsley, ardent aficionada of fantasy and science fiction, refreshed both my memory and my imagination in her analysis of the manuscript. Moreover, I have been companioned throughout this literary journey by a task force of metaphysical gadflies, led at different times by Tamara Diaghilev, Mara, Ari Lacelle, Cynthia Secor, and Helen Stewart.

Frequently, I have needed rescue from computer panic, and I've often lacked expertise in specific areas such as astrology, firearms, the geography of Los Angeles, how to play the violin, how to survive in the publishing world, Judaism, the Koran, Mandarin, medical terminology, police practices, and the scope of human sexuality. I thank the following people for coming to my aid in one or more of these matters: Bryce Travis, Carlin Diamond, Nancy Ellis, Esther Faber, Susan Feldman, Emmy Good, Dick Graham, Maggie Graham, Matthew Holtz, Loraine Hutchins, Tony King, Joann Lee, Lyndall MacCowan, Marilyn McNair, Jack Power, Teri Rogers, Sam Sapoznick, and Susan Smith.

As well, I offer a special thanks to all the anarchists, animal rights activists, capitalists, developers, environmentalists, hunters, loggers, militarists, pacifists, political radicals, ranchers, religious fundamentalists, and vegetarians, who, in my ongoing dialogues with them, have toughened up my thought processes and deepened my appreciation of diversity.

I have lived surrounded by a community of women—Peggy Cleveland, Morgaine Colston, Jean Crosby, Esther Faber, Bonnie Gordon, Jane Gurko, Susan Leo, Ana Mahoney, Carol Orton, Penny Sablove, Mary Anderson, and Diane Syrcle—which has provided the atmosphere of support and patient understanding that these books have required in order, at last, to be born.

The metaphysics ultimately embraced by the protagonists of *The Kanshou* and other Earthkeep books has its best articulation in the teachings of Abraham, available at Abraham-Hicks Publications, P.O. Box 690070, San Antonio, Texas, 78269 (830-755-2299). Abraham teaches joy, and it is the gift of joy that I wish for all whom I here finally acknowledge with gratitude: the readers of Earthkeep, in Aristotle's terms the "final cause of" or "that for the sake of which" these books have been written.

". . . such hands might carry out an unavoidable violence
with such restraint, with such a grasp
of the range and limits of violence
that violence ever after would be obsolete."

—Adrienne Rich
Twenty-One Love Poems, VI

PROLOGUE

[2087 C.E.]

Four dynamic circumstances shaped the initial decades of the new millennium on the planet, Little Blue.

First, within a single forty-eight-hour period in 2021 of the Common Era (C.E.), every non-human animal on the planet died.

Humans handled the practical effects of this dramatic disinheritance with comparative ease: their loss of a source of food, fuel, and fertilizer; their need for marine-oil substitutes and for alternate methods of seed and pollen transportation. At a deeper emotional level, however, the human species suffered a profound and apparently incurable despair. Animals had provided many humans with the rare experience of unconditional love and, for the more globally-minded, animals had been the model for a life of harmony with the rest of Nature which humans had been unable to sustain.

Second, an escalating wave of natural disasters spiked global warming, drought, and other weather cataclysms.

Third, a global vaccination campaign against recurring epidemic diseases resulted—by 2040—in women's reduced fertility as well as in the suppression of the Y chromosome in men. This plunged the human population to one-sixth of its 1999 size and fixed the ratio of females to males at 12-to-1.

Fourth, a global spiral of social unrest sparked food riots and street wars, as well as disruptions in global systems of electrical power, transport, and communication.

As social, economic, military, and governmental power shifted from men to women, new values, structures, and processes emerged. By mid-century, nuclear families were comparatively rare. The most common living pattern was still that of the extended family, honoring traditional kinship bonds. Women in such families usually embraced men as full partners in the human experience.

Almost as common were the tribes, nations, or communities of women-only citizens, who used ovular merging to produce girl-children among themselves or, alternatively, used men or semen banks for reproduction. Sexually, such women partnered with other women, sought solitary sexual gratification, or lived asexually. Some of them held to the belief of womanhood or manhood as self-identified, while others of them claimed biology as an immutable physical condition.

By 2060, the ascendancy of women had become the norm in all three of Little Blue's tri-satrapies or geo-political territories. Land, sea, and air divisions of the global peacekeeping force, called the Kanshoubu, were almost entirely female. Each Kanshou peacekeeper followed a code of conduct delineated in *The Labrys Manual*, and a large part of her responsibility was the confining of violent offenders ("habitantes") to the planet's 780 prisons ("bailiwicks").

Now, in 2087, a global movement has arisen in support of a law that would require the testing of habitantes in a neurological search for the organic cause of human violence. If such a cause is found, protocols can then be initiated for the surgical removal of that cause. The controversy rages throughout Little Blue over Habitante Testing and the Anti-Violence Protocols.

Despite the Animal Exodus, the ecocide, the reduced human population, the decline in human males, and continuing social unrest, a miracle has occurred.

Without the aid of wings or motors, women have learned to fly.

1
[2087 C.E.]

> *Violence* is that physical act which is
> done against another's will.
> *Harm* is the physical result of violence.
> Harm is harm, regardless of the intent
> of the harmer, as when the boy throws
> the stone in fun,
> but the frog dies in earnest.
> —*The Labrys Manual*

At Asir-By-The-Sea in the mountainous boot-heel of the
Arabian Peninsula, Jezebel Stronglaces—healer, seer, witch, and in
the tales of Tibetan Yagri, a sacred shape-shifter—woke to the
touch of Bess Dicken, her lover. She laughed, then slipped one
hand to the back of the big woman's neck, sending her fingers
upward through the wiry hair. With a twist, she fitted their long
bodies to the dimensions of the hard pallet, her other hand pressing intimacy into Dicken's back.

"Breath of Astarte!" Dicken gasped. "Jezebel, thirty girls and
three boys are waiting for us this minute, and you come along,
lighting these sacred flames—"

Jezebel smiled and melted into her lover's lax embrace,
pulling Dicken to her. "Guess we'd better get to that class, then."
She closed her eyes and began smoothing the heavy caftan that

covered Dicken's torso.

Jez's unicorn earring caught Dicken's eye. It was tangled in her lover's brown hair. Dicken freed it. "Aba says that coming this time last week would sure enough have been a problem." She wrapped a lock of the shoulder-length hair around her forefinger. "One of the children died. Real sudden. Whole school was upset." She pushed the curled hair to the end of her finger where she willed it to spring off into a corkscrew. "But they're back to normal now. So our visit is timed just right." The hair defied her efforts, falling back into a loose straight strand. Dicken sighed, conceding victory to the hair.

Reluctantly, Jez opened her eyes. She drew Dicken into a last long, voluptuous embrace. "So," she sighed, lightly slapping Dicken's back, "to work! Can these children handle the Standards?"

Dicken's lips had fallen into a concentrated grazing of Jez's collarbone. "All three," she mumbled. She frowned and cocked her head momentarily. "Well, English and Spanish at least." She began to nuzzle the hollow of Jez's throat.

"Dicken—"

Dicken's voice softened to a sensuous whisper. "The Mandarin's harder," she breathed, invitingly.

"Dicken!" Jez laughed. She took her lover's shoulders and held her at arm's length. "Bess Dicken, what language will we be speaking in this schoolroom today?"

Dicken looked hurt. "None of the Standards, my ladylove. Today we get to practice our Arabic!" She swept under Jez's arms and fell again to feasting on her lover's ear.

"Good!" As Jez lifted Dicken from her erotic concerns, her hand encountered the silver bangles circling the big woman's neck. "Look at this!" she teased, fingering the necklace. You've gone native! My Dicken will dance the nuba and pluck her pubic hair!"

"No time soon!" Dicken sighed, at last abandoning her amorous efforts and drawing Jezebel to a sitting position. "Asir's a wonderful place, no doubt about it. But just to visit," she added. "You notice? Everything is either real sticky, real sweet, or both."

Jez stretched. "So today's lesson is on 'sensing imbalance'?"

Dicken struggled to her feet. "That's it. And Aba says they have their hearts set on watching you demonstrate the belly antennae." She kissed a wisp of grey by Jez's temple and moved to the doorway where harsh sunlight framed her substantial body. "The schoolroom's a big pavilion, straight north," she said. Then she blew another kiss and disappeared.

"Tell them I'm on my way," her lover called after her, leaning back against the mud wall of the small hut. She sat motionless within a long intake of breath. Exhaling, she lay on her stomach in prone posture, arms to her side. She breathed deeply, her eyes closed.

Imperceptibly at first and then more swiftly, her body forsook the pallet and rose a few inches into the air, then a foot higher. She extended her arms over her head in imitation of a diver and sustained this position, her mind feasting on the image of hovering hummingbirds. In slow motion, she reached for her trews and softshirt. Still suspended above the pallet, she drew the shirt and pants over her body, spinning to supine position to secure the drawstring.

Now fully clothed, she doubled her knees to her chest in a quick motion and became upright just a foot above the floor. She exhaled and descended until her feet slipped into her sandals. Then she closed her eyes and briskly followed the scent of Dicken's presence out into the brightness of the Arabian afternoon. She did not open her eyes until she reached the pavilion.

Aba-Nuwas, who would be fifty years old next fall, sat with her students near a scrawl-board inscribed with these words: Honesty, Respect, Responsibility, Service. She scanned the faces of her young charges. All of them were in the sitting or kneeling postures that their meditation cushions or stools allowed them, their eyes closed. To a child, they were absorbed in thoughts of animals.

Aba's eyes sought the path beyond the open walls of the pavilion for the arrival of the two flying women from the Nueva Tierra Tri-Satrapy. She herself had had no experience of flying yet, but most of the women she knew were spooning partners. All the children had seen pairs of flying women at one time or another, dipping in and out of the sunlight above Shuqaiq or the Port of Newbirk. She knew that some of her students had secretly tried their hand at spooning and flying, none with any success— except, perhaps, girls who had celebrated their first moon and who had found a deep bonding with another girl or woman.

Though she had never met the near-legendary Jezebel Stronglaces, Aba did not fear the fire that was rumored to leap from Jezebel's fingers or the sandstorms the Bedouins had seen her conjure. Both Jezebel and Dicken would be comfortable and welcome in Aba's schoolroom.

The exercise was approaching its limits for young minds. Aba reseated herself within the large double circle and eased her voice into the long holding of an Ending Sound. Without haste, other voices joined hers until all the children were softly intoning an open-throated "ah" sound. Largely monodic, the sound nevertheless found a sweet harmony or two, flowed and complexified, wove in and out of a chorus of young voices and built at last to a full and formidable roar. Then, abruptly, by the intangible

4

common consent of all those participating, it ceased altogether.

The students burst into laughter, as did Aba, who then called for stretches and physical movement. The talking and shouting children were propelled by their high spirits, running and rolling over the planked flooring, bending in and out of the stools and pillows. They spilled loudly outward to the edges of the pavilion.

Gradually, Aba restored order, hustling students back to the circle and arranging writing boards for the more formal part of the afternoon. "Settle now," she urged them. Bibi, who steadfastly resisted peer pressure to remove her heavy kaffiyeh, even during play periods, pulled at Aba's sleeve. "What, Bibi? Yes, a promise. You can all write at the terminals before we dismiss today. Whatever you remember. But now, it's time for all of us to listen." Even as she engineered them into a tight group, Aba kept her eye upon the path beyond the schoolroom. "What places did you go?" she asked. "What animals did you talk to? What things did you learn?"

"I went with the elephants," said Zari, barely four and the youngest child there. "They took me all over the tri-satrapy."

"And you weren't afraid?" This from Shaheed, barely fifteen and the class's oldest student.

"Nah," Zari told him. "Why did they leave, Aba, why?"

"We just aren't sure, Zari," Aba replied softly.

Qatalona, an older girl, rose to the occasion. "They went by their own decision because they were tired of being hurt and humiliated and imprisoned and killed."

Students dropped their eyes and toyed with their sashes or studiously examined their writing boards.

"That's what most believe," Aba said. She took a quick inventory of the plummeting spirits around her. "But that's not why we do the meditation, to feel bad all over again about the Exodus. Many people even believe that if we talk to them in our memories and rituals, we may persuade the animals to return to Little Blue."

Kamasa, another older student, fingered the curl that wandered down her forehead from her booshi cloth. "Well," she said, "it makes me *feel* better to think of the animals. And not just *feel* better. I think I will *be* better. A better person, I mean." To her right, Masudhe Ratuda rolled her eyes heavenward. Kamasa gave Masudhe an elbow in the shoulder. "It's true, Masudhe! *You* may not believe it, but the whole lesson we learned from the Exodus was that all of life is connected. A long time ago, we felt everything that every other being felt. But we got separated, and that's how it became so easy to misuse animals."

Masudhe put her head down on her writing board, sighing loudly. She raised it again with a wide grin when Kamasa shook her. "Listen to me, Masudhe! You know I'm telling the truth—"

"You are telling the truth, Kamasa," Aba assured her. "Every person has been deeply affected by our loss of the animals." She felt the hush fall again. "Anyway," she continued, in a thinly disguised attempt at enthusiasm, "we're all historians, too. We study the old films and holos so we can understand what this world was once like. And we study the animals because remembering them is so often joyful."

Amid the nods, Bibi asked, "Do you remember the animals, Aba?"

"I'm not that old, preshi!" her teacher laughed. "But if I could remember them, what would I be called?"

"A Rememorante Afortunado!" came one reply. "No, an Afortunada! A Rememorante Afortunada!"

"Yes," said Aba. "One of the fortunate ones who remember. And we were all a kind of Afortunada today, weren't we, as we visualized the animals?" Aba scanned the faces of her students. "Now let's hear about some other visits. Laroos, how was your time with the animals?"

Like the skilled conductor of group life that she was, Aba drew out each child, encouraging the responses, helping each one to help the others hear and be heard. Gradually, the mood softened. There was laughter again and wonderful poignant descriptions of wilderness prowlers, far-flying birds, modest molluscs, and mighty whales. The children's fantasies were better than any book or holoscene, Aba thought.

Medhi had just begun his excited story of desert horses when, from the path beyond, Aba caught the glint of sunlight on Dicken's necklaces. As students turned to stare at the newcomer, Aba motioned Dicken to an empty stool across the circle.

"They came like the wind, over the dunes and through the low passes," Medhi continued. "Hundreds of them, slick and shining in the moonlight, their hooves stirring the sand that hid their galloping legs. In a cloud of silver dust they flew! And as they sailed by me, moving up toward the sky, they nickered and called to me, 'Come and ride with us! Hey, Medhi, come! We will carry you!'"

"Medhi, you're a poet!" Laroos announced.

"Did you ride, Medhi? Did you?" Zari desperately inquired.

"As the big horses thundered by me, I saw one I could mount. She came up on my right." Medhi stood and moved toward the center of the circle, pointing to show how the mare approached him. "Lady Eminence, may I ride you? She tossed her head and rolled out of the herd toward me." Medhi crouched and moved his gaze over the entire circle, his voice rising. The other children crouched with him. "She was so graceful that she didn't even stop as she dipped her head and caught me under the belly—"

"Oooh!" A simultaneous gasp.

"—and swung me up onto her back!"

"Aaahhh!" The whole class unbent with him as he straightened to take his place on the withers of the mighty beast, astride and triumphant, his left hand clearly grasping the mane, his right high above his head.

"As we swept across the sky, I could feel the whole herd around us, roaring in front of me and behind me like a big river! Like the sound of a waterfall! I could hardly breathe for the speed, and as we got higher and higher, I looked down, I looked down—"

Smiling mouths were open with expectancy. Zari put her hands over her eyes.

"I looked down, and I could see the world beneath me! I could see the Earth from her back! There were cities and forests and mountains and plains and oceans and islands and icecaps and deserts. Oh, what a ride! We could soar up to the stars! We could dive down into the Red Sea's waves!"

Medhi's voice became a near whisper. "And once, loping ever so softly just above the treetops . . . ." He paused and looked around at his audience. "What do you think I saw?"

Devotion, the child beside Aba, jumped to her feet. "You saw all the other animals!"

"Yes!" Medhi swirled and held his hands out to her.

Devotion rushed to his side. "There were bullfrogs on mossy logs and turtles crawling in the mud!"

"Yes!" said several children.

"And axolotls laying their eggs!" Medhi added.

Another child nearly shouted, "And seaslugs and piddocks!" Medhi motioned her to the center of the circle.

"Marmots and otter shrews!" A fourth joined the inner group.

"And hyenas and camels!" All the students were straining now to add their favorites.

"And trunkfish and gundis and blue wasps and egrets!"

"And termites and hoopoes and rhinos and rooks!"

"And cormorants and ostriches!" shouted Aba.

"And flatworms and tomb bats!" added Dicken.

"Kinkajous! Spoonbills! Sticklebacks! Eels!"

"Tapirs! Wombats! Horseflies! Storks!"

"How about Marsupialia?"

"Yes!" came the cry.

"And Dactylopteriformes?"

"Yes!"

"How about Homo sapiens?" a new voice asked.

"Yes, yes! Even us!" Medhi breathed, squeezing Devotion's hand.

A small riot greeted Jezebel Stronglaces when she entered the pavilion. As Dicken drew her to her side, Jez found herself for some unexplained reason loudly cheering the human race.

Aba, breathless and smiling, took control once more. "Class, our visitors from Nueva Tierra have arrived." The students took stock of the newcomers with open curiosity.

"They are Bess Dicken," Aba went on, "a Natural Resources Director in her satrapy, and Jezebel Stronglaces, a teacher of nonverbals, frequency reading, and universals. Jezebel has agreed to do some exercises with us this afternoon." Vigorous tongue clicks and some clapping greeted this introduction. Jez and Dicken nodded and then joined in the clicks to signal their applause of the group.

"But first," said Aba, "how did you like the story of Medhi's horses?" The responses again were excited.

"I'd give a lot to ride one!" Shaheed rocked his torso back and forth, his eyes bright toward the sky beyond the pavilion.

"Me too!" agreed a small girl. "One of Medhi's horses, flying to the moon!"

Shaheed rubbed his hands on his pants. "I'd like to ride real horses! Show them how to do tricks! We could ride anywhere! We could race them . . . ." His deep voice faded into the uncomfortable silence that had suddenly surrounded him. His eyes found

Jezebel's, and Jez realized that he was actually a young man, probably of the central desert tribes who came late to schooling, if at all.

"Race them, Shaheed?" Raka Khabin asked.

"You mean like 'taming' them?" one of the other children whispered.

The silence stiffened. Then Bibi said, "Why, Shaheed?"

"It's an act of dominance to *ride* a horse," piped up Qatalona. "It's *violence*."

"Medhi rode the horse in his story," countered the boy.

"But he asked, Shaheed," urged Qatalona.

"Riding without asking is what got us in trouble in the first place," declared Bibi.

"But even if you ask, you can't tell when they're saying it's all right," Shaheed insisted. "How do you know if they're saying yes?" No one looked ready to answer him. "Besides," he went on earnestly, "all horses liked to be ridden. That was their *use*—to hold riders and pull wagons!" Shaheed stuck out his jaw. "My grandfather rode the horses, and he has told me so—at night in the tents when we wait for the storms to pass—he has told me!"

Kamasa shook her head. "Usefulness isn't what gives a being its value," she said slowly. "If that were so it would be okay to mistreat lots of humans." There was some appreciative stirring in the class, a click or two of tongues. "Anyway," she went on, "would *you* like to be ridden?"

"No, of course not," Shaheed replied. "But I'm not a horse. Horses were made for riding."

"And what are men made for?"

Aba broke into the nervous laughter that followed. "Shaheed, are you taking a position outside your heart? Or do you truly believe what you're saying?"

Shaheed looked down. Then he raised his head. "I don't

know, Aba. I just know that when Medhi was telling his story, I felt like I wanted to ride the horses, to make them do what I wanted them to do." He looked down again, then up to meet Aba's eyes. "Maybe it's okay for animals to serve human beings. A whole world used to believe so."

A young woman spoke from the side. "Shaheed, you've said things like this before. You need to explain."

Sounds of agreement rose from different parts of the group. Aba quieted them. "We can do something interesting here," she said, glancing toward Jezebel. "Let's aim for clarity, and let's try to understand Shaheed's feelings, even if they are different from our own." She looked at the boy. "Would you feel comfortable with such a discussion, Shaheed?"

Surprisingly, Shaheed nodded. "I would like to try to explain," he said. Then he looked at Jezebel. "And I want you to be our moderator."

All eyes turned to Jez, who looked briefly at Dicken and then at Aba. "If you trust my good will, Shaheed, then I'll be glad to do that."

There was a small burst of chaos and anticipation while the group shifted cushions and stools.

Zari pulled at Aba's sleeve. "Can we *persuade,* Aba? Will Shaheed try to *persuade* us?"

"I don't know, preshi," said Aba. "Perhaps."

Jez closed her eyes and took a deep breath. "With the best that's in each of us," she said, finally, smiling her readiness to begin. "Shaheed?"

The boy shifted on his stool and then straightened. "Well," he began, "if the animals were still here, I think it would be all right to tame them."

Kamasa spoke without rancor. "You mean it's okay to 'dominate' them?"

"Right," Shaheed replied. "I mean it's fine to use animals for human purposes."

"Why, Shaheed?" Jez prompted.

Shaheed pointed at the words on the scrawl-board. "Well, first, because of responsibility. Beings of greater intelligence have the *responsibility* to train other beings; second, because it's *efficient*; and third, because it's *natural* for animals to be used by humans." Pleased at his summary, Shaheed became more animated. "Look. Those who are more intelligent always have to train those who are less intelligent. That goes for parents and teachers training us, for farmers who trained horses and oxen. . . ."

The students questioned Shaheed respectfully. One or two, like Masudhe, even took his part at times. Jezebel limited her interruptions to summaries and clarifications.

Dicken, impressed by the process, found her tongue clicking with others in approval of Kamasa's distillation: "It all comes down to whether you're going to respect other beings or not." It was at that moment, however, that the measured discussion changed its entire character and direction. To Dicken's alarm, Kamasa was following up her statement with a direct accusation of the young man who had begun it all. "Shaheed," she said, "as long as we have people like you around who don't respect others' freedom and dignity, people who believe it's okay to dominate other beings, then we'll always have violence. How can we ever have a peaceful world if you're always wanting to tame horses?"

The outburst was as passionate as it was unexpected. Jez raised her voice over the vocal response that ensued. "Personal attack, Kamasa—"

"Look," interrupted Shaheed, loudly confronting Kamasa, "I'm getting bullied just because I was honest! I had a strong reaction to Medhi's story, and I said so out loud. Obviously you don't like that, Kamasa. But what am I supposed to do with those 'impure' feelings? Hide them? Pretend I don't have them? Commit myself to the nearest nonviolence center for rehabilitation? If you want a perfect world, you have to figure this out: what are you going to do with people like me?" His words echoed through the hills, over the coffee fields, out to the distant ocean. Silence and stillness fell over the pavilion. On a parallel level, Jez assessed the shimmering softselves of the children and the wild buzzing of excitement there.

Shaheed's voice was a whisper on the air. "What are you going to do with me, Jezebel?" he repeated.

Jez re-centered herself. Breaking her gaze with the boy, she caught Dicken's almost imperceptible nod.

"Aba," she said evenly, "I think it's important for us to talk about Shaheed's question. It concerns, after all, the human violence that has plagued us for thousands of years. The Central Web will soon be making a decision about this very matter."

"Many believe that violent feelings could be controlled by brain surgery," Aba added in explanation to the class. "Jezebel is talking about a proposal for that surgery, which will go to the Central Web."

Jez smiled ruefully. "If we discuss this now, we probably won't have time for the exercises we planned on sensing danger." She cast her eyes over the company of young and serious faces. "What would you like to do?"

No one answered out of the hush. Then Laroos spoke. "Well, I wish I did, but I don't know the answer to Shaheed's question."

"Me either," said Medhi.

"I want to go home!" Zari had become a small round bundle of fatigue. At a signal from Aba, Raka took Zari onto her lap. Jez reached out toward the child with an easing enfoldment. Zari acknowledged the touch with a fret, then relaxed into Raka's arms.

Aba sensed the will of the students. "Get comfortable, class.

Shaheed, come sit by me." She held open an arm.

There was another shuffle as the class tightened its double circle. Dicken took a place between two of the quieter girls. She held out a hand to each and smiled at their prompt response. "We are ready, Jezebel," she announced, holding up their two smaller hands.

Jez took a deep breath. Aba nodded to her.

"Let's try this for a starting point," said Jez. "What happened in 2044?"

Medhi spoke as he raised his hand. "That was the year the economy turned. When all the governments reported no more scarcity. With the big population drop and the women in power, things finally changed. Nobody was hungry anymore."

"And we invented the transmogs," Raka added, "so we can make almost anything we want."

"And people don't fight over *things* anymore," nodded Medhi.

"But people do still fight," said Bibi.

"That makes the point, doesn't it?" asked Aba. "Our patterns of violating others are deeper than hunger or greed."

Jezebel nodded. "So," she said, "we still need to keep human beings from hurting each other and from hurting animals, if they were still here. What can a society do to keep that from happening?"

"Teach them to be good," said Devotion, to a chorus of nods and clicks.

"Love them from the start," said Raka. "Love them in the womb."

"And if they're loved, they won't want to dominate other beings," another girl added.

"But we're not the only ones who are violent," Bibi protested. "Animals dominated and killed each other."

"Right, Bibi," said Qatalona, "but they had to do that to eat."

"Survival of the fittest," Shaheed commented cynically.

14

Qatalona locked eyes with him. "What humans do to each other—and to Nature—is more than just for survival, Shaheed. It's often cruel. The animals weren't cruel. And a volcano isn't cruel."

"Fine," said Jez, pushing onward. "Now, how do we define violence?"

Kamasa held up her hand. "Violence is doing something to another . . . to another *being* against its will."

"That's a good working definition, Kamasa. In fact, it's the one that the Femmedarmes use, and all the Kanshou. Let's say, since the animals are gone, that violence is doing something to another *person* against her will. All right? So you're telling me that if we all love our children, they won't grow up to do things against the wills of other people?"

Heads nodded. Brows furrowed. Then Laroos objected, "But loving them and raising them right doesn't always work. They may turn out violent anyway."

"Especially men," an older child added.

"It's in the testosterone," said Kamasa.

"Since there are fewer and fewer men, maybe the problem will disappear on its own," said still another student.

"Look," said Masudhe suddenly, "laying it all on men can't make Shaheed feel very good. Or Medhi. Or Obatum," she added, indicating the only other boy in the class.

"I'm okay," Shaheed snapped.

"Focus," said someone from the outer edge of the circle.

Jez stepped in. "Back to Shaheed's question. Figure that it takes a while for the whole world to catch up and start educating their children. In the meantime, what does a satrapy or a demesne do with the people who dominate others—who kill someone else, for instance?"

"Well, we don't do capital punishment anymore," Laroos

said. Encouraged by Jez's nod, she remembered aloud to the others. "When things settled down after the epidemics and people had enough of everything they needed—and when there were not as many people to need things—then Kitchen Table and all the other courts realized that they hadn't pronounced a death sentence in over thirty years. They decided to take it off the books. And then the Central Web outlawed it officially."

"Well said," Dicken noted. Laroos flushed with pleasure.

Jez met the eyes of a black-clad girl on the edge of the group and heard her name in her own head. "You want to say something, Nahala?"

Nahala's voice was soft. "In some places, when someone kills another person, everybody just loves him more, pays more attention to him—unless he does it again, and then they kill him. They don't believe in prisons."

"Better to die free," Jez said, "than to live a slave."

"So now instead of capital punishment, we have the bailiwicks," said a voice. It was Shaheed's. "And that's what else you can do," he continued. "You can put violent people in a bailiwick."

"Bailiwicks are prisons," someone added, "like before Earthclasp."

"No, they're not! Prisons covered only a block or two. A bailiwick is sometimes a whole city. Thousands of acres."

"Or a whole island."

"It isn't even like you're being held against your will. You get to go all over. Not like a cage."

"But how big is a cage?" asked Aba.

"A cage is anything that takes away your freedom."

"But it's not really a cage unless you've explored it all and can't go any further . . . and then you realize you don't have freedom after all."

"In a prison, you don't get to have your friends with you," Devotion sang out, "but in a bailiwick, even your family can live nearby."

A child who had been silent was suddenly eager to speak. "And if you've been in a bailiwick for a long time, you can get out for a day or two if you have someone to be your guardian. Like a mother."

"That's only if you've changed, if you've been re—" Bibi struggled.

"Rehabilitated."

"Rehabilitated," echoed Bibi.

"The bailiwicks don't rehabilitate you," Shaheed asserted.

"Some do," Aba replied.

"In the Riyadh bailiwick, there are the Moving Men." Obatum spoke with authority. "They're men who have been cured and then live with violent people to help them change. My father's a Moving Man," he added proudly.

Jezebel was unconsciously counting the nods and the querulous looks, assuring herself of the group's sustained interest level. Zari, on Raka's lap, was in dreamland, and two other smaller children leaned sleepily against older girls, but the free discussion had gripped every other child.

"There are whole experimental bailiwicks," Dicken was saying. "In one, for instance, there's no technology beyond hand tools; the idea is that technology alienates and alienation is the perfect precondition for violence."

Laroos looked at Dicken. "Is it true that some habitantes get to live like free citizens? If they report in regularly?"

"That's right. They're part of 'controlled placement' programs," Dicken answered.

"They're called 'minor offenders,'" Laroos went on. "They get spread out all over the population—one or two in every town—

17

so they don't get together and make trouble."

"My old-old-grandmam says she never met a man she couldn't handle if he was all by himself," Kamasa said. "It was the men in twos and threes and more that scared her."

"The dangerous ones were those in groups," Bibi agreed. "Clubs, lodges, fraternities, armies. Aba had us studying that."

Without looking at them, Jez read the anxiety levels of the three boys in the class. Only Shaheed offered cause for concern. She set a quiet watchcurl around him and turned back to the speakers.

"Jezebel," Qatalona said suddenly, "say about the sex-healers."

"You probably know more about them than I do," Jez replied, glancing at Aba for any objection to the topic. Aba shrugged lightly and nodded with a small smile. "This part of the world is famous for sex-healing," Jez went on. She looked at a girl to her right who was sitting on the floor. "Will you tell me your name?" she asked, pushing her inflection toward the downcast eyes and moving her intent into the outskirts of the girl's energy field. Gently, she drew the girl's gaze up to meet her own.

"I'm Hawa Khashoggi."

"And you're from Baghdad?" When the girl looked surprised, Jez pointed to her sandals. "I could tell by your madass. Such fine threadwork comes only out of Baghdad."

The girl beamed. "I lived there until last year, and yes there are sex healers there. A whole colony of women who are committed to sexually pleasuring the . . . the violent offenders."

"Amazing." Raka leaned forward. "Does it work?"

"I don't know," said Hawa. "I hear that the women enjoy it," she added, smiling. Several girls suppressed giggles.

"Nobody knows yet, Raka, whether it works or not," said Jez, "but it's one of the 'controlled placement' programs. The theory behind it is that if male sexual energy can be channeled into physical release, then urges to violence subside in direct proportion." She felt Shaheed's increased attention before he spoke.

"Are there colonies of such men," he said, the strain obvious in his voice, "for the healing of criminal women? Or maybe these women also feel a responsibility to be sex-healers for convicted women offenders. Do they?"

Kamasa exploded. "Why don't you say it outright, Shaheed? You want to know if there are women who are convicted of violence? Well, yes. Yes! The answer is *yes*! But there are precious few compared to the men! It's the *men* who have always torn up the Earth; it's the *men* who always push their johnnycocks into somebody else's face! It's the *men*—"

"It's the *men*," Masudhe's voice topped Kamasa's, "the *men* who have had to do all the changing in the past hundred years!"

"Masudhe, you are such a lickspitting toady!" Kamasa screamed. "Come off it!"

Shaheed shot to his feet and squared off toward a livid Kamasa. He sought an invective to shred his adversary once and for all. Then, without warning, his tongue turned to jelly.

"Shaheed! What are you doing?" asked his Inner Self, a dazzling presence hovering behind his eyes. Without hesitation he whispered back, "Something not worthy of my heart!" In that moment, his Inner Self opened wide its arms. The boy closed his eyes, turned, and stepped into the embrace.

Jezebel had been riding the waves of anger from the two older girls. When Shaheed stood, she made a decision and pushed toward him an enfolding shield that thrust his anger back toward his own deep center. She watched him charge toward Kamasa and then stagger. In a protracted moment, he drew himself up and stood galvanized in an unexpected silence. His lips moved. Then his shoulders slumped and he closed his eyes.

The class sat frozen. Jez sent a blessing to the Goddess for

Shaheed's powerful Inner Self. Then Aba rose and stepped behind her student, her arms extended. While the group watched, stunned, Shaheed turned and sank into her embrace. He stood holding her, surrounded by his classmates' sighs and exclamations.

Jezebel Stronglaces looked from face to face. She found concern among the students and a healthy dose of respect for Shaheed. Masudhe and Kamasa were still puzzled and uneasy. When she saw Kamasa reach out to lay her hand on Masudhe's knee, Jez released a breath she hadn't known she was holding. Masudhe did not quite smile, but extended her little finger. Kamasa took it with her own, and with a mutual squeeze, both the older girls subsided into a chastened armistice.

The class was recovering from the eruption. One sweep told Jezebel that the curiosity was still high and the willingness unconcealed. Dicken's short nod lent her a sweet assurance. She drew a restorative breath.

"Well," she said, "so far we've talked of three ways to handle violent people. First, we can execute them. Second, we can confine them in bailiwicks where they may or may not be rehabilitated. Third, we can put them in controlled placement programs. We've missed only two alternatives, both pretty obvious—"

Qatalona preempted her. "You can just send them away, Jezebel."

"Good. Exile them," Jezebel nodded. "But to where?"

"The middle of the ocean."

"The moon colony!"

"A satellite circling the globe!"

"That all takes too many guards. How're you going to keep them from getting out? And coming back to be violent again?"

"Maybe that's what the people from other galaxies think of us," mused a previously silent student. "They're afraid we'll discover stardrive and escape our solar system, and that then we'll take over the universe and ruin it just like we almost did Little Blue."

"Well, we might," said Raka. "To them we may be just like *habitantes*. And Little Blue is our bailiwick!"

Jez was keeping her extensors in light touch with Shaheed, Kamasa, and Masudhe. The girls had entered another terrain, apart now from Shaheed. They were not yet ready to participate again. Two more conversational turns, she estimated, and they would be drawn in once more. Shaheed was another matter.

Jezebel Stronglaces, whose mistrust of the male biology was well known and understood over all nine satrapies, found herself struggling with an unfamiliar empathy for the dark beanpole of a young man whose eyes rose once more to meet her own. Mingled with his rage, his shame, and his confusion was the unmistakable pulse of good will. That pulse rode straight to her heart.

He raised his hand. The mildness of his manner startled her. "And there's the last option, isn't there, Jezebel? The one that proposes getting rid of all violence completely."

"Oh, Shaheed," Qatalona objected, "nobody believes we could get rid of violence completely!"

"Jezebel Stronglaces believes it," he said softly, keeping his eyes on Jez.

"What, Shaheed? Repeat." Qatalona bent toward him.

"Jezebel Stronglaces believes it!" Shaheed placed each word like a cannon shot into the air. Then, before anyone could respond, he rose to one knee. "They're going to try to cripple or kill anybody who is still violent, aren't they? That's what the Testing and the Protocols are all about." His voice, even softened, remained accusatory. "And you want them to do it."

Jez found one long breath. "What have you heard, Shaheed, about the Protocols?"

He sat back on his cushion. "I've heard that scientists want to change violent people into peaceful ones. By performing surgery on their brains."

"That's accurate," Jez told him. "Anti-Violence Protocols would involve brain surgeries that would inhibit an individual's physiological tendency toward violence, and perhaps the violent tendencies of their children." She searched the attentive faces around her. "But physicians and researchers aren't even sure yet that there *is* such a violence center in the brain. To discover that center, they have proposed surgical experiments upon bailiwick habitantes."

Aba-Nuwas silently explored the temper of her students. They sat in unblinking concentration, sorting information, grasping for meanings, and absorbing the implications of Jez's words. She spoke without disrupting the tension.

"So there are two moral questions here. First, is it right to use habitantes for experimentation in the search for a physical or organic cause of violence? And second, if an organic cause is found, can we justify the use of the Anti-Violence Protocols on violent offenders against society?"

Jez scanned the room, noting Shaheed's rueful grin. Some eyes met hers. Some heads nodded solemnly. "The fundamental question is that of the Protocols," she explained, "but the Central Web will probably take up the matter of Habitante Testing first, figuring that if some physical cause is found, violent people who want to change could choose the surgical procedure—even if the Web decides that no one should be forced to have the operation. After all, if we haven't looked for the cause, violent people who want to change won't have that option. Does that make sense?"

"And that's what all the fighting's about," Laroos mused.

"That's the heart of the present controversy, yes. Whether it's right to use habitantes for the studies."

Shaheed's spoke evenly. "Whether it's right to use habitantes *against their will.*"

Jezebel looked across the wide abyss that separated her from Shaheed. "All our lives are going to be affected by this controversy," she said to him, "but you could be affected more than most."

His dark eyes regarded her without faltering. "Because I think about taming horses."

Jez nodded slowly.

"Never," he whispered. Then louder he said, "I would *never* agree to let someone tinker with my brain!" No one moved. Or breathed. "So would you force me to have the surgery, Jezebel?" He waited. "Would you? Where is all your nonviolence then?"

Deliberately, and with Shaheed's tacit permission, Jezebel put long legs on her softself and unhesitatingly strode the narrow plank of tension between them. She moved behind him and merged tentatively with his waiting softself. She saw what he saw, felt what he felt. While a cold wind of doubt whipped around them both, she opened her mind and heart.

She was a clean-cut, sharp-edged warrior whose self-knowledge and identity had been won at great cost. She raised her sword of Selfhood against the sea of faceless uniformity that rose inexorably on every side, luring her into its bottomless depths with promises of peace, harmony, and love. She defied it, striking at it with her sword and crying, "I abhor your sameness! I do not choose to be like you! I stand apart from you, alone and free!"

Thus, on that bright mountain-desert afternoon, in the wraparound shoes of a lanky Yemen boy, Jezebel Stronglaces learned something of the fear, the loneliness, and the pride of Little Blue's male minority—once its ruling force. She took up residence again in her own body, ready at last to answer his question. Around her, the class sat transfixed, watching a silent drama, the dimensions of which they could barely imagine.

"Shaheed," she began.

His chin moved upward.

"Shaheed, if you had proved yourself to be a violent man, and if we knew that through surgery you could be changed into a non-violent man, I would insist for the sake of society—and yourself —that you be required to have the surgery. Even against your will."

Nothing moved in the pavilion, neither breeze nor breath.

Jez held the young man's gaze.

Then, ever so slightly, Shaheed nodded. Once.

Jezebel spoke again. "Because of who you are and because of what I have learned from you today, I find inside myself a wish that I could believe differently. But I doubt that I ever will. I would lie if I told you otherwise."

Shaheed's countenance expressed neither guile nor rancor. Jez held his eyes.

Someone's body rustled into movement. Then, as if rising from a dream, many bodies began stirring softly.

Aba sighed aloud. Zari was back in her lap again, now bright-eyed and smiling. As the teacher straightened on her stool all eyes turned toward her, those of Shaheed and Jezebel among them. "We have lots to think about," she said, capturing any still straying attention. The circle of students drew more tightly together. Aba spoke to their guests. "Jezebel and Dicken, you've given us a great gift today. We'll be doing the hard work you've laid out for us long after you have gone." Her voice took on a formal tone. "Our thanks to you both," she said.

Slowly, tongue clicks and knee slaps from the whole group began escalating into full-bodied applause. The students clapped and clicked for half a minute before Aba found the sound she wanted. She shifted her Zari-bundle to her other knee and began a sustained chanting of each word as it came to her. "This has been a fine afternoon," she intoned, "filled with surprises."

Jez took her turn immediately, chanting, "I give my thanks to you all."

Dicken shifted the rhythm to a singable beat and rallied the voices around the optimum pitch. "Praise for the lessons of this bright day!" she sang.

"Praise for the lessons of this bright day!" the students repeated. They swung into a litany of gratitude for every event of the afternoon, particularly for the galloping of majestic wild horses across their sky.

Aba shifted the gratitude to a chanting of the name of each student, a ritual obviously so familiar that it brought forth a rich variety of rhythms and pacings, whirrs and buzzes. When each student's name and that of Dicken and Aba had been sung, it was Shaheed who stood up and chanted above all the rest, "Jezebel!" His voice—and the laughs and clicks that followed—ended the afternoon.

2
[2087 C.E.]

Midair explosion of R-18C bimodular cushcar just off ocean
side of Ciudad Bolivar Hoverpath now attributed to combustive
detonation of explosive cargo. Firearms, cribs/canisters of
ammunition, grenades; Grade 6 trinitrotoluene, pyroxylin, and
solanas rockets, all proscribed by law.
Occupants instantly killed: two men, one woman.
—*Report to Tri-Satrapy Center*
0125 10.13.87 ASBR.cog.sen 36.caracas.NTSur

On the other side of the world, a woman in uniform sat in an
office twenty floors above the City and Bailiwick of Los Angeles.
She had short, thick, salt-and-pepper hair that fell across her forehead in curls. Her eyes were solid brown except when the sun
struck her face, and then they revealed specks of light that
brought summer fireworks to mind. Her cheekbones rode high,
and a small silver ring suspended a rampant unicorn from her left
earlobe. Her skin was the color of a highly polished pecan. Below
her trim solid torso, smooth-muscled legs set her an inch shorter
than most of the women in her charge. When she smiled, people
looked up in astonished joy.

Zella Terremoto Adverb, Magister of the Vigilancia and thus
also the chief executive officer of the Nueva Tierra Tri-Satrapy,
was called "Zude" by most and "Zudie" by a precious few. She was

one of the rare Kanshou (or Shrieves) on Little Blue privileged to wear the colors of any one of the planet's three peacekeeping forces. As a graduate of the Hong Kong Amah Academy, she had worn the red tabard of the Asia-China-Insula Tri-Satrapy's Amahrery, and during her two-year service as a Femmedarme in the Africa-Europe-Mideast Tri-Satrapy, she had worn the green tabard of the Femmedarmery. But her greatest dedication was ever to Nueva Tierra's Vigilancia, and her daily dress was thus in the cobalt blue of a Vigilante.

This night she wore the black rhyndon comfortsuit and the black breeks of every Kanshou, regardless of tri-satrapy. For the occasion of her expected Amahrery visitors and to acknowledge her own experience as an Amah, she wore over the comfortsuit a deep red open-throated smock, the semi-casual garment of the Amahs.

Here in Zude's office behind hanging plants, small murals of blue and silver accented the contoured walls of grey. On one back-lit panel, a hand-woven net of metal squares or fighting meshes seemed poised for combat, hanging three-dimensionally off gleaming steel rings. In another recessed panel, a violin sat upright, its bow leaning lightly against its fingerboard. A prominent inset of the complex desk unit was filled by the taxidermy of a crouching calico cat, curved neck slightly turned, yellow eyes flashing. Draped over a chairback was the long cloak of tekla in Vigilancia blue, its clasp emblazoned with the Magistry insignia.

Zella Adverb sat within her desk unit staring at the report of the cushcar explosion. "Outlaws," she muttered, "on their way to big trouble. And one of them a woman."

"And why not, Captain?" retorted a voice from her past. *The lanky habitante in light-green coveralls added a jeer to her voice. "You think women are too pure to bust a man's head in?"*

Femmedarme Captain Adverb shook her head. "No." Then she

asked, *"And you experience a Crossover?"*

"A what?"

"Do you find your anger escalating with successive minor irritations until at last you cross over from restraint to full-blown violence?"

"You bet," said the long-legged woman, savoring a familiar satisfaction. She smiled. *"Where I come from, nothing, not even tribal law, stops a Crossover. How about you, Captain?"* she inquired conversationally.

Zude was silent. Then she said, *"Yes, I've felt that."*

"Then why aren't you sitting here, and me in your chair?"

Zude studied the woman. *"I don't know, habitante. Just luck, I guess."*

A voice in the present filled the office. "Magister?"

"Ah, Flora." Zude straightened, shaking off the memory.

"They've just landed on the roof. Two Flying Daggers from Sydney: Amah Matrix Major Rhoda Densmore and Amah Jing-Cha Longleaf. They brought with them in their gert a woman from Mexico. She's called Bosca. All three are waiting in the down-room."

"Fine, Flora. Have Captain Edge bring them to me with whatever they want to drink. And stand by."

She looked over the room, then crossed to a wallpocket, removing from it a box of cigarillos. She hesitated, then placed the cigarillos on the circular table, together with an ashtray. She dimmed the lights and activated the depaque control for a full wall view of the vast twinkling city below.

◆

Amah Jing-Cha Longleaf's comfortsuit usually adjusted easily to extraordinary climate or weather changes, guaranteeing that her body's optimum temperature was never disturbed. But tonight she was freezing. Last week's hops across the Pacific,

gerting with Rhoda from ship to ship, had given her a quick chill
or two, but nothing quite equalled this night's trip through that
unexpected cold desert air.

She was following Bosca and Rhoda now and their Vigilante
escort down into the Nueva Tierra's Shrievalty Building. One by
one, they stepped into a downchute and floated to a floor far
below, emerging into a large multi-levelled rest area for Vigilancia
personnel and their families. Singly, in pairs, or in groups, women
and children read, ate, drank, played, talked, viewed flatfilms.
Longleaf could see the head of one smiling woman protruding
from the end of a robomassager.

The Vigilante who greeted them was square-faced and pale,
even for a white woman. "You have quarters here at the
Shrievalty," she said, "with food and hot baths after you see the
Magister." She handed them cups of hempbrew and tea, then dis-
appeared. Longleaf sank down onto a thick couch beside Rhoda.
Bosca, sensing her chill, placed a gigantic shawl over her shoulders.

Of the three of them, Bosca was clearly the native of this continent, a woman as aptly prepared for the cold desert nights as she
was for the dry heat of its days. She had insisted on making the
flight between the two Gerting Amahs in a cotton robe that
hooded and gloved her, keeping her warm all the way from the
Mexican heartland northwest to the city she had longed to see
since childhood.

Rhoda's voice broke into her reverie. "Bosca, here's Captain
Edge." The three visitors forsook their cups and fell into step
behind their imperious Vigilante guide. Rhoda adjusted her belt
and checked her uniform for impeccable presentation, smoothing
the tekla of her neck cowl as she blessed again that extraordinary
synthetic textile—if in fact it *was* synthetic, since nobody knew
for sure.

Before they stepped into the upchute, Rhoda asked,

"Captain, I forfeited a 'weapon' to the roof-keepers. Can you tell me where it is?" Edge withdrew a cotton pouch from the back of her sleeve, feeling the objects inside it. "That's it," Rhoda nodded.

"I'll check them out," said the Captain, "and have them ready for the Magister." Then she added, "Is there a name for these items?"

"They're called 'ballbakers.'" Rhoda replied, with a small shrug.

The upchute deposited them in a bare hallway. To the surprise of the visitors, no door sighed open, no iris widened. Instead, the small wall facing them simply began to disappear, gradually revealing a low-lit room. Beyond it, a giant window hugged a vast pattern of lights. Zella Terremoto Adverb stood in silhouette between them and her city, tonight bare of harbor fog. She stepped forward from the shadows.

On an almost tangible level, the first twenty seconds of the encounter would determine the course of the entire meeting. It would set the tone and establish the myriad psychic and psychological parameters that would couch the exchanges that were to follow.

For her part, Bosca saw the fog-naked city, stretching for miles behind the Magister's imposing figure. "I'm the City of Angels," something sang from a gentle congestion in her throat. Quietly, she sang back to it, "Sprawl and fester all you please. You're still beautiful."

Jing-Cha Longleaf was thrust unexpectedly inside a silver-grey room where green plants hung in lush pockets of life. When she saw the long-haired calico cat in the lighted desk inset, she involuntarily touched Rhoda's arm and expelled a low exclamation. The Magister had preserved a reality from another era. Zude's face was still shadowed beyond Longleaf's capacity to be sure, but she felt a kind of assurance from that part of the room and decided to trade some of her apprehension for a shade of trust.

Rhoda registered surprise that the Magister was not seven feet tall, reassured Longleaf by leaning toward her, and turned slightly in the direction of the Vigilante behind them so as to hold that formidable figure in her peripheral field of vision.

Captain Edge kept her first level attention on the woman whose rank pips designated her as a Matrix Major. She prepared to move toward the transmogrifier as soon as opening formalities among the visitors were accomplished.

In the beginning seconds, Zella Terremoto Adverb saw before her two well-conditioned but wary Anglo women and a darker woman impossible to describe . . . except, Zude marveled to herself, except that she loves my city! Zude raised both hands just above her head, extending to the visitors the womb formed by her thumbs and forefingers. Her guests were one beat behind her in returning the high formal Kanshou salute.

"Amahs, we welcome you to the Vigilancia," Zude said, "I'm Zella Terremoto Adverb, Magister of the Nueva Tierra Tri-Satrapy."

"Thank you, Magister," Rhoda replied. "We are Amah Matrix Major Rhoda Densmore and Jing-Cha Longleaf, or Rhoda-Gert-Longleaf, from the Asia-China-Insula Tri-Satrapy. We've come not as emissaries of Magister Lin-ci Win, but with her support. And this is Bosca, who sheltered us in her Mexico home."

Bosca came to her unnecessary salute belatedly but vigorously. She spoke as she lowered her arms. "I'm a visitor, Magister, and not a part of these negotiations unless you want me here."

Zude was abrupt. "Would you like a tour of the city?" To Rhoda, that voice still belonged to a larger-than-life presence.

"Is there time?" Bosca asked.

"With our monitors, there's always time." Zude smiled

warmly. With a touch of her hand, she raised the room's general illumination and the circle of light over the round table. "We can show you any public part of this city, ride above it or underneath it, move you through it as slowly as the Earth turns or as fast as a rocket."

"Are there flowers?"

"Fields of them, for as far as the eye can see. Bluebells, pansies, exotics."

"And the ocean. Can a visitor see the ocean?"

"The beach is one place you should go in person, particularly the part we've begun reclaiming. You won't find a structure for miles. No souvenir vendors or food kiosks."

"Then I'd like to accept your offer."

"Fine. Edge, take Bosca to L-9 and have Lieutenant Nan give her the whole show." The Captain nodded. Zude continued, "And arrange a hovercraft for a beach trip tomorrow."

Edge nodded again. She had placed full cups from the transmogrifier on the round table. She turned now to gesture Bosca toward the wall where they had entered. The wall dissolved once more, and Bosca nodded a quick thank-you to Zude before she disappeared into the hallway by the downchute. The Vigilante started to follow her.

"And Edge," the Magister's voice stopped her. "Check my schedule. Find out when I am free so I can pilot the hovercraft and conduct Bosca's tour of the beaches."

As the wall reconstituted itself behind Bosca and Captain Edge, Longleaf shot her lover a covert glance of astonishment. Rhoda widened her eyes almost imperceptibly and shrugged ever so slightly. They watched the Magister who stood smiling at the repaqued wall.

Zude turned and glided toward the table, her extended arm inviting Rhoda and Longleaf to sit. Longleaf physically felt a shift in the air as the Magister moved. Zude seemed more to conquer space than merely to walk through it.

The window had repaqued itself, replacing the vista of lights with a holo perfectly matched to the room's cushion-like walls and ceiling panels. Zude stood between her visitors as they sat at the table.

Rhoda broke the silence. "You are a violinist, Magister?"

Zude glanced toward the instrument in its display nook and smiled briefly. "A fiddler, Major. And that a very long time ago." Without pause, she declared, "It's always good to see Amahs. I miss Hong Kong sometimes more even than my birthplace." She adjusted the remaining chair. "Are we in a rush? Or may we share a such-and-such?"

"We've no time limit, Magister," said Longleaf.

"Then by all means," Zude replied. She sat and noncommitally offered them cigarillos. Predictably, both women declined.

Longleaf spoke. "Before we begin, I must tell you that Matrix Major Densmore is the official spokeswoman here. I have the kind of mind that will be able to reproduce this meeting verbatim, and with paralanguage and nonverbal counter- and sub-texts if requested. That's my function."

Zude nodded. "Our parallel to your talents is a flatfilm recording, which at this moment is immortalizing us all on micropiezoplates. I assume you do not object?" Neither did. All three women settled, significantly more comfortable now and ready for the such-and-such. There was another silence. "Your choice, visitors," Zude said.

"Let's acknowledge our mothers," Rhoda decided, catching Longleaf's eye and subsequent nod.

"Very well," said Zude.

"My mother was Rowena Densmore," Rhoda began. "I remember her as pretty and strong, with lots of friends. She took care of me and my brother in Nueva Tierra Norte until she died of radiation poisoning from the Warrenton waste storage site that took so many lives. We lived in Lower Eastern Corridor, just below old D.C. in a complex of over a hundred families.

"I remember her best in the crisp white uniform she wore with her seniors in the nursing home. She ironed those uniforms herself with an old electric because she didn't trust the cleaning service, and the regulation permapress fabrics were too limber for her. She insisted that a limp uniform did not show enough respect for the old people. Every night I'd stand beside her on a styrostiff chair and squirt the starch for her while she ironed." Rhoda paused.

"I remember . . . just before she left for work that last time. She was feeling ill, but struggled to keep her spirits high. Her starched collar scratched my face when she hugged me and adjusted our mom-calls. Even after our aunt took us halfway around the world to Sydney, I still kept that little mom-monitor to remember her by." Rhoda closed her hands in the gesture of completion.

Zude activated her exhaust chute and lit a cigarillo. She smiled through a puff of smoke. "My mother . . . Sylvia Isabel Romero, called 'Queta.' From a Tuyan tribe in the selvas, Eastern Colombia. After their village was appropriated for soybean production, her family moved by rail, river, and muletrail to Barranquilla. She and her husband and my brothers worked for a cocoa company. Cutting, drying, roasting, skinning the nibs. Packing and loading boats.

"She lived with my youngest half-brother and his family. Was almost fifty when she had me. She never said who my father was, but she told me stories of the animals, which she remembered very well. Those stories fed my spirit. They still do." Zude's eyes shifted to the calico cat in her desk unit. Then she resumed her narrative. "She joined the Church so I could go to school. I taught her to read. When I was fourteen, I left home and worked my way up the Caribbean side of the isthmus to Mexico City." Zude smothered the cigarillo against the bottom of the ashtray. Longleaf and Rhoda sat without moving.

"I had dreams of sending for her when I made a fortune, but things didn't work out that way." Zude leaned forward on the table. "It was my mother who first told me about spooning. I was eight. I used to crawl onto her cot with her. She would turn me away from her and then fit herself to me, holding me from the back. I remember once wondering how her holding me so close could feel so good on such a hot night. She laughed like she did whenever she read my thoughts. Then she said, 'The Motherkin say that if you truly love a woman and then sleep with her in this way, in a spoon, you can walk in her dreams and fly with her to the stars.'"

"No!" exclaimed Rhoda.

"Your mother!" Longleaf said.

Zude nodded. "So I wanted to fly with her right then. She told me we couldn't do that but that I might find such a love one day." There was a silence. Then Zude resumed. "I carried her words with me. Right into the arms of my first lover." All three women laughed softly. Zude folded her hands and turned to Longleaf. "And to complete our circle . . . ."

Longleaf shook her head. "I can't feature my mother ever telling me anything of that sort. She still lives just outside of Sydney in the Blue Hills. Her name is Florence Scarborough, and she was taught to be a European lady — formal dinners and fancy dress balls. My most vivid memory is of a scene on our patio when I was about seven. My father had been dead more than a year, and my mother was constantly crying to my aunt about what a horrid place the world had become because now there were no men for her daughters to marry.

"That day she went on a real rampage. She blamed the navies of every country in the world for bringing the epidemics to Australia. Then she blamed the prostitutes, the Mafia, the gays, and the government. I made it all worse by running up to her and tugging at her hand and telling her that she should stop crying because Sissy and I didn't want to get married anyway, men just gave you diseases, and Sissy and I were going to love only each other and live to be two hundred.

"There she was, with her greatest fears materializing before her eyes: no wedding parties for me or Sissy, no grandchildren for her. Sissy and I have further distressed Mother since then—Sissy by choosing to live with the yurt people instead of with our mother and aunt, I by entering the Kanshou Amah Academy."

After a moment, Rhoda sighed. "My mother, clean and crisp," she said.

"Mi madre," said Zude, "Rememorante Afortunada."

"My mother, the perfect lady," said Longleaf.

No one broke the long silence that followed until Rhoda sighed again. "Well," she said, "that's the such-and-such."

"That's the such-and-such." Longleaf and Zude repeated, almost in unison.

Zude took their cups to the transmog for refills. "And now to the business of the day."

"That's harder," Rhoda said.

"It always is." Zude set Longleaf's tea before her and Rhoda's hempbrew in front of her. Three auras pulled back to more formal but still cordial distances, and a field of mutual concern rested among the three.

Rhoda leaned toward Zude. "Magister, you've probably heard about the outbreaks of male violence in New Howrah and Greater Chendu, in the bailiwicks."

"I know about the bailiwick uprisings there. I don't assume that the violence is male." Zude sipped her coffee.

"Those circumscribed in the bailiwicks are overwhelmingly men."

"But not exclusively."

"No. Not exclusively." Rhoda exhaled audibly, trying to soften the brittle texture that began to surround them. "But these outbreaks seem to be especially intense. And fairly well organized."

"Oh?" An exploding cushcar filled Zude's mind. She suppressed the image and focused on Rhoda's words.

"I don't know if you know it . . . Magister Win kept it under close wraps . . . but riots in New Howrah and Greater Chendu were followed by even more severe uprisings in Kandy and Singapore."

"I did not know they were counted more severe."

Rhoda leaned toward her. "They are severe enough, Magister, that whole demesnes of women are demanding immediate Habitante Testing—"

"Double-damn," Zude muttered, not taking her eyes from Rhoda.

"—so that research on the Anti-Violence Protocols can get underway."

"They're so sure!"

"So sure, Magister?"

"So sure that research will reveal a physical, discernable center of violence!" Zude overarticulated the words.

Rhoda glanced at Longleaf. "Yes," she said to Zude, "they're of that persuasion."

Abruptly, Zude stood up. "Insanity!" she breathed. She strode toward her desk unit.

"They want a final ridding of violence, Magister," Rhoda declared, "and to them the solution is the use of neurological inhibitors on any man convicted of—"

The words shot out of Zude's mouth: "*Person*, Major Densmore, on any *person* convicted of a violent act!"

Rhoda flared, almost rising from her seat. "Magister, with respect, you are ostriching! Over 95 percent of violent acts are still perpetrated by men!"

"I don't care if it's 99.9999 percent, Major! The jury is still out on the question of female violence potential. Until we can determine *without question* the incompatibility of violence with the female psyche, then our language must reflect that reality!" *The image of the coverall-clad habitante held up two thumbs. "Brava, Captain!" she cheered, her laughter filling Zude's head.* Zude cleared the vision and laid her gaze hard upon the Amah who confronted her.

Rhoda did not flinch. With her eyes still fixed on Zude, she spoke evenly. "I stand corrected, Magister. Charge my language to the fact that my duties have been exclusively with women for over two years. That makes inflated statements about men easy utterances."

"I suppose so," Zude nodded, still discomfited. "Amahs," she said, walking toward them, "with rapidly increasing frequency, I am besieged by organizations throughout this tri-satrapy who want Habitante Testing enacted immediately."

"Magister—" Rhoda began.

Zude reclaimed her chair, her hand raised in a gesture of deterrence. "I'm also besieged by those who feel that such testing would be a disaster, that the price in human freedom would be too great. Habitantes have rights, Amahs! And even if some organic basis for violence is proven, there still can be no excuse for any tampering with the brain of a violent offender. I daresay you already know my position on all this."

In the pause that followed, Zude studied her two Australian

visitors. All three of them were carefully dodging the thousand volatile aspects of the planet's most controversial issue.

"Kanshoumates," she continued, letting her inchoate feelings guide her, "we've been drawing near a pointed and dangerous cusp in our talking. Magister Lin-ci Win and other protofiles would have us obliterate violence. But we cannot obliterate it if, in the process, we destroy the rights of any person. Both the Habitante Testing and the notion of violence inhibitors constitute for me an abrogation of individual rights. It's no wonder you find me touchy on this subject." She paused. "We need to be more direct with each other."

Rhoda and Longleaf exchanged a look, unprepared for the Magister's candor. Rhoda took a deep breath and asked, "Are you asking for true-talk, Magister?"

Zude's eyes opened a fraction of a centimeter wider. "I am."

Still stunned by Zude's deliberate vulnerability, Rhoda adjusted her subvention belt, trying to ease its pressure on her waist. "Magister, do you feel comfortable with Longleaf as our witness and facilitator?"

"Fine."

All three women shifted and settled, though a measure of tension remained. Longleaf began, "There are three preliminary agreements and three behaviors required for true-talk. The agreements include equal commitment to struggle and self-examination in dialogue, suspension of rank without fear of retribution, and good will that avoids the exploitation or abuse of any being or thing, whether natural or artificial."

"All granted." Rhoda and Zude spoke almost simultaneously.

Then Zude added, "That last agreement will be difficult, since it's precisely the agenda of the people you seem to represent here. In my view, they wish to exploit or do violence to a whole group of people."

40

"You mean they want to exploit violent . . . people?" Rhoda asked.

"Exactly," answered Zude.

Longleaf spoke decisively. "We suspend the agreement about good will for the present, since it is substantial, as part of the discussion." She continued, "The first of the three behaviors states: 'I will say all of the truth as I know it that pertains to the matter at hand. I believe my partners in true-talk will do the same.'"

"Granted." Rhoda and Zude again spoke in unison.

"Second behavior: I will acknowledge the shortcomings of my position and the virtues of the counter position."

"Granted."

"Last behavior: I will articulate and attempt to understand and appreciate the point of view that opposes my own; I will give this viewpoint respect-in-disagreement."

"Granted."

Zude addressed Rhoda. "So you will present a case and receive my response."

Rhoda smiled in spite of herself. "Yes, and—dare I use the word?—I will *persuade* you if I can . . . ."

Remarkably, Zude smiled back. "And I you, Major. If I can." She lit another cigarillo, adjusting the exhaust chute. "Take us back to the cusp, Jing-Cha."

"Before we return to that point, Magister," said Rhoda, "would you ask Captain Edge to bring us the package I turned over to her staff?"

Zude moved to her desk and tapped a message into one of the consoles there. She resumed her seat. "Jing-Cha?"

Longleaf recited. "Amah Densmore had just said, 'They want a final ridding of violence, Magister, and to them the solution is the use of neurological inhibitors on any *man* corrected to *person* convicted of a violent act.'"

"Thank you. I wish to respond."

Rhoda nodded.

Zude pressed the edge of the table, activating a large screen in the cushioned wall by Longleaf. From what looked like a dense graphic, she isolated and magnified a statistical report. "There it is, Kanshoumates. We now have on Little Blue 780 bailiwicks, colonies which confine within their boundaries habitantes found guilty of violent acts." She filled the screen with the three tri-satrapies in sequenced carto-sections, highlighted to demonstrate the bailiwicks' locations. "That figure includes central cities, like this one, where the colonies are characteristically surrounded by free citizens."

She shifted the screen to the tables again and scrolled to comparative calculations. "Each bailiwick holds an average of 1,282 habitantes, some as few as 500 and some as many as 4,000. As you indicated, the habitantes are in large majority men, even when we count the people, in large majority women, who choose to live there with convicted habitantes.

"All told, we're looking at about a million habitantes and approximately 120,000 people who choose to live near them in bailiwicks, from Thule to the Falklands, from Ouagadougou to Fiji." She paqued the screen and leaned back in her chair. "Let's assume the highly unlikely possibility that a violence center is discovered in the human brain." She extinguished her cigarillo. "One million people. If I understand you, you're suggesting that all of them, at least those convicted, should, against their will, be subjected to the surgical procedures that are supposed to render them docile and law-abiding."

Rhoda hesitated, wondering, in spite of the true-talk, what trap might lie ahead. "Yes. Perhaps with the promise of freedom or a reduced sentence if they have the surgery. It would not be against their will, Magister. They would have a choice."

Zude looked toward the entrance wall. Captain Edge appeared, deposited a small package in front of Zude and disappeared.

"A choice, you say," Zude repeated. "A choice of what? Surgery or death?"

Rhoda did not answer.

"And how many do you imagine would choose to be so altered?" Zude persisted.

"Magister, when the benefits to society are understood, I suspect most of those convicted would choose to be relieved of their drive to destroy or injure."

Zude grunted. "If they were choosing it over death, maybe. But maybe not. Maybe even the freedom to die unaltered, uninvaded, to die as one's own self, is more precious than living as a citizen, harmless and docile." Zude rose to her feet, pacing again. "And consider the consequences of such research for future generations in the issue of Infancy Protocols. Suppose through the widest stretch of the imagination that we could determine which infants might 'carry' the violence center and which not. Then we impose on newborns a neurological requirement that vastly alters their lives—"

Rhoda interposed, "Like the transfusion of healthy blood for diseased blood, Magister? Like endocrine transplants? Like in-utero organ rehabilitation, gene substitution, lymph regeneration, all the techniques—"

"Major!" Zude snapped. "What the pluperfect hell do you think the biotech riots were about? About control of epidemics, yes, but far more than that! What kind of history are they filling you with at the Hong Kong Academy these days that you don't know about the cyborg disasters and the genetic engineering fiascos? You—"

Longleaf stood. She moved to Zude's side and placed her

hand on the Magister's arm. "Personal attack and associational slur."

Zude looked at her. "Right," she grunted. "Right. Delete. I wish it unsaid." Both she and Longleaf sat again.

Rhoda nodded. "Magister, on this matter my feet point with yours," she encouraged. "I understand the reasoning behind banning such research and behind the moratorium on cloning. I am in sympathy with the public's loss of confidence in biotechnology."

Zude raised an eyebrow.

"*But* we are speaking here of benefits to all humankind. If research were to be authorized and a violence center discovered, then we could make ethical use of our knowledge and take a giant step toward an advanced, nonviolent civilization, toward a reverence for life from the moment of our birth." She looked toward the cat figure by Zude's desk unit. "And if we rid ourselves of violence, Little Blue might even be populated again with animal beings."

Shaking her head, Zude contended, "Amah, you can't talk about the Protocols and reverence for life in the same breath. Reverence for life interferes as little as possible with another's freedom." She paused for several heartbeats, looking far down the familiar discursive path that now rolled out before them. Then she changed direction entirely. "You say you come with Magister Lin-ci Win's knowlege, even though she has not sent you. I'm fully aware of her support of Habitante Testing. Does she plan some strategy for convincing the Central Web?"

"I don't know the answer to that."

Longleaf touched Rhoda's sleeve. "First Behavior."

The Matrix Major blushed as she turned back to Zude. "Magister Win would, of course, want your support with the Central Web, though she realizes that's unlikely. Still, she hopes a new development might influence you." Rhoda picked up the

44

cotton pouch that Captain Edge had brought in and emptied onto the table two three-inch wooden shafts, each terminating in a delicate and sharply pointed crystal. "Have you ever seen these?"

Zude shook her head. She examined the crystals. "Are they tuned?"

"Precisely. But not charged. Captain Edge will tell you that they are monoclinic staurolytes with a wildcard vector that can operate as far away as twenty feet. They burn out hairs, vocal bands . . . and testicles."

Zude looked at her.

Rhoda picked up one of the shafts. "They're called 'ballbakers.' In a rash of recent incidents in Singapore, they have been used to castrate men. The woman in possession of these told us that, if the Amahrery continues to stall on the matter of neurological violence inhibitors, renegade women will do it themselves and in their own way. By castration."

Zude's fist hit the table. "Revenge!" she breathed. "Insane, mindless revenge!" She pushed her fingers through her hair, then stood abruptly. "Forgive me, Kanshoumates," she said, pulling in a deep breath, "but I have trouble understanding anyone who thinks that burning off a man's balls will make him docile."

Rhoda shot a glance at Longleaf, then turned back to Zude. "I would agree, Magister, but you will admit that the symbolism of the act carries with it a powerful message."

"I'll admit no such thing!" Zude shot back. She leaned on the table. "Such women don't want a nonviolent world, Major. They simply want to punish men. And to participate in the escalation of the violence . . . thus, I might add, damaging their own argument that men are the violent sex!"

"Whatever the case," Rhoda replied, "Magister Win believes the spreading use of these devices triggered the uprisings, at least in Kandy and Singapore."

Zude leaned toward Rhoda. "Lin-ci Win sent these crystals?"

Rhoda looked at Longleaf. "Insofar as she sent us at all, she sent them with us as evidence of the new extremes that citizens are moving toward. She is being pressured, Magister, to use her influence in hastening the Central Web to a ratification of the Testing and the Protocols . . . pressured by women from all over China and India. And by women from your own tri-satrapy."

Something with sharp corners stirred in Zude's stomach. "What women?" she asked steadily.

"Jezebel Stronglaces has brought together most of the sentiment here in your jurisdiction. She allies herself with many in the Africa-Europe-Mideast Tri-Satrapy as well."

Zude stiffened. "I knew Jezebel Stronglaces. At the Academy."

Both Amahs visibly refrained from making full eye contact with each other. They waited in silence.

"Amahs," Zude continued, "if Jezebel Stronglaces is still the woman she was then, she would abhor such violence as this."

"Clarification, Magister," said Longleaf promptly. "Jezebel Stronglaces has not been identified with the women distributing the ballbakers. The majority of women who pressure Magister Win are not associated with the crystals either. Most are opposed to violence in any form."

Zude suppressed a sardonic rejoinder. "I understand," she muttered, sifting and sorting the new information. When she refocused at last on her two guests, it was with deliberate purpose. "Kanshoumates," she said, "I have to end this encounter. You've fanned the fires of change tonight, and I formally thank you." She straightened and smiled briefly. "Do we need any closure?"

Matrix Major Densmore studied the Magister. "Only to thank you," she said, "for the surprise—and the gift—of the true-talk."

Zude nodded.

"And for the such-and-such," added the Jing-Cha. "I thank you too, Magister."

Together the three women stood.

Zude moved toward the exit wall. "Then goodnight," she said. "Captain Edge will see you to your quarters here in the Shrievalty. Consider yourselves my guests for as long as you need to stay." She touched the depaque control that revealed the hallway.

When the wall re-established itself behind the Australian women, Zude walked to the desk unit that held the taxidermed cat. She rested her hand on its taut curved neck and closed her eyes.

Long minutes later, she swung into action, calling up desktop, wall, and ceiling screens for the files she was seeking with her fingers. "Flora!"

"Ma'am, Magister?" Vigilante Flora Arguelles's voice filled the room.

"Get me Magister Lutu on flatscreen. Tell her I must hear from her within three hours or I'll be in Crete by low rocket before sunset tomorrow." Zude's voice lost its sharp edges. "I also need Kayita and Ria. At home. They're waiting up for me. Set it up on holofone if you can."

When Flora beeped off, Zude threw one last toggle.

"Here, Magister," said the voice of Captain Edge.

Zude worked smoothly with her adjutant, conducting conferences with her three Vice-Magisters and then reaching two old friends in simul-call at Kanshou field posts in Shenyang and Paris, each of whom had been a legal advisor to her in the past. She set them to the task of polling every member of the Central Web as to whether or not Habitante Testing or the Anti-Violence

47

Protocols might reach active agenda status. "Explore any morally defensible technicality," she told them, "that could stop the Web from initiating this legislation."

She left off her study of the Central Web's roster of members to take Flora's relay of the message from Magister Flossie Yotoma Lutu. Magister Lutu would be free to talk early the next morning, L.A. time, by unmonitored priority holochannel. She would call Magister Adverb then. Under no condition was Zude to come to Crete since tonight Yotoma herself was being gerted to Rome.

Zude was in conversation with Aztlán's best crystal expert when Flora announced, "I've got your folks on comline three." Zude cut short the lecture on orgone accumulators. She pressed a strip under her desk and filled her office with the holoscreen image of an old woman's face—a highly agitated old woman. Behind the face—and trying to calm it—was a younger woman who struggled at the same time to control a small black-haired girl eager to get into the holopicture.

"Again, again," the old woman moaned loudly, "again you are not coming!"

"Zudie!" the child cried, wiggling with joy. When the young woman whispered in her ear, the little girl settled, still intent upon Zude's holo-image. The old woman continued moaning.

Zude waved a sound-damp into effect and widened the hololens to encompass her chaotic desk. She addressed the old woman. "Kayita," she soothed, trying to be heard over the sounds of distress, "Kayita—"

"Zella, you are wholly without honor, worth nothing to woman or child. Worth nothing to a man. Worth nothing. Why do you not come?"

Zude overrode the tirade. "Kayita, look at my desk, look at my office. Look at all the work!" She pointed to the disarray of cups, chairs, magnopads, papers, full screens, blinking lights.

"Hey," she said, snagging the image of Bosca out of the air, "there's a woman I'd like for you to meet, from Old Mexico—"

The old woman's eyes lit up. "Oaxaca? She is from Oaxaca?"

"Near there, at least. I'm sure she could tell us about Oaxaca. Why don't I bring her for a visit tomorrow?"

"Tomorrow? 'Tomorrow' you said yesterday. You said, 'Tomorrow I will sleep at your house.' It is tomorrow. And you sleep in your office. Again."

The younger woman pushed in beside Kayita, holding her, stroking her hair, talking both to her and Zude. "Zude, it's fine," she said.

"Fine?" burst in Kayita. "What is fine? Fine that she is not coming? We are her family. Like a mother I am to her!" she railed. "Zella, you come home tonight. Your bed is ready."

Zude interrupted. "I know, Kayita, I know." She addressed Ria. "I see generations one and three and half of number four. Where's the other half of four?"

"Enrique? He's sleeping tight."

"And number two? Eva?"

"She's at a class. And we'll all be here tomorrow. Bring your friend." Ria grabbed Regina to stop her plunge into a hololens.

"Zudie!" bellowed the child.

"Reggie," Zude beamed, "I promise, we'll go flying when I come—"

Regina's face glowed brighter. "Tomorrow! We'll fly! You and me and your friend!"

Zude swallowed abruptly. "Well, not that friend, preshi. But I'll fly with you soon."

Regina was soothed.

Kayita had lapsed into a grim silence. She peered at Zude. "You work too much," she rasped.

Both Zude and Ria laughed.

49

Kayita grumbled, moving out of holorange. "Big cocoroca. She says she is not coming tonight. She is not coming tonight. When God says no, the saints are helpless." She disappeared.

Zude shook her head. "I can't make it okay with her."

"She'll be fine," Ria promised, "bright as the sun tomorrow, knowing you're coming."

"And by then I'll be brighter, too, Ria."

Ria, her arms full, kissed the air in Zude's direction. Regina sputtered her affection with a loud lip flutter. Magister Adverb blew a gallant goodbye kiss toward them both.

Zude's longest and most wide-ranging strategizing session was conducted by intra-tri-satrapy conference with three trusted Vigilantes and friends: Captain Edge; Brigadier Vigilante Robin Echevarría, in charge of the tri-satrapy's bailiwick management and stationed in Buenos Aires; and Sky Commander Susana Femmesole whose staff in Old Albuquerque handled one of the tri-satrapy's three information centers. After Edge had played the flatcube of the just-completed meeting with Amahs Densmore and Longleaf for the advisors, Zude drew responses from each of them, especially in regard to the possible threat of the ballbakers.

Within an hour, the group had evolved a plan of action for data-gathering throughout the tri-satrapy. It called for the activation of tempsquads, polling groups which operated in highly tuned personal contact circumstances. These groups would spot-interview carefully selected cross-sections of the population to determine the "temperature" of the citizenry on the question of Habitante Testing and the Anti-Violence Protocols. When Echavarría and Femmesole signed off, Zude called up from her personal files the names of free citizens and officers in the other two tri-satrapies who could shake loose the results of similar polls outside Nueva Tierra. She copied their preliminary assessments of the inquiry and handed the magnopad over to Edge.

When Edge's departing footsteps had died, Zude took up her vigil again by the depaqued wall overlooking Los Angeles. Her thoughts were no longer of violent skirmishes within the tri-satrapy or of crystal ballbakers, not even of Kayita or her chosen children. Instead, Magister Adverb summoned the memory of an earlier world and a younger heart. She traced in her mind the curious turns of Fate that had crossed her path with that of Jezebel Stronglaces. Many years ago, they had come together and then separated—painfully and irrevocably.

3
MEETING
[2041-2069 C.E.]

> Said Caterpillar to Maria, "How do you manage with only
> two legs? Isn't it tiring, bouncing back and forth like that?"
> "Yes," answered Maria, "but alas, it is my human condition."
> *Question*: What does this mean? *Response*: I both abhor violence and
> practice it daily, for I physically restrain the freedom of those who
> would harm others. I thus live with this human contradiction,
> consoling myself with the reminder of the Precepts of the
> Kanshoubu: that as Kanshou I serve a Greater Good by protecting
> others with my own violent acts; that as Kanshou I at least practice
> the Principle of Least Necessary Restraint in the violence that I do
> commit; and that if my Kanshoumates and I do our jobs well, we
> may ultimately bring about a nonviolent world, a world in which
> Kanshou will not be necessary.
> —*The Labrys Manual*

Jezebel Stronglaces was born Jezebel ("Bella") Engracia Dolalicia
in 2041 C.E., near the eastern shores of Lake Michigan. The bearing mother for the ovarian transplant was Alicia Tuatha Sands,
one of the revered far-seers of the Spooner Ensconcement called
Lakemir. The nucleus donor was Ola Adelia Nariño of Cozumel,
whose duties as a Vigilante Sea-Shrieve kept her from full partic-
ipation in the affairs of that community.

Though a female separatist society, the Lakemir Spooners did
not embrace the rigid strictures of Mother Right colonies who
saw men as dangerous and to be protected against. The Spooners
maintained commercial relations with surrounding towns and
regularly elected their representative to the demesne web. As Bella
would learn, the Lakemir women did not think of men at all.
Within the meadows and forests of their ensconcement, men

53

simply did not exist.

With Lakemir's other villagedaughters, Bella Dolalicia worked the ensconcement's orchards and began an early political education in the company of the older women responsible for governance. Her deep commitment to the female culture surrounding her helped her through the early loss of both her mothers and the frequent mild-to-severe seizures which began when she was four and continued until she was thirteen—at which time they disappeared altogether. She lived with her mothers' comadres until, at thirteen, she became Jezebel Dolalicia, an independent minor.

In all her endeavors, Jezebel sought a mental and spiritual discipline that would enable her to control not only her voracious mind but the unorthodox psychic gifts that frequently emerged without her bidding. Her seeking led her to the Yucatan, where she mastered languages and transmogrifier manufacture and where she apprenticed to a Mayan herbalist. When the daughter that she and her lover, Myrtha, had so carefully planned for died shortly after Jez gave birth to her, Jezebel dedicated herself for two years to the austere practices of a Tsangpo convent. She subsequently took up the formal study of physics in Beijing, where she also worked to make transmog technology available to rural areas. In 2068 C.E., Jezebel Dolalicia sought the discipline of Hong Kong's Kanshou Cadet Academy, preparatory to a peacekeeping career as an Amah of the Asia-China-Insula Tri-Satrapy.

———————◆———————

Though the child of a heterosexual union, Zella Terremoto Adverb never learned her father's identity. She was born in midsummer of 2042 C.E., in Barranquilla, Colombia, to Sylvia Isabel Romero and was raised with her brother's children in Barrio Santín of that city.

Even before she started to blockschool, she began to learn everything she could about Vigilantes, Amahs, and Femmedarmes and
what it meant to follow the Kanshou Code. When she was eight, she
watched two Vigilantes subdue a crowd of drunken rowdies with
nothing but their persuasive voices and the judicious use of their
batons. "Principle of Least Necessary Restraint," she reminded herself, as if the Shrieves themselves had left their voices inside her.

Endowed with a finely-tuned sense of justice, enthralled by
the women who in her eyes were the keepers of justice, and utterly
convinced that she would someday be one of those women, Zella
Terremoto Adverb consciously molded her young life. By the time
she was fourteen, she had organized broad-based grassroots resistance to the interference of outside commercial interests in
Colombia's demesne affairs and had turned down an appointment
as teen representative to the newly forming Barranquilla Demesne
Legislative Web. That same year, she left home and headed north
for the Reclaimed Territory of Aztlán, where she worked in bailiwicks and pursued her studies in Kitchen Table tribunals. It was
there that she began her lifelong efforts to change bailiwicks from
explosive ghettos into places where habitantes' survival, security,
and social needs were met.

Using her carefully saved credits, Zude travelled the planet by
rocket, hovercraft, ship, and spoon to visit bailiwicks all over
Little Blue. In 2067 C.E., along with 800 other women who had
reached the age of twenty-five or older, she entered the Kanshou
Cadet Academy in Hong Kong, intent upon making its training
her second nature.

———◆———

When, on that cloud-covered midwinter Hong Kong day,
Third-Form Amah Cadet Zella Terremoto Adverb laid her dark
brown eyes on the tilted head and lean body of the oldest of the

55

entering chelas, Fourth-Form Cadet Jezebel Dolalicia, some sleeping animal awoke and uncoiled just below her navel. When on that
same day, Amah Cadet Dolalicia turned from the transmog with
her cup of tea and saw outlined against the grey face of Victoria
Peak the transfixed form of Cadet Adverb, she straightened her
head and heard the whisper of her Source Self, *"She's the one."*

Amah cadets, including chelas, had three nights monthly
when they could use their credits away from the Amah Academy,
free at last of the rows of cots in the dossrooms. During the nearly
two years that Jez was at the academy, she and Zude spent those
nights together in one or another of the city's rooming houses or
under the stars on the banks of the Xi Jiang's waters. They flew
together over placid lakes and turbulent seas, touching Celebes
mountaintops and the reefs of the old Philippines. They danced
in Taipei's botanical gardens and hung their drenched uniforms
on the struts of Jakarta's drawbridges. Wherever they placed their
bodies into the spoon of afterlove sleep, they trusted willow and
plum tree, orchid and hibiscus to hold the memory inviolable.

As their passion grew into legend, they endured the day-by-
day rigors of the Amahrery's training. They molded their bodies
and minds into weapons of authority and order—Jez with hesitation then determination, Zude from the outset with exhilaration
and keen satisfaction. They vied with each other and, together,
against others; they ran, climbed, swam, flew, shot, slashed,
crawled, dived, and leapt; they calculated, measured, memorized,
analyzed, conjugated, recited, formulated, discussed, negotiated,
strategized, and argued. And, like all Amah cadets, they celebrated
at every opportunity.

The rational, practical Zude despaired over her lover's active
imagination, even once going so far as to insist to Jezebel that unicorns were not real. Jez succeeded in convincing her that unicorns
might, with the proper open-heartedness, become real, and to

that end she presented Zude with a custom-cast pair of silver earrings, each in the form of a rampant unicorn, mane-flared and horn held high. They always had pride of place among the tasteful piercings that decorated Zude's ears.

———————◆———————

One idyllic evening by the South China Sea, Zude stood in the academy's weaponsyard after target-and-evasion drills. Sweating from her exertion, she pushed a cleaning rod through her dartsleeve and watched the falling sun drench the top of the hardwood fencing. All along the fencetop were mounted the warrior weapons of the thousand-armed Durga, Invincible Hindu Warrior Goddess—sword, ax, kukri, arrow, javelin, katar, spear, trident, noose, discus, mesh, and pike. Just to her left and topping the archway that led to the Contemplation Garden beyond blazed the Sumerian Eye Goddess, flanked by statues of man-eating Valkyries whose raven feathers merged into the bodies of mares. The idiography across the arch came from the early women of Hong Kong, themselves saviors of their nation's culture. In Zude's rough translation it said, "Humanity can do better, and women will lead the way."

Zude squinted one eye and peered down her dartsleeve with the other. "And what a polyglot we are," she mused aloud. "Study and philosophize in English, shop and do laundry in Mandarin, make love and quarrel in Spanish." She wiped her brow, automatically checking her earlobes for her unicorns.

Jezebel was leaning against the upper gatepost, one of her faraway looks immobilizing her face. If she hadn't just observed her lover laying in rank after rank of dead-center blowdarts, each one with an exclamation of triumph, Zude would have sworn that Jez was crying.

"Hail, Intrepid Markswoman!" she called.

Jez turned. She *was* crying. Zude gathered her sweat tunic, her darts, their quiver, her cleaning rods, and the sleeve. She joined her lover, sitting on the bench just below her. She reached up and took Jez's hand. They were silent for half a minute.

"Good match this morning," Zude said casually. "With Ciab."

Jez looked askance at her lover. "How did you know?"

"How . . . ? I didn't," Zude confessed. "I was just commenting."

"It was awful." Tears welled up again in Jez's eyes. "Zudie, I came close to hurting her. Really hurting her, I mean." She wiped her face with her sleeve.

Zude rested against the bench's back. "But you *didn't*—"

"I don't mean physically," Jez insisted. "I mean I could have stripped her mind, levelled her intention!" She struck the fence pillar. "I wasn't in control, I almost . . . ." She pushed off from the post and paced. "What if that had been some man I was trying to restrain? I managed not to hurt Ciab, but how do I know I wouldn't use my . . . my weapons if I were restraining a *man*? If I were an Amah?"

As always, Zude avoided any direct discussion of Jezebel's psychic powers. "Bella-Belle," she said softly, "you wouldn't hurt an offender, not beyond Least Necessary—"

"You don't know that!"

"Look, you didn't hurt Ciab. All of us—"

"She's a woman!"

Zude blinked. "Even if she'd been a man—"

"If she'd been a man, I might have wiped him out for sure! I could have done him irreparable harm! Oh Zudie," she slumped onto the bench, "that's exactly the trouble, don't you see? Ciab's a woman, a *temporary harmer*. That's why I didn't hurt her. Any violence in a woman is *conditioned* violence, and the deepest part of me knew that. A woman can be helped because she's not violent by nature. It's *men* who've got violence in their genes!"

"Jezebel, that's—"

"I know, I know! '*Any* offender is only a temporary harmer,' says the holy Kanshou Code. But if I don't believe that, how can I be a Kanshou? And I *don't* believe it about men, Zudie. Men are totally at the mercy of their biology! Look at wars and crime. Look at who is in the bailiwicks. It's *men!*"

Zude's lips tightened. She focused on the toe of her boot.

Jezebel waved her dartsleeve. "They can't help it," she shrugged. "It's hard-wired into them. At rock bottom they love cruelty and dominance." Jez paused, her eyes like cold stone. "They're killers," she said slowly. "Maybe we ought to just drain the testosterone out of them the minute they hit puberty!"

"Jez!"

"Why not, Zudie?" Jez was calm now. She pulled the sweat-band from her head.

"Because we don't know that's true, Jezebel," Zude rose and paced. "Because there's not a shred of scientific evidence to support that crazy idea, because—"

"Then let's find it, Zude. Let's find that scientific evidence!" Jez catapulted off the bench and stood toe-to-toe with her lover. "Let's do some hormone control on the men in the bailiwicks, on the killers and the rapists and the abusers, like they used to do on alpha males in the baboon colonies. Let's find that little spot in the male anatomy that secretes the testosterone and—"

"You won't find it, Jez! You won't find anything in the male anatomy any different from—"

"We'll find it, Zude," Jez shouted, "and when we do, we can stamp it out in all men!"

"Jez!" Zude's voice topped her lover's.

The volume of the confrontation brought two concerned

cadets to the edge of the weaponsyard. When they identified the scene and its familiar participants, they moved on, shaking their heads and smiling.

Zude was incredulous. "What an act of violence, Jezebel! You want to invade the very identity of a human being and force him into being like you, maybe even making a zombie of him! Don't talk to me about men's history of cruelty and violence! Look to yourself, Jezebel!"

"Wrong! It would be violence maybe, yes!" Her voice softened. "But only once, only for right now, until the chain of violence is broken! Zudie, it may be the only way. We're women, and we'd do it with love and with full understanding of what we're doing! We'd be forcing men to give up their violence only until we get the initial cause eradicated. After that, social conditioning could take care of it all. It would be worth it, Zudie! One act of violence that ends violence forevermore!"

"Never, Jez, never." Zude stepped away from her lover. She ran a hand through her hair. "The whole idea is wrong from the start, wrong all along the way."

"Violence for a Greater Good, Zude," Jez said quietly. "Like the Kanshou are violent when they restrain an offender. Violence for a Greater Good."

Zude turned. "Touché."

Jez sank to the bench again. "I feel better."

Zude let her breath settle. "That's good," she whispered, dropping to the bench beside her lover. She pulled out a cigarillo, reconsidered, then folded it back into her pocket. They sat, again in silence. "We'll never agree on that one, Bella-Belle," Zude said.

"I guess not." A moment later, Jez added, "Zude, did you wonder why Ciab forfeited when she had me pinned?" Before Zude could reply, she went on. "I was so scared because I'd realized I could hurt her that I just surrendered to her. Gave up my power. I mentally held out my arms to her."

"And she rushed into them." Zude shifted and stretched.

"She got off me. Same difference." Jez gave a wide pinch or two with her thumb and forefinger to Zude's trapezius.

Zude closed her eyes, dutifully practicing the unfamiliar art of receiving. After a moment, she managed to observe, "To make that work, you risk losing your whole identity. Do you know how dangerous that is?"

"For you . . . yes. But does it occur to you that identity remains, even in surrender?" Jez moved both her hands in deep strong movements on Zude's neck. "Anyway," she added before Zude could reply, "that's not why you couldn't do it."

"No?"

"No. You're just too *scared* to give over your power." Jez gave Zude's muscles a parting squeeze and began to gather her gear.

Zude was unruffled. "Bullseye," she said. "I'm not just scared. I'm smart. Power's not meant to be given over. It's meant to be used." She touched Jez's hair at the wet temple. "And you know that too, my love. I've seen you do it. Even when you're empowering someone else, you still hold back a wild card, in case she blows it and you have to rescue her."

Jez's lips tightened, and she lowered her gaze. When she looked at Zude again, her eyes were sad, but she smiled. "Bullseye," she said.

Zude gave her head a short jerk of satisfaction. Still, something remained unsaid. Carefully, she took a deep breath, put her hands around her knee, and leaned back in a balance. "So how can you hope to be a Kanshou, Bella-Belle, if you want to give away all your power? You're a cadet in one of the three great Kanshou Academies of the world. You've signed on for a four- or five-year lesson in how to win, how to disarm, how to overpower a violent offender." She sat up straight and searched her lover's face. "What are you doing here, Jezebel?"

Jez's eyes roamed the weapons along the fencetop. "I've been asking myself that very question, Zudie," she whispered. She stood up, kissed her stunned lover firmly on the lips, and wound her way down the path.

Zude's eyes followed her to the turn. Then she lit the cigarillo and inhaled its poison.

◆

Cadet Jezebel Dolalicia did not share with her lover the escalation within herself of knowledge that came unbidden to her, of unorthodox skills that she acquired effortlessly. She didn't talk, for instance, about a particular encounter with Fourth-Form Amah Cadet Sarawak Ardis, The Banjar.

Ardis claimed a birthplace dead center on the equator in the high mountains of Borneo and an early education on the rubber plantations where her mothers flattened bulky latex slabs into thin sheets for export to Shanghai. She boasted with a wide grin that her prognathous jaw was built for devouring white women and offered to prove that to Jezebel early in their acquaintance. Jezebel declined the offer to be devoured, claiming that her brown blood disqualified her. She and Ardis nevertheless sustained a flirtatious comaraderie and commiserated frequently over sore feet on parade weekends.

Then, one day, Jez was on the dentist's couch enduring the irritating but painless dislodging of a deeply impacted wisdom tooth. The sonar waves were playing over her cheekbones and tantalizing the edge of her sinuses. She felt the tooth break free. Then, just as Captain Yuan lifted the offending molar out of the small incision she had made, Jez was suddenly blasted in her belly with a wave of panic and a sense of imminent danger. When she began shaking involuntarily, the concerned Captain Yuan consigned her to an observed recovery room. There, Jez focused on the terror and found to her astonishment that she was in clear mental communication with Ardis The Banjar, three miles away.

"Jezebel!" The voice was ragged. "Is that you?"

Jez formulated a silent question, "Where are you?"

"For the Great Goddess's sake, I'm at the top of the practice 'scraper on a construction girder. Looking at Food Street thirty stories down. I'm the last one up here, and I'll be here until I faint."

"You won't faint, Ardis. When you fly you don't . . ." Jez caught herself. "I forgot. You don't fly."

"Right. I'm a lowly Foot-Shrieve cadet."

Jez felt the stiffness of a tall figure clinging to upright steel. She tried to send warmth, ease. And practicality. "Is the cable ladder there?" she asked.

Ardis's grunt became an affirmative.

"Is it secure?"

A long pause, then, "Everybody else went down it."

"Reach for it, Ardis."

Even the mindstretch seemed to come between gritted teeth. "Jez, there's too much nothing between me and the ground. I can't move."

Jez felt the swirlings in Ardis's head. "You don't have to move, Ardis. Just breathe. Breathe hard. Now tell me about rice fields and rubber plants. Tell me about Borneo."

"Wish to Oshun I was in Borneo—" The mindstretch was a whisper.

"The swamp and the mangroves, Ardis. Tell me about the thickets of mangroves."

Ardis calmed. Jez began seeing images of deep jungles and intertwined mangrove vines. She also felt the bursts of Ardis's self-condemnation for her cowardice, for her foolhardiness at thinking she could pass this test, for her attempts to hide her fear of heights. "I thought I had it licked," she panted. "Lucked out on the preliminary exams. Had them fooled."

"Mangroves, Ardis. Jungles. Rivers."

"Rivers. Let's swim the Barito Fork." Ardis eased again. Jez sent swirls of strong air, winds to lean upon, images of rolling waters to buoy up Ardis's tense body. And Ardis relaxed enough to reach for the ladder and place her foot on it. She let Jez talk her down the wiggling rungs, over slick girders to the rough walls, over rough walls to the crowded street below. Down to relief and gratitude. Down to safety and pride.

Abruptly, Jez lost the contact altogether. She sat upright on the cot in the bare recovery room, dumbfounded by what had taken place. She left the dental office in a daze.

Neither she nor Ardis acknowledged the incident in their daily comings and goings. But Jez received a small package two days later by express gert from Borneo. There was no card, but inside lay a reddish brown conical berry. It held, she discovered, a mangrove seed.

Some months later, Jez and Zude were both off-duty but still in uniform as they stepped out the door of Maud's Again and rounded the corner to the rolling walkway. The evening air vacillated between swelter and unseasonable cooling. It was cool again now as Zude hesitated at the on-step. Jez raised her hand to take Zude's elbow.

"I'm fine," Zude announced to the world. "One gin swirl and you treat me like an invalid!" She leapt immediately to the middle corridor and, to prove her steadiness, caught Jez's hand as she joined her. They angled smoothly onto the fast strip, Zude balancing her arm lightly on the hand bar and speaking loudly against the wind.

"Love, those Irish girls were wonderful," she said, shifting the pack that sheltered her fiddle case. "I never saw such bow work— or such clogging!" She pulled Jez closer to her. "Did you bribe them to ask me to play with them afterwards? Tell true, now. Did you?" Abruptly, she raised a finger and a thumb in half-womb response to three chelas approaching on the opposing roller lane who were sending them the same salute.

"Negative," Jez answered, offering the chelas her own belated acknowledgement. "I asked them if they'd be winding down after their performance, and if so, could they use another fiddle. They said, 'Of course, of course.'" She gave Zude a squeeze. "Particularly when I explained that I was treating you to a wish day." Jez patted the fiddle case. "Guarna seemed in good shape, too. So you both loved it?"

"A perfect ending to a perfect day, Bella-Belle." Zude swayed a little on the fast-moving walkway as she planted a kiss on Jez's cheek.

"Far from ended," Jez corrected her, "unless you're too schnockered to enjoy some more." She kept her arm on the rail behind Zude, steadying her by leaning on her.

"Never!" Zude proclaimed. "Where are we headed, my jewel? Toward what new adventure do we speed?"

Jez sighted an upcoming liftlane. "Toward a new and special den of iniquity over by the shipyards," she answered, "called the Fools Rush Inn. Are you compos mentis enough to swing?" When Zude began an outraged response, Jez sprang onto the liftlane. "Then come on!"

Zude vaulted onto the stepped track after Jez, barely clearing the guard rail. They rose up and over the low buildings toward the dark sky. With a whine of acceleration, massive hidden pumps whisked them higher, story after story, along the cold windowless wall of Hong Kong's Education Administration Center. A rising wind accompanied their ascent.

They waited atop the building while swinging cables passed them at intervals of fifty feet. Jez stopped their passing in order to help Zude secure her grasp of one of the cableclasps. When she tugged on the cable, the swings resumed their flight over the twinkling city below them. One loud yahoo of exultation as Zude lifted her feet, then she sailed off into the blackness. Jez followed her on the next cable, and together they swung laughing and bellowing over Hong Kong toward the sea.

The Fools Rush Inn mimicked in every detectable detail a nineteenth century hotel of the Old American West. In its clamorous saloon, two lighthearted Amah cadets sang along with the chorus lines, caught gaudy garters, and carried frequent beers to the inexhaustible piano player. When at last the saloon's patrons dispersed, Jez and Zude climbed the red carpeted stairs to the privacy of their cool, low-lit room, where the embroidered sheets of the four-poster bed were turned back in welcome.

"Mother's Blessings!" Zude exclaimed. She was charmed: by the chiffonier, the dark wood walls devouring the light of oil lamps; by the tall bulky wardrobe and the flowered thunderjug under the bed. She dropped her pack and turned to Jez.

Jez stood without moving, her bright eyes holding Zude in a sheath of patent desire. Zude's own eyes fastened upon Jez's neck, the small birthmark just below the left earlobe. It pulsed in a customary assurance of Jez's carnal excitement. Zude blinked slowly, her lips halting just short of a smile.

Then the space between them collapsed, lost in a burst of emancipated ardor and the engagement of two wills, each pushing, each pulling, in the arousing tilt for primacy—so familiar yet ever so unpredictable. Each was peak and each was valley, each was crest and trough, each the matter of the universe and each its dynamo.

Suddenly, and by tacit mutual consent, they broke apart.

With eyes locked, they breathed their fire and restrained laughter while they removed dangling earrings—first Jez her laminated feathers, then Zude her silver unicorns, placing them ceremoniously, and by touch only, on the marble top of the washstand. Their gaze still unbroken, they ritually flung off the breeches, buskins, and tabards of the Amahrery and parted the thin arm-and-torso seams of their rhyndon bodystockings. They stood then, shining bodies bathed in yellow lamplight, a tableau of classical athletes poised in expectation of some decisive moment.

Jez moved first. She feinted to the left then swept up and under Zude's credulous response to embrace and immobilize that astonished body. Zude's howl acknowledged the affront of being bettered. She closed her eyes, let her lover's tongue discover her own, and sank with undisguised anticipation down to the meager resiliance of the room's big rag rug.

She was a lake in a high meadow, welcoming the steady tapping of a spring rain upon her surfaces, the gentle expansion of her depths with the filling of her edges. Near her was a second lake, also swelling to the visit of the rain, to its tiny insistent pressures and its covert bid to annex every bank.

She leaned toward lower land where her borders were disappearing, urging her fullnesses in that direction. A companion outpouring from the other lake joined her on the friendly mountainside, merging their abundances without hastening their waters. They were a stream a-borning, bound to roll together toward distant valleys, to touch newborn embankments, to tease clumps of earth from rocks and roots for the seasoning of their progress. But the angle of their descent would be modest, and their journey would be long and slow.

Jez's face above her was curtained by long hair, her eyes a sparkling green where the lamplight crept through. She was watching Zude's face as she made love to her.

A sweet ambition swept through Zude. She raised her head and drew Jez's mouth toward her lips. Her kiss asked for a change in priorities. "Jez," she whispered, "I want to make love to *you*. Now."

"Zude—!"

"It's my wish day, remember? Anything I want, you said." Zude drew them both to a sitting posture, hushing Jez's protest with a finger to her lips. "'Anything,' you said." She knelt and urged her lover onto the bed, then covered the outspread body with her own. "This is what I want."

"Zude, I—!"

"Sh-h-h!" Zude's lips formed soundless words by Jez's ear. "We'll do this one together," they assured her. The body under Zude eased, and she whispered carefully, "Open to me, Jezebel."

Jez lay long and golden in the lampglow, invitation stretching upward from her every highlight and shadow. Zude began by touching her only with her breath, then with tongue and fingertips, until the stream began again its slow expanding movement down the sloping meadow. When at last she set her hand at its proper angle between the eager thighs and gave her fingers their appropriate berth, Jez gasped, and the stream leapt forward in a sudden drop to terrain more rugged and steep. It charged sharply downward now, its broad white waters alert with purpose.

Zude moved her fingers in rhythmic caresses that never varied in tension, speed, or angle. She could move this way forever, she knew, in this particular fashion of loving Jezebel's body. And Jez could stay forever trembling on this edge before the ecstasy.

From far away, Zude heard the roar that summoned them both: the voice of the approaching waterfall. She knew precisely the touch that would sweep them inescapably to its brink and out over its roaring waters. Carefully, she reached with her tongue for the mound of flesh that was both the core of Jezebel's rising desire and her deliverance from it. At her touch, a sharp cry burst from Jez's throat and mounted in a sustained crescendo. The rising of her own climax matched Jez's cry. She kept the movement of her fingers steady even as her tongue stroked the mound itself.

They plunged headlong toward the waterfall, colonizing rain and rivulet, engulfing any log or boulder that challenged their exuberance. In the instant that Jez's body testified that it could no longer resist its explosion, Zude abruptly halted all motion and resolutely clasped with her full hand the pinnacle of Jez's exultation, catapulting at the same time her own excitement to its zenith. Together, they hung suspended over raging torrents of cascading waters, scorning for ageless moments the plunge into drenching release.

Then, on wave after wave of wonder, they rode down together toward the sea.

Almost an hour later, the night was becoming a swelter again. Jezebel sat in a rocker by the white-curtained window, her feet perched on a wooden stool. She swirled the remains of a stout brandy around in her glass. Zude lay on the bed, her arms behind her head, her sleep shirt clinging wetly to her skin. She watched the changing contours of her lover's face.

"I'm still holding you, Jezebel," she said in a low voice.

"You always hold me, Zudie. Always," Jez smiled.

"I do," Zude agreed. "I do." She wiped her face on the bedclothes.

"Here," Jez said, turning to the window. Gently, she summoned a cool breeze from the offshore waters. It came sweeping into the room to lift her own loose sleep tunic with short flaps and ripples.

"Love, how do you do that?" Zude whispered.

"Sh-h-h," Jez whispered back. She closed her eyes. The breeze billowed into a mild but persistent gale, reaching out toward

Zude's damp body. It lifted the folds of cotton from her skin and suspended them in a fluttering, balmy surcease of her discomfort.

Zude watched, hardly daring to breathe. The billows died down, depositing on her torso the dry folds of her thin cotton shirt. Zude shot a glance at her lover, then deliberately flipped onto her stomach, daring with her sweaty back an encore of the performance.

Jez smiled, her eyes still closed. Her lips puckered only slightly, and the breeze obligingly wafted forward once more, lifting Zude's shirt from her back and dropping its cool dryness over her body again.

Zude lay still except for the tapping of her fingers on the bedclothes. Her voice was muffled. "Impossible," it said. Then she pushed up to her elbow and turned to her lover. "I never know what to say when you do something like that, Bella-Belle."

Jez finished off her brandy. "A little 'thank you' will do fine," she replied.

"Of course," Zude whispered. "I thank you."

"We both have our secrets, Zudie," she said.

Zude nodded. "We do." She shifted to a sitting position against a long bolster and a pillow at the head of the bed. Seconds later she remarked, "It should be dawn."

"In another hour," Jez answered. "Fifty-six minutes, to be exact," she added lightly.

Zude didn't question her statement. "Time goes slowly when you're having fun," she observed.

Jez nodded, rocking contentedly.

Zude retrieved her own near-empty brandy glass from the bedside table. She downed its contents and sat looking at Jez for a moment. Then she set the glass back on the table. "I have a secret to share too, Jezebel," she said. When Jez cocked her head, Zude continued. "Is it still my wish day?"

"It is," Jez assured her. Then she grinned. "Until dawn."

"You'd give me a massage?"

The rocking slowed. "Zude, I asked if you wanted—"

"No, no, love," Zude assured her, "I'm not talking sexual." She paused. "I'm just inquiring . . . . So, you'd give me a massage?"

"Zude, that's a crazy question—"

"Bear with me," Zude said. "If I wanted you to really pound my muscles, go in deep, relieve some tough tensions . . . I figure you'd do that for me . . . ?"

Jez stopped rocking. "What are you getting at?"

"There's something in my pack," Zude gestured. "There, strapped to Guarna."

Jez extricated the violin case from Zude's pack and liberated from it a short thick stick protected by sharp-scented flannel. Zude's nod urged her to unwrap it. Jez unfolded the rounds of lightly oiled cloth, and into her lap rolled a finely-wrought handle of carefully tooled black leather. Extending from one end of it were a dozen or more flat strands, each also of leather and about eighteen inches in length. They were wrapped around the handle. Jez picked it up and examined it. Then she flushed and snapped her head toward Zude. Her eyes were ablaze.

Zude was off the bed in an instant, forestalling any words from Jez. "A beauty, isn't it?" she enthused. "A museum item, in fact." She knelt on one knee beside Jezebel. "Feel it, Jez! That kind of work was rare even a hundred years ago—"

"I don't want to feel it, Zude." Jez sat like a statue, holding the object, looking steadily at her lover.

"Wait, love, wait. I know what you're thinking—"

"Oh?" Jez's voice was without emotion. "Then help me, Zude. I'm not quite sure why I'm sitting here holding a . . . a whip. And I'm not sure what I'm supposed to be thinking. Perhaps that this is an instrument of punishment? Originally invented, they say, for the control and abuse of animals? Made, in fact, of the skin of animals, Zude, yes? And later adapted, if I'm not mistaken, for the control and abuse of humans . . . of slaves, right? Is that what I'm thinking?"

Zude let a silence lengthen. "Mockery doesn't become you, Jez." She sank onto the wooden stool by Jez's chair.

"You want me to whip you. Is that it?"

"You make it sound like an indecency."

"That's what it is."

Zude's arms were on her knees. "I've clearly miscalculated. I'd thought we'd reached a special place tonight." She leaned toward her lover. "Jez, in all our days together, this is the first time I've broached this with you. It's something I've wanted for a long time."

Jez's eyes became stone. Zude felt the heat drain from the room. She shivered in spite of herself.

"I'm sure you have other friends who would oblige you in this . . . desire."

"Lots of them," Zude agreed lightly. "But you are my beloved. And I've wanted this intimacy to be between us."

Jez held out the whip. "To me, this means violence and suffering and humiliation and degradation. To you, it means something different; it means making a travesty of those things, just so you can get bigger and better sexual kicks." She threw the whip into Zude's arms. "Go find your friends, Zude. But don't bring their obscenity into my reality, especially not into our lovemaking."

"You're neck-deep in a swamp of ignorance," Zude sighed. She stood and tossed the whip onto the stool. She held out her arms. "How can I talk to you about this? How can I get you to listen to me?" When the stiff figure in the rocker did not respond, Zude folded her arms across her chest. "How courageous are you, Jezebel?"

Jez's eyebrows raised. She looked askance at her lover.

"I dare you to test your courage," Zude's words gathered volume. "I dare you to go to a party with me next Saturday, a party where—"

"Where I can watch depraved women play sex games with each other in public?" Jez sat up straight, and her eyes were alive again as she overrode Zude's immediate protest. "I can't believe you're saying this to me! Here I am telling you that you've just breached any respect we've had for each other, and you want me to come to an orgy and see more of . . . of *this?*" She picked up the whip and waved it. "Zude, the parody of pain is unconscionable, particularly the public parody of it! Pain is *not* erotic!"

"And who are you to say what another woman feels?" Zude shot back. "Pain *may* be erotic for her!"

They glared at each other across the tiny room. It was Zude who broke the silence, turning to lean on the tall bed poster. "Jezebel, you could do with a little less heavy judgment on other people's lives," she said tiredly.

Jez slumped back into the chair. "Begging your most illustrious pardon, Cadet Lieutenant Adverb," she said wryly, "it's not just a few 'other people'! The mindset of the whole planet suffers from those master-slave set-ups, those dominance games. That behavior affects us all!"

Zude threw up her hands. "Jez, Jez," she cried, kneeling again by the rocking chair. "Bella-Belle—"

Jez jerked the whip down to her lap in a hard clenching of her hands. She turned her head away from Zude, her eyes closed tight. Zude reached out, but Jez shrugged off her touch and shot to her feet. "You have some strange notions about sex and intimacy, Zude," she said steadily, almost brandishing the whip. "I've never challenged you about that, and you've never pushed me about it. I've always assumed that you took it for the adolescent behavior that it clearly is—"

"Jez!" Zude began.

Jez stopped her with a quick and firm blow of the whip handle to Zude's shoulder. "Hear me out!" she ordered.

In that moment, a look passed over Zude's face. Jez's eyes widened and froze on the spectacle of her own gesture and the display of Zude's unequivocal reaction. At that sight, unbidden blood surged to her cheeks and a fierce burst of satisfaction flamed through her body. She fingered the whip, her breath rising slowly toward some long-hungered promise. Then, without warning, brand new eyes embraced the scene. Her stomach turned to bilge water.

"Forget it!" she cried, flinging the whip at Zude. She lunged toward the bed. "Forget it!" She began gathering her clothes, tugging on her breeks over her naked body.

Zude stared at her in silence. When Jez froze in the midst of dressing and met Zude's gaze, her lover said quietly, "Come with me, Jezebel. Come to the party with me."

They stared at each other, unmoving. Then Jezebel thrust her chin forward. "I'll do that," she said. "I'll go with you to your party." She sank to the bed. "But I need some sleep now, Zudie."

Both women sighed. Then Zude doused the light and settled by Jezebel under the thin sheet. A breeze swept lightly over their bodies. "We're okay, love," Zude whispered, "aren't we?"

Jez put her arm around Zude, turning her onto her own supine body, maneuvering Zude's head onto her shoulder. "We're fine, Zudie," she whispered back, holding the strong body tight against her. "We're fine."

Moments later, tensions eased, they lay in spoon and sang together an incantation, ancient and forever new, for the sleep of loving women:

"I seek the darkness as of old
With you I trust the Earth to hold
and cradle me in worlds untold,
to dare the death within our slumber.
    "I sink and unencumbered spin.
    I swoop the caverns of the wind.
    I number those who are my kin
    as all who do not cage another.
"Come, woman, partner of my rest
we join our lives in sisterquest
and plunge the hidden learningfest
where all of life will surge before us."

Jez awakened slowly into Hong Kong's pre-dawn hush. She lay beside Zude on her back, idly monitoring her lover's soft snores.

Then she gasped, suddenly aware that her body was rising upward, being lifted by strong hands straight through the ceiling of the room, through the roof. On her left, a wild-haired old hag held her close to her side; on her right, a younger woman clasped her equally close. They carried her between them, upward in their flight pod, high above the city and toward a rising sun.

"You're too antsy, girl," cracked the voice to her left. Jez turned to find bright black eyes studying her. "You got to let up," the old woman snapped, pressing her mouth into a tight line as she squinted at her.

"Who are you?" Jezebel asked.

"You can think of me as a guide," said the younger woman to her right. Jez turned to see a Jezebel with greying hair and the same smile that greeted her in every mirror. "I'm your Future Self," the woman added.

"And I'm her Ganeshananda," rasped the old woman at her other side. "That's a helper, somebody who removes obstacles for you.

Tonight, I'm here to help with the transportation," she added with a toothless grin. Her body banked right to turn the flying spoon southward over the sea. They soared higher. "You been getting mighty disconnected lately, girl," the old crone said. "We figured you could do with a little high fresh air."

Jez nodded. She folded herself closer into the warm embrace of the women, letting the cool dawn clear her head. "You're just in time," she said to them conversationally as the flight pod sailed over the sun-drenched sea. "I need a guide right now. Something to help me with these . . . these contradictions!"

The Future Jezebel laughed. "I remember. You keep trying to resolve them." She raised her arm, and the flight pod angled westward, trailed by the new day. "You can't resolve them, you know. You just live on them."

"Hold them and love them," croaked the crone, "and let them be!"

"But I'm an Amah cadet," Jez protested, "and a hypocrite! How can I wear that uniform?"

"Wear the uniform as long as you can. Then you'll no longer wear it," said her Future Self.

"So I'll just 'know'?"

"You'll know," the Future Jezebel assured her. "Trust your sacred powers. They can do no harm. Only if you disconnect from who you are could you misuse them."

A loud cackle broke the sound of the wind around the flight pod. "Hold on," shouted the crone. Her hand shot upward, and the flight pod swooped into a high backward roll. Jez gasped, watching the coastal hills spin below her. Jez caught the smile of her Older Self and let it mellow into a full-throated laugh. The three women laughed their way back toward the east again, driving into a blinding sun. They banked and dipped over shorelines and lush gardens, and when Hong Kong lay below them, they plummeted into its lap.

"Bella-Belle!" Zude was shaking her. Jez opened her eyes. "You were laughing! Are you all right? You were almost hysterical. Jez!"

Jez smiled and wiped her cheeks. "Zudie," she said. Then, as noises of a waking city wafted through the window, she wrapped herself in her lover's arms and drew her once more into sweet sleep.

———◆———

In a three-storied warehouse crammed with women representing all stages of dress and undress, all varieties and periods of costume, all shapes and sizes of props and accessories, all levels of technology and imagination, the women of Hong Kong gathered for a party. It was a sex party. And it was a party where, among other modes of interaction, dominance and submission opportunities filled the menu. Amahs, cadets, non-military citizens, and visitors from coastal caravansaries mingled—and performed—in a provocative concoction of street-fair celebration and intensified interpersonal drama.

Ardis The Banjar hung at a face-down angle, suspended thirty feet from the floor at the center of an intricate webbing of hempen lines. She held court there with floor-level admirers who marvelled at the warp and weft that sustained her.

"Ardis," Cadet Jezebel Dolalicia called up to her, "there's a lot of nothing between you and the ground!"

"Jezebel!" Ardis beamed. "It's true. But it's so easy when you know how!"

Jez's eyes played over the stalls and vendors that lined the lower level, the piercing and tattoo artists, the ranks of sex toys and exotic fabrics, the banquet of edible ice sculpted into female forms, the raucous parlor games. She walked through the crowds in the company of her Future Self, a palpable Presence who held her hand in assurance of serenity and openness.

Occasionally, that Self whispered, *"Breathe, Jezebel."*

On one of the darkened upper levels, she wandered as a welcome voyeur through lume-pockets of sexual activity. There, typically, she could watch a single woman's expression of sexual desire and the excited gratification of other women who bent their every effort toward the full satisfaction of that desire. The hand of the Future Jezebel held her steady, gifting her with tolerance and even, at times, appreciation.

At one moment when she stood with other voyeurs observing such a scene, her eyes fell on her lover far across the room. Zude was the center of a group of cadets, exploding with them in rowdy laughter at some oft-told tale of academy life. Deliberately, she turned back to the lume-scene and imagined her lover, splayed naked in thralldom, like the woman there. Zude in bondage, and hungry.

It rose again, that thrill of mastery and flame, summoned from such unfamiliar wellsprings. And hard on its heels, the horror and the sickening self-loathing. Jez flailed backward to the support of an upright girder. Wildly, she flung out her arm again, reaching for the Presence, for the woman she knew she would become. Instantly, her Future Self responded with the handclasp of support. In that moment, Jez gained her internal victory. Her body eased.

"How can I," she said aloud, "how—"

"Rejoice," said her guide.

"But I'm not—"

"You are both. You are all. Rejoice." The figure beside her moved. *"Come. There is more."*

In the company of her new-found guide, Jez weathered the evening's intermingling of sex and violence. The explicit and abhorrent message seemed clear. "Women," it said, "can be violators, too, and this is the way we shall treat each other: with men's weapons, men's uniforms, men's power, men's arrogance, men's titillations. We play here in this domain of men, and we enjoy it. We are masters of it." Her control served her to the last dregs of the party.

It was close to the witching hour of three when she and Zude emerged from the darkened pier building where the party had taken place. Through the trees, they could see small boats bobbing at their moorings. In their accustomed walking posture, elbows bent with forearms locked and fingers intertwined, they wound their way through the bowers of wisteria that marked a path by the harbor.

Zude broke the silence. "Bella-Belle, I need to hear from you." When Jez did not respond, she continued. "You see, love, it's not violence. It's about consent. Nothing is done against another's will."

Jez shook her head, disrupting the evenness of their walking. "I'm breathing," she sent to her Inner Guide. "I'm breathing, and I'm in control." Aloud, she said calmly, "Zude, it's not enough to say that violence is what's done against our will. That's a hollow definition for me. Consent isn't the key."

Zude didn't push her. Still ecstatic at Jez's apparent openness, she chanced some levity. "Confess it, best beloved," she teased. "You got off tonight on some . . ." She caught herself. "Jez, I mean—"

Jez had halted their progress. She stood looking at Zude. "Yes," she said evenly. "Yes, I did." Neither breathed. "And I was sickened by that, by my reaction." She moved away abruptly to the support of a nearby cypress tree. When she turned back to Zude, she was flushed. She spoke through a flood of tears. "Zudie, don't you see? What went on in that warehouse tonight was just an imitation of men's control games! I don't want that between us!"

Zude moved toward her lover. "They're not men's games, Jezebel. They're *human* games!"

"Wrong!" Jez exploded, the thin fabric of her composure finally torn asunder. She warded off Zude's move to touch her. "And who the hell are the Kanshou anyway, that they spend their lives fighting men's violence in the streets and then glorify it here? How can they pontificate at the academy about the horrors of slavery . . . and about men's abuse of animals . . . and then put the very women they say they 'love' in cages and collars and leashes and chains? Zude, I don't want to turn into that!"

She struck the tree with her fist. Then she looked at Zude, her voice soft. "And you think Amahs and Vigilantes and Femmedarmes are going to rid the world of violence? Never, Zudie! They're taking us right back to where the men had us in the first place!" She leaned, head down, against the cypress.

Breathe, whispered her Future Self.

In that same moment, Zude bent close to Jez's ear. "Jezebel," she said softly, "we have a room at the Hideaway. I'd like to go there with you now." She took Jez's hand. "No roles, no toys, no games. Just you and me."

Jez lifted her head and searched Zude's face. Slowly, she straightened, then yielded to the breath imprisoned by her rage. It blew freedom through her guarded body and rarefied her thickened mind. It sent her, a zephyr of desire, into Zude's astonished arms.

When they had moved clear of the cypress trees, Zude stepped behind her lover and drew the long body tight against her own. They bent their knees and closed their eyes, breathing themselves into an intimate alignment.

"By all the dreams we've walked together," said Zude.

"By all the love with which we've filled the vessels of our lives," said Jezebel.

They intoned a harmony, tumbled inward, and touched familiar reaches of a vista that opened to the stars. They lifted Earth-free feet and leapt above the rolling boats to sail together over Hong Kong's twinkling lights.

4

Cadets and Sea-Shrieves aboard a light transfer craft were down-
loading ancient munitions from a cargo vessel for the Kowloon
Military Museum when a midship explosion set off serial on-deck
fulminations. The conflagration that followed threatened the cargo
vessel and attending personnel.
Unexpectedly, rolling harbor waves poured over the cargo ship,
rolling it to a near-capsize but extinguishing the flames completely.
One of the eight cadets cast overboard had to be resuscitated, and
six more were treated for burns. Miraculously, no lives were lost.
Two eye-witness reports concur that almost simultaneous with
the explosion, Third Form Amah Cadet Dolalicia "summoned
waves of water" from the calms of Hong Kong Harbor, shaped
them into a wall that rose above the ship, and thus drenched the
conflagration.
—*Amah Academy Service Log 1423,* October 3, 2069

Dossroom Three of the Tsui Building was cantilevered into the
willow trees that flanked the gateway to the Hong Kong
Amahrery Cadet Academy. In the winter afternoon light, leafy
patterns flung themselves through the skylights onto forty crisp-
cornered cots footed by forty red lockers. Forty dress uniforms of
red and black hung in plastasis to the right of forty stiff pillows,
and forty long windows separated the areas from each other by a
few feet. Above each bed, neatly concealed ceiling chutes held
drop shelves of wardrobes and toiletries. Idle glolobes, with focus
or spread capacity, hung suspended in midair over each bed.

Animal figures, astonishingly lifelike and in a variety of postures, graced almost half the beds: stalking tigers or wolves, eagles
or hawks in full flight, dolphins, foxes, turtles, snakes, bears, and

a number of other species, including one spider. Some were full-sized, others reduced in size but no less imposing. They guarded their modest human fiefdoms with the dignity appropriate to their status as totem, companion, or spirit-guide.

The floor chronometer barely whispered its pulse.

From the upchute, arguing voices resounded in the empty dossroom.

"Just tell me how you did it, Jez, and I'll leave you in peace!"

Jez shot out of the chute with Zude just behind her. "Psychic bench presses. Mass hypnosis." Jez strode down the central row of silent cots to her own berth. She began working her way out of her ryndon comfortsuit.

"And when the dust clears at the dock and everybody's back here talking about it forever, what do I say?"

"You say what you saw. Zude, you're not my keeper!"

Zude caught Jez by the shoulders and turned her toward her. "Right. I'm your lover!" She shook her. "Remember me?"

Jez pulled away from her and began climbing into a woodswarmth tunic.

Zude leapt in front of Jezebel, flinging her arms wide. "*Listen to me!*" she shouted. Jez froze. Zude pointed to herself. "I'm your Faithful Zudie, and I've been traipsing after you for weeks! But every time I think I've caught you, you just pat my hand like a nanny and then discorporate like a cloud!" She leaned toward Jez. "I bring you a kiss-cola and a rose because you're off on a 90-k trek, and all I get from you is a glassy-eyed stare. Then to top it all off, this afternoon I watch while this strange woman, who is supposed to be my best beloved, picks up half the South China Sea and puts out a fire that otherwise could have killed eight people!"

Zude paused. Jez held her gaze.

The willows had stopped waving. The chronometer hushed. Neither woman breathed. Nothing stirred in the sunlit dossroom.

Seventeen silent witnesses regarded the scene with wise eyes.

Jez's shoulders rounded. She dropped her head.

Zude's hand hovered an instant by Jez's shoulder. Then she sank to the cot, her arms resting on her wide hipbones, her limp hands filling the emptiness between her thighs.

"You're going."

Jez released a soft whimper. Then her arms stiffened, and she threw her head wide to the ceiling, moaning in an upward glissando to a full-bodied roar.

Zude closed her eyes. The breath she exhaled rasped awkwardly and then flooded like a wild tributary into Jez's rising wail. The sounds ceased simultaneously as the two women collapsed sobbing into each other and into the narrow space between the cots, wrapped in a familiar holding. On the white tiled floor of Doss Three, they sat rocking back and forth until the sun had tilted another inch in the sky.

When at last they could look at each other, Jez freed one of the twin rampant unicorns, which was caught up in her lover's black hair. Zude lowered her eyes and then closed them, leaning back against the bed, her body lifeless for perhaps the first time in its waking life.

Jez's whisper reverberated in the empty dossroom. "Come with me, Zudie." She pressed Zude's limp hand.

From the bottom of her belly, a cynical laugh rose silently out of Amah Cadet Lieutenant Adverb. Then she gave the laugh its voice. "Come with you? Me?" Large tears began rolling down her cheeks. "And what would you do with me, Bella-Belle? Carry me with you from fair to fair, the Beautiful Witch Jezebel's bonzai handmaiden, who holds her greatcoat while the miraculous lady performs acts of wonder?" The tears poured effortlessly now, drenching Zude's tunic. "Maybe I could get a job dispatching flexcabs to bring the old and the infirm to your magic healing shows."

Jez flushed. "Unkind, Zudie."

Zude nodded. She pressed her forehead to Jez's and whispered, "True. It was unkind. Erase, please."

Jez placed Zude's hands on her own brown head and then took Zude's head in her own hands, completing the ritual. "Erased." They held their brows together for a long moment.

Zude wiped her hand over her face, then on her loose-fitting pants. Jez caught a wet tear on Zude's chin. She wiped it on her own tunic.

"Zudie, it may sound crazy, but I'm reaching for a part of you that questions all this just like I do."

Zude opened her eyes.

"All this," Jez whispered. "The academy. The Kanshoubu. And all that they stand for."

Zude searched her lover's face.

"Look," Jez said, "I'm not leaving because I have some place to go. I don't know where I'll go. I'm leaving because I can't stay here. Every day I'm putting up another wall against what I truly know within myself, blanking out options, limiting possibilities." She wiped tears from her own eyes. "Killing my spirit." She pulled herself close to Zude's face. "And, my love, you're doing the same thing."

Zude grew completely alert, moving into a verbal protest.

"Hush." Jez put her finger on Zude's lips. "Zude, my best beloved, if enough of our friends, our academy cadets, were to throw away their weapons and look deep inside themselves, they would discover powers that would put to shame the combined military arsenals of this planet's entire history."

She shifted so that Zude would have to look at her. "Zudie," Jez whispered. "I've seen you touch bigger parts of yourself, just like I have. They scare you senseless, but you know they're there. You fly, for the Love of Inana! You fly! Where do you think that power comes from?" She scrunched closer. "Every time a spark of nonrational power sneaks up on you, you snuff it out. You talk about my psychic gifts like I'm something special. But in your gut, you know that it could have been you who picked up that water today and saved our friends." She drew her hands through Zude's black hair, soothing the head backwards. "The only difference between you and me is that I let it in. I practice it, and you don't."

Zude took Jez's hands between her own. "You've been frustrated, I know. I'd have to be blind not to see it."

"Why won't you come with me?" Jez persisted.

Zude flared. "I understand why you've decided to go. You've got a path to follow, and so have I. Two roads to the same place."

"Not the same place at all!" Jez drew in her sprawled legs. She knelt on one knee and drove her words at the figure beside her. "You're obsessed with having a world that's *just*. I want a world that's *healed*. Not the same thing at all!"

"Healing, healing, healing!" Zude tiredly pushed herself to a kneeling position on Jez's level. "You can heal all you want, Jezebel, but if we don't agree to some mutual respect, some justice, then we're going to keep on spilling blood."

"And a ton of your justice won't guarantee a drop of love or compassion! Or a whit less cruelty from violent men!" Jez moved squarely in front of her lover. "And what if you had your just world, Zudie? What if there were all the individual freedom and self-determination that the Kanshoubu is charged with protecting? If it isn't grounded in compassion, it'll be hollow as a drum. The healing, the love, the compassion, the empathy—however you name it, it's first. It's fundamental and most important. It's sine qua non. It would make your justice unnecessary."

"That's enough, Jez," Zude said quietly.

"Zude, you—"

"I said that's enough." Zude's voice drained the warmth from the pools of sunlight on the floor.

Jez stayed still, watching Amah Cadet Lieutenant Adverb get to her feet. Then, in the silence, she pulled herself up and sat wearily on the bed that neighbored her own.

Zude dusted her breeks, her swipes across the black cotton cloth the only sounds audible in the large room. She picked up a toppled elephant and set it upright on the bed.

She spoke evenly to Jezebel. "Jez, do you remember the Oath?"

"The Oath? Zude, every Shrieve—and every cadet—walks her day within the Kanshou Oath."

Zude nodded. "The Oath that every one of us will make a lifetime commitment to when we become Kanshou, the Oath that every cadet—Amah or Femmedarme or Vigilante—studies as her prayer for peace, as the guidance she'll live by for the rest of her life."

Jez waited.

Zude began the recitation of the Oath's final phrasing. "While I honor the Kanshoubu and its component forces—the Amahrery, the Femmedarmery, the Vigilancia—and while I set my feet . . ."

Jez took up the recitation, ". . . and while I set my feet upon the principles of the Kanshoubu and my hands and mind to its practices, I hold in my heart the vision of a world where peace-keeping forces are unnecessary." She paused.

"Go on," Zude urged.

Jez stood, propelled by the words themselves. "Thus my primary and unalterable purpose in becoming Kanshou will ever be to render obsolete my own profession and the Kanshoubu itself." Her voice was strong, her eyes focused beyond one of the narrow windows.

Neither woman spoke for many seconds. Seventeen witnesses waited calmly.

Zude drew a long breath. "Show me any man's police force, any man's army, in all of military or social history that has named that as its purpose: to make itself obsolete." Jez turned slowly to face her. Zude continued, "That's radical, Jezebel. It may never happen. Certainly not in our lifetime. But the vision, the *intent* is there."

She took Jez by the shoulders. "Love, you're right about the choice the Kanshoubu has made, the choice to contain much of today's violence with the old male methods. And sometimes I think that we've turned out to be the most effective peacekeeping force in history only because we've handled men's tools better than the men did. We're stronger, smarter, and more sophisticated. We have more courage and less need for ultimate control. But you know, just as I do, that *it's because the Kanshou are women* that we've changed the image of peacekeepers all over the world. Our purpose has honestly been different from men's. And that difference shows. Police aren't feared anymore. We're trusted. And respected. In some satrapies, we're even loved. That's different, Jez. Qualitatively different from the ten thousand years of men's law-and-order. At least admit that."

Jez sank to her own cot. "Granted."

Zude sat and faced her lover. "You may have the better way, Jezebel, the better purpose. But I'm still an Amah cadet. I believe in the Kanshoubu and in what it has done to heal and to keep the Earth. War is history, the air's clean, drugs are controlled, the ozone's healthier, hunger is obsolete, and 'development' is the dirtiest word on the street. Little Blue is slowly revitalizing. We're beginning to govern ourselves, from within ourselves and among ourselves. All of us. The global village is discovering itself." Zude paused. "The Kanshoubu is at the heart of all that. The

Kanshoubu is the most decent thing to happen to this planet since the days of the worship of the Ancient Goddess."

"I can't argue that, Zudie," Jez replied. "It's just that, good as the Kanshoubu is, it's not good enough for me right now." She started to say more, but at that moment a shaft of sunlight fell upon Zude's big hands. Jez froze, then dropped to the floor in front of those hands, seizing them with her own. She covered them with kisses and blessed them with tears. She sobbed. Then, in the stretch of her last cry, she straightened and stood. Zude rose with her.

The sun had left the dossroom altogether.

Jez moved to her locker and opened it. She pulled out a heavy, hooded, canvas jacket. Then a worn rucksack, fully packed. She slid into Zude's arms again, her lips close to Zude's ear. She closed her eyes and pressed out the words slowly, one-by-one: "I do not want to go without you. I do not want to live my life without you. You are my heart."

"Then don't go."

Jezebel Dolalicia and Amah Cadet Lieutenant Adverb kissed. Silent witnesses on other beds delicately dropped their gaze.

Then Jez broke from the embrace and picked up her rucksack and jacket. She headed for the down pole.

Zude's voice stopped her. "Jezebel." Zude stepped toward her with something in her hand.

Jez felt a tiny object fall into her palm. One of Zude's earrings. A silver unicorn. Her eyes sought Zude's, and her lips tightened.

"If you ever need me, send this and I'll come."

Clutching the earring, Jez turned and spiralled down the exit pole.

When on that warm winter afternoon Jezebel Dolalicia, clad in soft cotton woodswarmth, turned her feet away from the Amah Academy of Hong Kong, she invoked the Disciplines Survivory of her craft to carry her through immediate times. By day, she walked with unhurried steps toward the colding north. By night, she bedded in way shelters and set her dreams to work on releasing Zella Terremoto Adverb from her constant thoughts. She marked each day with wonder and gratitude, sought the wisdom of her Future Self, and as she walked, she chanted the litanies for Loss and Forgiveness.

In China's coastal cities, she fired kaolin pots, sang her way into sanctuaries and stupas, repaired electronic breakdowns, and on occasion gave spirited lectures on physics to university classes. In the hills and recovering forests, she performed small mental feats of cloud-gathering and metal-heating and often offered herself as pain-soaker for those who needed such cures. When her food credits drooped or her canvas and tree-gum boots wore thin, she begged permission to glean and grind her own grain, to cut and sew for the filling of her own needs. She avoided the transmogrifier and other convenient hard-tech options, for they called up too much memory of Hong Kong.

During the first months after her departure from the academy, Jezebel articulated no purpose for her life. Rather, she opened to the will of her Source Self, turning her feet toward any beckoning whim or hunch and following wherever it led. She sensed that some destiny awaited her and that her developing capacities and insights would eventually engage in a satisfying use, but she refused any temptation to speculate about an ultimate goal. She breathed deeply and took notice of the largesse of every moment.

In the late spring of her first year away from Hong Kong, Jezebel embarked on a pilgrimage of curiosity, rich and solitary. She signed onto a crew captained by Patrice of The Seven Seas and set out on a square-rigger bound for proving its mettle on the widest of waters. In Samoa, she found a new peace. Over the Pacific Basin, she lost all fear. In the Peruvian Andes, she understood for the first time why it was the power of women that was transforming the globe. In Santiago, she hallowed the lessons of her travel by becoming Jezebel Stronglaces.

Sometimes, and particularly when the stars sprinkled themselves into memories of dancing brown eyes or when she awoke with her hands stroking a cold emptiness, Jez admitted to herself that she sorely missed the wonders of spooned sleep and the comfort of a warm body wrapped around her. Most of all, she longed for the dreamwalking, that precious gift of womanlove wherein she could wander measureless worlds within another's sleep and wherein that other could roam with her the networked pathways of her own undiscovered countries.

She began to see more clearly the tasks of her every day: to sharpen her unorthodox skills, to develop new powers, to appreciate the boundless dimensions of women, and to understand the enigma of men. Toward what end she still did not know, except that the journey itself must be her home.

She spent several seasons with sub-Pacific communities, bent upon coaxing into existence a low-level animal life form from the tolerantly whispering ocean floor. In Ouagadougou, she became adept at reading truth-glows around a speaker. In Kanazawa, she learned to develop her ki as she slept. In the shrill grasses of the Kinangop Plateau, she practiced the refinements of wind shaping. Near a tributary to the great Irrawaddy, she at last mastered her shape-shifting and practiced it by becoming one after another of the lush plants of central Burma. She learned to think of plants as "bound movers" and of humans and the departed animals as "free movers."

As season followed season and year followed year, Jezebel's feet touched every continent and roamed the deepest interiors of Little Blue's every satrapy. In communities of women, or of women and men, she slipped into the appropriate tribal custom and used her special skill in sleep transference to learn the language.

Shortly thereafter, she trained for two years in a hospital satellite, developing nul-gravity psychic surgeries. It was there, when she saw the marbled Earth hanging in space, that she fully appreciated the spiritual transformation of satellite riders who saw their home world from that distance. It was Astronaut Kasey Shelton who had first called it "Little Blue." Jez at last understood why the name had caught the imagination of its inhabitants.

Jezebel knew by now that, even among extraordinary women, the gifts she possessed were extraordinary. And because she was courageous and honest in her regard for Things Which Are True and because she struck a level of intimacy with all she touched, she drew into her company large numbers of people, overwhelmingly women. They sensed a destiny in her gait, or they basked in the cadence of her voice. Some of them swore in their secret selves to be forever by her side.

The paradox that was to harry her throughout her life then began to crystallize: how to use, for the benefit of all, the powers she found galloping to fruition within herself, and at the same time how to avoid the historical paradigm of leadership with its rationalizations and subtle assimilations, its eventual and inevitable misuses of power.

"Do not worship another person," she would advise those who would deify her. "Your authority is in yourself, not in me." Or she would encourage, "Let us learn together, making an atmosphere that calls up gifts from all of us, for all of us."

Wherever she went, Jez conscientiously gathered about her a group of women who trusted her, whom she trusted, and whom other women trusted. Together, they addressed the matter of Jezebel's power, trying to understand how that power could be shared and used with greatest effectiveness. Together, they sought every person's appropriate use of personal power and the reconnection of the human family with All of Life. They worked for the elimination of violence, frequently debating its cause and the question of whether or not violence was gender-related.

About 2085 C.E., women worldwide began organizing for the once-and-for-all eradication of violence, and they clamored for leadership. They hoped for a woman who had charm, intelligence, energy, imagination, the appropriate convictions, an unfailing regard for those she worked with, and a charisma that would call forth loyalty and dedication. Almost against her will, Jezebel Stronglaces became that unanointed leader, the linchpin in a widening wheel of global activism.

In 2086 and preparatory to a formal proposal to Little Blue's Central Web, the Consorority of Neurosurgeons revealed to demesne news services in every part of Little Blue a plan to use bailiwick habitantes in the search for a violence center in the brain. Thus, the controversy over moral issues that had brewed for decades in laboratories and academies was now exploding in the cities and hamlets of every satrapy. Jezebel Stronglaces, her heart alive at last with hope for her species and for her planet, lent her considerable influence to the forces demanding Habitante Testing and to the ultimate legalization of the use of Anti-Violence Protocols on convicted social offenders.

When Cadet Lieutenant Adverb saw Jezebel Dolalicia walk out of the Amah Academy and toward the northern mountains, she did not question the finality of that action or her own response to it. With determination and calm, she immediately delegated her daily and weekly duties, wrote a formal memorandum to her commanding officer, and put herself on temporary—if unsanctioned—leave.

She disappeared first into the hands of Viana Painstalker, who pushed and pummelled her body until it was open enough to allow the release of her anguish and anger. Weeks later, when Painstalker and her attendant sound healers finished with that body, Zude cleansed herself for weeks with fire, water, and thousand-foot bungie drops over a Gongga Shan gorge. She breathed ammonia culled from Jupiter's clouds, chewed the acidic mulch of Mendocino oaks, and cursed womankind in clarion shouts from a raft adrift in the Taiwan Strait. Finally, she submerged herself in warm amniotic fluid at the New Life Center and dreamt there that she had swapped her lungs for gills, that she could sit at the bottom of the tank forever if she so chose.

She emerged only when concerned friends lured her out with an invitation to drum for three days on Victoria Peak in the city-wide rejoicing to the Approach of Spring. With the invitation was an unspoken understanding that the name of Jezebel Dolalicia would not be mentioned.

Upon her return to the Amahrery, Zella Terremoto Adverb acquitted herself as no other cadet had done in any academy—Hong Kong, Los Angeles, or Tripoli. She achieved multiple honors before she was graduated into the Kanshoubu in 2071. She served a year in Calcutta with the Amahrery and two more in Cairo with the Femmedarmery.

In 2074, Zude was summoned to Los Angeles, main seat of the Nueva Tierra Norte Satrapy (and of Aztlán Siempre), to serve as Steward of Bailiwicks for the satrapy, an office designed to exploit the best of her dedication to the transformation of bailiwick policy and conditions. Wherever her ambition had taken her and with whatever accomplishments, Zude's first priority had been always to implement her model of "contained violence" in the administration of bailiwicks. So in Nueva Tierra Norte, she advocated for and, where possible, mandated changes that allowed each bailiwick to be endowed with its own life, to function as an independent organism; she sought relationships of peaceful co-existence between each bailiwick and the environment of free citizens surrounding it.

Her reforms earned her the rank of Matrix Major and the high regard of both Kanshou and citizens in the Nueva Tierra Sur, Central, and Norte Satrapies. During that time, the Vigilantes under her command—Foot-Shrieves, Flex-Car Shrieves, Sea- and Sky-Shrieves, particularly the Flying Daggers—took every opportunity to demonstrate their pride in their leader and their unswerving loyalty to her person.

In 2080, after negotiating the success of a series of humanizing (and risky) innovations in Vigilancia policy and practice, Zude dared to place her name in candidacy for the position of Vice-Magister of the Nueva Tierra Norte Satrapy, an office soon to be vacated by the widely-loved Guygavin Mahaney. In an unprecedented move and on first consensus consideration, the Heart appointed Adverb to the position, the youngest Shrieve ever to sit so high in the Kanshoubu. Thus, with her companion Vice-Magisters in the Nueva Tierra Central and Nueva Tierra Sur Satrapies, Zude at the age of thirty-eight stood only one step away from her tri-satrapy's highest executive office that of Magister.

As she continued her career as a stateswoman, Zude increasingly understood on a profound level the rare gift of trust that Little Blue's citizens bestowed upon its public servants, particularly upon its Kanshou. At every level of her rise to power, she honored that trust by a constant searching out of the needs of her subordinates and of Little Blue's citizens alike. Every morning before she rolled out of bed, she recited her mantra from *The Labrys Manual*: "Where are they going? I must hasten after them for I am their leader!"

In the first year of her Vice-Magistry, one of Zude's close friendships expanded into a large extended family. To her deep satisfaction, her life began to take on the rich textures and dimensions of children, grandparents, sisters, and cousins.

In that same year, Flossie Yotoma Lutu, Magister of The Africa-Europe-Mideast Tri-Satrapy, invited Zude to attend as her guest Crete's annual Aviary Celebration, a computer-modelled performance of thousands of birds from around the world, especially programmed that year for interaction with human spectators. Once, as a teenager, Zude had briefly met and admired Magister Lutu. But Magisters usually kept their own society and their own political associations, and Zude felt she hardly qualified either as friend or colleague of enough long-standing to be tapped by Yotoma. Yet there it was, that formal invitation, cleverly engraved within the comcube. Zude accepted and flew to Crete, Yotoma's unofficial seat of government. She was enchanted by the Aviary Celebration, but more important, she began to establish on that evening a political and personal liaison which was to inform her life from that moment onward.

In the years that followed, Zude and Yotoma regularly sought each other out. They were never lovers, but Yotoma, Zude's elder by over 30 years, became a mentor to the young Vice-Magister, coaching her in the subtleties of the cultural differences that can create or destroy genuine understanding. Among Zude's most precious memories were those of the secret excursions that the two women enjoyed in busy streets and bars or on farms and seafronts. They would sneak from the confines of a meeting room in Cairo or Oslo or Shreveport, and in elaborate disguises, they would spend hours or days incognito in conversation with women, children, and men whom they otherwise would never have met.

Though they agreed upon the things that ultimately mattered, like justice and peace and the incomparable allure of an absinthe-spiked cola, their relationship thrived upon adversarial discussion and debate. Under what conditions, they would ask each other, should one of the planet's many separatist communities be obliged to relate to the whole society—when a flood threatened it, or when one of its citizens' tobacco smoke polluted others, or never? Should taxation or tithing be the minimum requirement for citizenship on Little Blue? Should there be trisatrapy protection for barter cultures and gift societies who were trying to survive in the face of an automated credit economy? Should transmogrifiers be introduced in areas where techless tribes were resisting assimilation into the fast-moving techful world? How much surveillance should the Size Bureau exercise over any business or governmental group? Under what conditions, if any, should a Kanshou be allowed to save a person from suicide?

They frequently marvelled at the smoothness with which the world's diversity interfaced with the superstructures of global government and economic intercourse. "Flossie," Zude would pant as she pummeled masses of teflofoam in a rousing pattern of aerobic performance at Yotoma's private gym, "are we just . . . lucky? Figure how many . . . hundreds of different cultures . . . and sub-cultures we've got on this planet . . . how many thousands . . . of languages . . . and dialects . . . ." Zude took a deep breath then vollied rapid-fire punches. "Artifacts! Customs! Costumes! Foods! Behaviors!" Then another breath, followed by another concentrated blast of punches. "We ought to be fighting more than we are!"

"Plenty of air," Yotoma would pant from her pot of plastimud, "plenty of water . . . a transmog on every corner . . . why fight?"

"Differences, Floss!" Zude would give a final accelerated set of blows to the teflofoam. "We've always . . . fought over . . . differences!"

Flossie would speed up the lifting of her feet from the suction of the viscous mass below her and pant all the harder. "Haven't you noticed, Adverb? We've got . . . a new take . . . on differences. Ever since . . . the animals, ever . . . since they left. These days we . . . ," she would groan aloud in a final effort, ". . . these days we . . . we *worship* differences!" And in near collapse, she would shake her feet free of the plastimud.

Later, as they floated in cool zero-gravity laxchambers and clung to puffy support pillows, Flossie would mumble, "Maybe it's all just magic."

"Godgossip!" Zude would mumble back.

"You're short on imagination, Adverb," Yotoma would observe, her hands almost indistinguishable from the old bear's skin she drew around her for warmth, "and you have so much to learn!"

It was no surprise to anyone, least of all to Zude, that when Elizabeth Cloudstar, Magister of the Nueva Tierra Tri-Satrapy, climbed a peak in the Himalayas and declared herself spiritually free of political endeavor, her mantle should fall upon the shoulders of Zella Terremoto Adverb. There were others who outranked Zude, but none quite so respected by the citizens and the Kanshou of all three satrapies in Nueva Tierra. Added to that popularity was the blessing of Magister Lutu and the fact that the ratifying bodies—the Central Web and the Kitchen Table—were too distracted with more pressing matters to block Zude's election. At an unprecedented early age, not yet 44, Zude rose to the Magistership. She was the chief executive of one of the three major geo-political entities on Little Blue.

The friendship between Adverb and Yotoma became ever more lively and more public. No politically minded citizen ever failed to tune to the flatcasts on which they were both scheduled to appear for fear of missing a rousing intellectual altercation between the two.

Equally as public as their legendary disagreements was the absolute concordance of the two Magisters on the matter of Habitante Testing and the Anti-Violence Protocols. This political question, now rearing its global head, could, from their point of view, threaten the individual freedom of every citizen on Little Blue. Both were clearly and uncompromisingly committed to the obliteration of that threat.

5
BOSCA
[2087 C.E.]

> Nose smells. Lips taste. Ears hear. Eyes see. Fingertips discern.
> Honest maidservants in the House of Knowledge. Then
> Imagination, that insidious slattern, creeps into the
> Householder's bed. Before dawn, her house crumbles.
> Question: What does this mean?
> Response: Measurable and verifiable sense data must be the
> foundation of my action as Kanshou, for imaginative or
> intuitive assumptions about another's intent mislead me. Neither
> I nor the Kitchen Table can determine a harmer's intent or limit
> his autonomy unless his intent is made manifest to my senses, as
> when he displays a weapon or raises his hand in attack.
> —*The Labrys Manual*

"So," Zude shrugged, "the whole desalinization industry really grew out of sewage disposal techniques." She angled the cushcar gently over the sun-bright waters of the Gulf and parked it in a hover so she could look at Bosca while she warmed to one of her favorite subjects.

"We usually name three pivotal phenomena in the transformation of the Los Angeles Basin. First, for all the reasons you already know, its population was quickly reduced to a mere three million or so."

Bosca nodded. She and Zude were exquisitely cool in the hovercraft, even in the warm rays of the sun.

"Second," Zude went on, "California finally solved its eternal water problem." Zude spoke behind her hand, in an aside. "Actually, it was witches who came up with the formulas, though

101

nobody would admit it."

Bosca smiled with her.

"The resulting desalinization processes surprised even the fine minds that had designed them."

"But not the witches," Bosca added.

"Correct. Not the witches." Zude looked at Bosca, realizing that the woman was listening intently. Momentarily distracted by that discovery, she hastened to continue. "So the waters of the mighty Colorado and other eastern rivers could then be used for the restoration of inland lakes and streams, the ones that had been drained in the first place to answer the water supply needs of Los Angeles' huge population. Los Angeles finally got the chance to live up to its potential as one of the world's most beautiful garden spots."

Bosca pivoted her padded chair back and forth in a small arc. "And third?"

"The third big cause of change was the increase in the number of hydrogen-enhanced, solar power plants we had in orbit around Little Blue, providing clean energy for the whole globe. That's still expensive, but with the shift to Earthclasp mentality, funding isn't a problem. And pollution is a thing of the past." She sat back in her chair. "There you have it."

"Good story," said Bosca.

In the silence, Zude found herself nodding and smiling with her guest. The silence grew longer, until Zude's comfort boundary was breached. She cleared her throat and busied herself with the craft's controls.

"There," she said, pointing back toward the shore. "That's the view I wanted." Before them, spanning the area from high cliffs down to low beaches and harbors, an explosion of color filled the horizon. The hills vibrated with reds and oranges, blues and purples, all nestled in hanging gardens of green intricacy. Steps and small white buildings peeped now and again from the splendor, leading the eye up and back to the taller trees, to streams, and even toward the waterfalls in the Santa Ana hills.

Bosca gasped. As far as she could see, there was nothing but life and growth and color. "Magister . . ." Deliberately, she corrected herself. "Zude, I could spend my life here!" Then she turned to her pilot. "I'm exaggerating. But not much. Is it tropical? Did you change the soil? Where . . . ?"

Zude laughed. "Largest botanical reserve in Aztlán Siempre," she boasted. "Every indigenous species and thousands imported. If you're serious, I'll drop you off there this evening. It has become quite a meditation retreat. Accommodations adequate, if quaint."

Bosca did not answer. Her eyes were fixed on the gardens. Magister Adverb studied her guest. They had spent the morning covering ground as familiar to Zude as the palm of her hand; yet, in Bosca's company every step had revealed some brand new way of seeing, some discovery of the obvious-made-profound. Bosca, she realized, was a true innocent who gloried in every moment as an adventure of the soul.

Zude quietly checked their status and then closed her eyes, sinking into the firm embrace of the cushcar's contour seat. A spectrum of duties wove through her mind—the Size Bureau's Arctic Proposal, negotiations between rail and rocket, yesterday's cushcar explosion near Caracas, some unusual population figures from the Upper Mississippi Demesne. And, of course, Jezebel . . . and the swirls of questions surrounding the Protocols and Habitante Testing. She couldn't shake the ominous feeling that she was enjoying the lull before some coming storm. She felt Bosca looking at her. She opened her eyes.

"Yes," her guest was saying, "I'd like to go there tonight, Zude. But your family, your Kayita. You told me . . ."

Zude nodded as she consulted the floor chronometer. "We'll

head in soon and visit them. I'll see that you get to the gardens after that." She moved the hovercraft back into motion and out to sea again. "We'll just whisk you once or twice around Catalina," she added, giving a full even thrust to all twenty-four of the air jets that supported them. The cushcar rose. She engaged the horizontals, and they swept toward the southwest.

The trip was full of ideas, opinions, and shared interests. When Bosca suggested that true community is a complex harmonic singing-together, like crystals that form by resonating with other crystals, Zude actively wished that her friend and colleague, Magister Lutu, could meet this woman. When she herself shared her own failure to achieve enlightenment from ayuhuasca, the sacred drink of the Peruvian soul vine, Zude found her hand on Bosca's shoulder, vibrating with a laughter beyond her own, new and rich.

They had just finished speculating about the unusual number of children they knew who swore to regular conversations with extraterrestrials and had just begun to explore the notion of soul counterparts when they were treated to an unexpected show. Flying Daggers, a division of the Vigilancia's Air-Shrieves, filled the sky ahead of them. Scores of Vigilantes, flying in pairs, their capes in graceful flow behind them, climbed and swooped in precise formations as they practiced complex flight maneuvers.

To Zude's delight, the Daggers recognized the insignia on her personal cushcar and immediately peeled off into a mass surrounding of the vehicle. For several minutes, they established a v-shaped escort for their Commander-in-Chief. Zude failed in her attempts to reach the Flight Commander by audio-hail and had to be content with returning the smiles and waves of the Vigilantes just outside their windows. At last, the airborne women swirled gert-by-gert around the cushcar to offer farewell salutes.

"That was amazing," Bosca exclaimed when the Kanshou

were out of sight. "Before I met Amahs Densmore and Longleaf a few days ago, I had known women who were spooners—not in the military, you know—but I'd never seen a Sky-Shrieve up close. And now . . ."

"Now you've not only flown with a gert but had your own personal air show."

"Is it true that the gerts have to be lovers to fly together?" she asked.

"Yes," Zude answered, "or they have to have been lovers." She glanced at her passenger. "Sometimes women who were lovers twenty years ago can still fly together. And occasionally, those who are lovers right now can't. Nobody has distilled the formula yet, but we know that the elements are the sexual relationship and shared sleep. Mostly, we don't ask questions," she grinned.

Bosca nodded. "I've heard of women—actually up north from here—women who could fly alone."

"Rumor," said Zude. "Don't believe it." She shook her head. "If there were such women, then the Vigilancia would be busy recruiting them. Think what a boon it would be to have Kanshou who could fly solo!"

Both women lapsed into silence. Zude busied herself with a slow circling of the island, then banked and altered course slightly, seeking smoother ocean beneath them. "Tell me about—" she said, just as Bosca turned to her to say, "Do you believe—?" They stopped, laughing at the momentary awkwardness and at a sudden mutual awareness that this behavior was a common one between people beginning to know each other.

Zude found herself blushing. "I was just about to ask about your community in the plains," she said.

"And I was about to go back to the subject of counterparts." Bosca raised her eyebrows. "Clearly, we were both uneasy with the silence."

Zude ventured a quick look at her passenger, then headed the cushcar toward the open sea again. "So what about counterparts. You mean soul-mates?"

"Sort of. But a little different." Bosca closed her eyes and adjusted her swivel to catch the sunlight. "Beings of the same soul-group who split up and incarnate into two or three different people at the same time. Or across centuries. The time doesn't seem to matter. The point is, their lives somehow influence each other, usually at critical moments."

"Guardian angels?"

"Not exactly."

Zude shook her head. "You've lost me, Bosca. I can't buy the body-soul split."

Bosca eased the padded chair back so as to catch more sun on her thin figure. "Zude, are you a materialist hold-out?"

"Am I—what?"

Bosca frowned, then said, "Ideas. Where do you think ideas come from?"

Zude settled the cushcar once more into a lightly-monitored circle over the grey-blue sea. "Ideas come from reality," she said earnestly, patting the bulkhead beside her. "This is solid, real. I can't walk through it. Our ideas, anything we think or believe, all of that comes from this solid world, from the way we perceive it through our five senses." She patted the bulkhead again, then looked at Bosca. "So no sermons about the spirit, please. The only 'spirit' I have is my body. Here 'tis." She slapped her thigh. "And when it dies, it dies. Poof! It just rejoins the nitrogen cycle."

"But Zude, where's your sense of magic?" She drew herself to an upright position. "You fly! I mean, you have flown with—you do fly with your . . . your . . ." She faltered.

"Why, yes, but—"

"Well, that ability contradicts physical laws. How do you

explain it?"

"I don't," Zude said sharply. "Nobody does. Although everybody tries." She shifted in her chair. "Bosca, there's a good explanation for why women can fly together. We just haven't discovered it yet."

"How about all the other things that defy logic and physical laws—those witches who found the desalinization formulas, for instance? Spontaneous healing? Levitation? Precognition? Some people can mindstretch—"

"Bosca, people are always exceeding themselves," Zude said, struggling for patience. "Once there was no such thing as a four-minute mile. Once we wrote with quill and parchment, but only because we hadn't yet discovered the information we needed in order to make writing easier. I'm not denying that we have undiscovered capacities. I'm just saying that what's knowable becomes known according to set laws. Maybe we'll all be able to fly someday or to mindstretch. But that won't mean that there's some kind of supernatural power apart from us that has suddenly reached out and endowed us! When mindstretching becomes common we'll have a physical explanation for it. And for flying," she added. She suddenly wanted to light up a cigarillo. She chewed on her lip instead.

"I understand," Bosca said. "You're a little old-fashioned, maybe, but—"

"Old-fashioned?" Zude exclaimed. "Old-fashioned? Bosca, that is about as current and as common a belief system as you'll find anywhere on the planet!"

"Relax, please, Magister Adverb." Bosca's voice was steady. "I just meant that it's pre-Earthclasp thinking. There's nothing really wrong with it. It's just sort of . . . a throwback. And a little limited."

Zude ducked her chin and eyed a distant cloud. "And clung to by a big part of the world all the more desperately, I guess, in the face of millennium spiritualism. Yes, I admit that."

Zude bore the silence for several of her own agitated breaths, then broke the tension. "I've never been much good at talking about spiritual matters, Bosca." She leaned forward, trying to catch her passenger's eye. Bosca studied the status panels that blinked and pulsed before them. Zude tried once more. "I'm certainly not good at spiritual growth." She sought Bosca's eyes again.

Then Bosca laughed.

Zude was vastly relieved. Heartily, she continued. "I have always been sort of spiritually incorrect. You know, always bored by meditation, always blocking the cosmic energy—"

"Always kind," Bosca observed pointedly. Zude shot her a glance. "I didn't expect it," Bosca continued. When Zude frowned, Bosca swiveled her seat toward her. "I never expected a Magister to be kind."

Magister Adverb was plainly disconcerted. Once more, she sky-parked the ship over the ocean. She studied her guest. "Bosca," she said, "I'm uncomfortable with this whole conversation. For all kinds of reasons. But I'll try to hang with it because it's apparently important to you. And," she shrugged both hands into the air, "who knows? It may be important to me."

"It is," Bosca said, her voice curtailing Zude's extravagant gesture. Zude froze. Bosca continued. "It is important to both of us." She held Zude's eyes.

Intimacy flooded Zude's veins. Her palms were sweating. "Bosca, I'm—"

"Zude." Bosca held up her hand. Then she dropped her eyes, as if all courage had failed her. Zude kept absolutely still. A breeze rocked the hovercraft, urging it out of its parked status. Automatically, Zude steadied the steering orb.

Then Bosca's voice lost any hint of hesitation. "Zude, I had no reason to come to Los Angeles. No purpose, I mean. It was a spontaneous decision if ever I made one. And now I know why I came." Zude said nothing. "Magister Adverb." Bosca turned her chair directly toward Zude's. As she did so, she gently pulled around Zude's swivel seat to face her own. "I came to ask," she said, "if I can be your friend." Before Zude could respond, Bosca elaborated. "Not your lover, and certainly not your co-worker, though there is some important work we have to do together. Not to intrude on any of your present relations. Just to be your friend."

The hovercraft hovered. Zude sat flabbergasted.

"Well," Bosca finished, matter-of-factly, "you can think about it." She sat back and smiled. "Will you tell me about this family of yours so I can at least call them by name when we meet?" She turned her chair forward again, toward the panorama of sea and sky. "They're all from Old Mexico?"

Zude blinked. Deliberately, she shifted her mind toward Bosca's change of subject. With only a little difficulty she found her voice and the hovercraft's forward impulse tab. "No," she said, "no, only Kayita. She left her brother leaning against a slot machine in Oaxaca sixty years ago. She's been looking for him ever since. Be ready to be quizzed."

"Zude, I have been to Oaxaca only once in my life—"

"It doesn't matter. What matters is that you're from Kayita's part of the world. You tell her about your home, about Tres Valles. That will be sufficient." Zude turned the cushcar toward land, explaining as they flew how her adopted family spanned four generations: Kayita, the matriarch; Eva, her daughter who would soon be back in Australia for two more years; Ria, or Gabriella, the daughter of Eva who lived with Kayita and the children; and finally, her chosen children, Regina and Enrique and their one hundred cousins, all of whom would undoubtedly greet Zude and

109

Bosca when they arrived.

They were approaching land, and the cushcar was decelerating with gentle jerks when Zude broke off her narration. She turned to her companion.

"What work do we have to do together, Bosca?"

"Work that you will refuse at first," Bosca replied.

"But only at first?"

"Only at first."

"Will you tell me what it is?"

"Will you promise to consider doing it?"

"I promise," Zude replied. "To consider it," she added hastily.

Bosca looked straight ahead and spoke calmly. "I'm being told by my Guides that I must show you the considerable extent and force of your psychic abilities."

Zude guided the cushcar very carefully, revealing nothing of the flood of memories that filled her mind. Harsh accusations and bitter quarrels, fierce arguments and sweet reconciliations. Swirls of frustration and pain—all of it set about by the words, over and over again: *"Yes you can, Zude!" "No I can't, Bella-Belle, I can't do it!" "You mean you won't!"*

Magister Adverb had no intention at that moment of submitting to any psychic development program.

She grunted in response to Bosca's announcement, then brought the cushcar over the beach, rocking her passenger a bit with the airjets' transition to the multicolored sands beneath them. She chose a route over smooth low grass that would allow them to sail at a height of about twenty feet. She locked into a free lane. "There," she said, pointing to a complex of low white buildings. "That's the South City Employment Center where Ria works. She's the daughter—"

"The daughter of Eva," Bosca recited, "who works in Australia, and birthmother to Reggie and Enrique, who have one

110

hundred cousins."

"Correct," said Zude, smiling in spite of herself.

Bosca watched the Center flow by.

When Zude dropped the cushcar in a whisper to the pad atop an adobe house, whoops of delight broke from the safety door, now open and expelling a herd of children onto the roof. They led Zude and Bosca to an old woman down in the patio, who eyed them carefully before pointing to two chairs. "Good," she nodded. "Now you will say about Oaxaca."

6

[2087 C.E.]

We bind him hand and foot under an eyeless hood similar to
our own masks and drive him under dark skies to the deserted
clearing in the high grove. He cries for mercy all the way, and
his sweatsmell fouls the flex-wagon. Spread-eagled on the sacred
ground, he hears the litany of his deeds against women. Shaqya
removes his hood, and Rutana draws down the fire for the
charging of the crystals. We chant our ritual-of–intent. I stand
guard at a distance as my sisters begin their work.
I hear only his screams.
—Barya's Speaking from *The Transcribed Tellings of
The Mothers' Resistance,* August 14, 2087

The pavilion lesson with Aba's students had left Bess Dicken
uncomfortable in a part of herself that she did not wish to
explore. Shaheed's desire to tame horses had reawakened her
memory of the hut on the Jamaican mountainside, where, when
she was ten, Panzon Wundu had raped her and bludgeoned her
mother. Accompanying the intertwining of the images of breaking horses and violating women, Shaheed's defiance still rang in
her ears, "What will you do with people like me?"

Typically, when she found herself this disturbed, Dicken
would commit her body to programs of strenuous physical chal-
lenge in which she would outlift stevedores, outsplit wood-
women, outclimb professional sheer-scalers, or outdance
dervishes. But that kind of chastening and clarifying was not
available to her in this village by the Red Sea, and she entered the

activities of the evening accompanied by a rising anxiety.

Bess Dicken did not stand easily in second place, particularly to a woman so light-skinned, a woman so universally simpered after, as Jezebel. A fierce love of freedom shot through her days, legacy of her bearing mother whose ancestors had been cimarrón or maroon, slaves who had fled both the Spanish and the English to live for centuries without recapture or interference in the mountains of Jamaica. Though she had lived in Birmingham with her donor mother since she was ten, Dicken had never lost the fire of that cimarrón heritage.

Moreover, Dicken was no stranger to the dynamics of leadership and personal power, having headed up such bureaucratic agencies as the mill board of Nueva Tierra Norte's steel manufacture and, later, that same satrapy's Hemp Standardization Bureau. She had attracted Jez in the beginning not only with her grace and energy (and her dancing) but with her commitment to making global electronic communication an efficient, convenient, and non-intrusive reality as well. It was Bess Dicken, who at that very moment held the unofficial but most widely trusted overview of Little Blue's every natural resource and who carried in her head the one hundred complex compucodes that could locate in swift seconds the repositories of styrene in Akron, for example, or of ilmenite in Rostov.

And yet, to the person of Jezebel Stronglaces, Dicken was glad to yield the conch, for Jez most clearly articulated Dicken's political purpose and fired her creative imagination. She understood that Jez looked upon her as her buffer zone of protective sensitivity as well as her love-and-learn-together; Jez had assured her that Dicken read her health, her needs, and her desires in ways no other had ever done.

Happily, Dicken's uneasiness subsided at the evening meal, when someone put a drum in her hands and urged her to join the village musicmakers. To appreciative clicks and applause, she also rendered her variations on seawomen's ballads and taught the group a hambone riff adaptable to any dactylic cadence.

Jezebel made her contribution to the meal by instructing villagers in the fundamentals of breathshine. With her guidance, Zari created a low flicker of light in an idle glolobe with only her breath, her mind, and her tiny hands. When Dicken and Jez at last departed for their spin with Asir-By-The-Sea's sub-demesne web, the foodcave was alive with the efforts of adults and children alike to coax into life whatever inactive glolobes could be found.

After the webspin, the visitors said reluctant farewells to Aba and the Asir websters. Jezebel was determined to fly that night across the desert's edge, down to Brandnew Salalah in Oman. She and Dicken would ziprocket from there to Bombay, where Central Webster Dhamni Diu Pradesh would host them for two days. They were readying their packs to the background of go-to-bed noises in the distant village when Dicken caught in her lover's voice the unmistakable edge of profound fatigue. Fatigue, when during these next weeks the two of them were bound for a gruelling tour of satrapy and demesne webs in all parts of the world.

She moved behind her lover, slipped her arms around her waist, closed her eyes, and released a long sigh. She rested her chin on Jez's shoulder. "After we see Dhamni in Bombay, let's take some rest time, maybe only a day or two, before we see Thurlanki in Tabora."

"Depends on how critical Dhamni thinks—"

"Depends on how much you want to push that fatigue . . . maybe even risk one of your old seizures."

Jez smiled. "What did you have in mind?"

Dicken shifted her weight very slightly back and forth, from one foot to the other; Jez's enfolded body swayed with her. "When I was doing my field time with the Teakwood Searchers," Dicken said, "I met a Rememorante Afortunada who took me to a beach that was a combination playground and shrine. Over a hundred giant tortoise shells were there, just lying in the sun. Some were oiled and polished to preserve them; others had little temples built around them. Some were beaten up and worn down where children had scrambled in and out of them. One was completely covered with small gifts and notes. The notes said, 'Please come back,' or 'We didn't mean to hurt you,' or 'I think you are beautiful, Ms. Tortoise.'"

Still holding Jez's hand, Dicken leaned against the room's makeshift table of crates and boards, then continued speaking more and more slowly. "There they were, all those shells, empty of life since the day the big turtles died in them. We climbed up on top of some that had been stacked together, and the old woman spread out huge red palm leaves for us to sit on. She taught me how to play the zeze. It was the holiest place I've ever been in. I want to take you there."

Jez stared at her lover. "Dicken," she said, framing the big face with her hands. "Where is this place? Is it near?"

"Very near. It's Aldabra Island. In the Seychelles."

"Right off the Tanzania coast. We'll go!" Dicken's face outshone the sun. "It's practically on our way back from Bombay."

"And," Dicken grinned, "we have a nice out-of-the-way mud hut here and a bright starry sky. I think we should stay here for the night. Fly out early tomorrow for Brandnew Salalah. We can still make Bombay by next day."

With a deep laugh, Jez kicked her pack aside. Dicken gave an extinguishing tap to the glolobe, plunging the earthen room into blackness. Starlight from the open doorway gradually made visible the outlines of Jez's naked body. Dicken shed her caftan and trews, then drew her lover down to the pallet, laughing her own deep anticipation.

In the affairs of bodily pleasure, Bess Dicken had made a goodly number of women happy; and a goodly number had made her happy as well. But nothing else ever gave Dicken the sheer joy she got from making love with Jezebel. In their best times together, they would arrive together at a "Crystal Gate," beyond which their loving was a highly conscious and mutual act, a place of tender and almost unbearable intimacy. Once entered, the Gate cast Dicken's softself into Jez's body and Jez's softself into Dicken's, so that each woman inhabited the extraordinary dual reality of being in every moment both toucher and the touched, both lover and the loved.

Now, in the chill of a desert night, Dicken began the precious ritual of gliding toward the Gate and the softself exchange, discovering all over again every niche and plane of the bared body before her. She found a pocket of extra-fine brown hair just behind Jez's ear, noted a starboard list in the tissue of Jez's erect nipple, drew her tongue down an intercostal channel, and calculated in the back of her mind the probable moment of Jez's inevitable burst into full-body sweat.

"Stop, love."

At first, Dicken ignored the whisper.

Then it came again. "Dicken, stop a minute. Something's out of kilter."

Bewildered, Dicken muttered, "Out of kilter?" Then she flared and pulled away from Jez. "Out of kilter!" She sat up.

Jez lay looking up at her. "Clearly," she observed pointedly. Then she, too, sat upright. She rested her hand on Dicken's arm. "One of us is not all-present." She closed her eyes.

All of Dicken's latent uneasiness from the schoolroom encounter rose up out of her pores. She held her hands over her ears.

Jez slid behind her, her chin on Dicken's shoulder. "Let's just back off a minute." She settled herself against the wall and held out her arms, making a place in them exactly the size of Dicken's throbbing head.

Dicken hesitated, then reluctantly stretched out again. She felt strong fingers massaging her scalp. When Jez pushed a stiff thumb into the tiny muscles that connected her skull to her neck, Dicken howled.

"That's what you're blocking," Jez soothed her lover's brow even as she maintained pressure on the delicate spot.

Dicken stiffened with a gasp. She felt her resistance ebbing away, and with it, her conscious control. *A scent of bixin assailed her nose and a red crystalline liquid dripped from a bibcock by her pallet, staining her cotton skirt. The floor was wet and slippery with piles of annatto seed pulp. Through the half-open door, a shaft of candlelight flickered and bounced.*

She was in the dye room—asleep, or so her Momah thought. How could she sleep with the man yelling, with Momah's cries? It was Wundu again, back from the cockpits.

Dicken crept to the door. Momah was lying on the floor among scattered dishes and pots. She held her arm over her face while Wundu kept hitting her with the flat of his hand.

"What you gon do, fancy woe-manna? You gon calla Kan-show? Huh?" He held her by her hair, jerking her whole body with his shaking of her head. "You gon make them take me 'way? What you gon do wi' me, woe-manna?" He brought his fist down from above, smashing against her temple.

Dicken felt the shriek rise in her throat as she lunged across the room.

"Bess, stay back!" her mother cried, staggering to her feet. "Get back, child!"

Wundu turned his soggy face to Dicken as she flung herself on him. "Hah!" With one mighty backhand, he sent Momah's thin frame sailing through the air, her head thudding into the corner of the stove. She fell limp. Then he turned his attention to the wild figure clinging to his neck and clawing at his eyes.

In a second, Dicken was on the floor with his thick bulk holding her motionless, his rank rum breath hot on her face. She heaved and writhed, trying to find air, pushing at his eyes with her one free hand. Wundu snagged her fingers between his teeth, twisting his tongue around them, sucking and biting.

Then he pinned her free arm and let his lips drag damply over her face. "Oh, Miss Prick Teaser, you gotta this coming oh, for so longa long time!" He shifted his weight to the side, puffing and grunting as he untied his belt with one hand and pulled one leg free of his pants, all the while keeping her immobile with his chest and his other hand, his wet face next to hers.

Dicken closed her eyes and screamed. She screamed with all the breath she could draw, one long scream drowning his foul talk, his moist whispers, as he struggled with his clothes.

"You wanna suck my cock, don you, don you, Miss Tease?" She spat at him. He guffawed and wiped the spittle across her cheek, adding his own slobber as he reached her mouth and tried to pressure it open with his teeth and tongue. Dicken twisted her head away, her mouth a tight line. Wundu fumbled under her skirt; then with an angry jerk, he tore her underwraps from her body. Dicken forced a curse through her raw throat. He was on her again, rocking and rubbing. She could feel his hand between their bodies massaging his cock. He panted, eyes closed, pushing faster and faster. "Oh, Miss Priss," he moaned, "you gon get oh sucha big meat! Gon fill you up, hard!"

Dicken felt him spreading her legs with his own, his grunts louder now, his fingers sliding and poking into her vagina as if he were trying to widen the opening. When Wundu changed his body weight so his cock could fit between her legs, Dicken glimpsed the immensity of what was in store for her young body. She rebelled again,

119

*trying in vain to throw him. As she felt the blunt weapon at the edge
of its intended sheath, she drew a long breath, stifled it, and sent her
awareness out of her body, upward and out beyond the hut and the
annatto trees, over the coconut groves, the streams, the vally sinks, up
past green mountains and the eastern coast of the island.*

"Dicken!" Jez's voice rode the distant cloud cluster. "Come
back to me!" Jez was rocking her, shaking her gently. Dicken swallowed; her throat was sore. Jez held her closer, humming a stilling
chant into her ear. Dicken opened her eyes. She heard herself
panting loudly.

"Jez!" She clung to Jezebel, heaving and shaking with her own
attempts at calm.

"Dicken, my love." Jez hummed and held and chanted.

When Dicken could speak, she gasped, "Wundu." Then,
"Fucker!" Her rage still shook her.

"I felt you leave your body," Jez said softly. "That's your
block, when you dissociate."

Dicken staggered up from the pallet. "So what, I should take
my memory back to the place it all happened and fix it!"

"Dicken—"

"Witch-woman, I just been there! I just been there and seen
it all over again!" She held her belly. "And this is what it gets me!"
Dicken threw her arms high. "So what you gonna do for me,
Jezebel? What's your cure? You go round fixing the whole world,
and now you gonna fix your own love-together!" She prowled.
"You gonna tell me like my Hoonah that it's all my doing? That I
brought this fucker into my world with my own negative vibes?
That if only I'd-a been in synch with my Source Self the whole
unfortunate incident would never have happened? That my vir-
ginity would-a been intact, and Wundu would not-a got away
scott-free, and my Momah would not-a spent the rest of her days
wandering up and down the plateau in a nightshirt eating tree

bark and singing hymns?"

Jez shook her head.

"Or maybe you're going to tell me to get inside old Wundu's experience and understand why he had to go round raping little girls and why I got to forgive him!" She laid both hands against the hard-mud wall, then rested her bent forehead between them. Cunning flashed over her countenance. "I know what you got up your sleeve! You gonna say, 'Why Dicken, you got to purely love that poor soul, putting it to you with his big dick! You gotta love him while he tears your insides out, so he can hallelujah see his sin and come on back home, come on back to Jesus!'"

Jez pushed herself up from the pallet. She put her naked body squarely against Dicken's. "Look—" she began.

Dicken wasn't finished. Her mouth was a sneer. "You never been raped, Jezebel. It was the most demeaning, humiliating, enraging thing I ever felt! It was hell, pure burning hell! That violation is forever!"

"Not so, Dicken!" Jez levelled at her. "It's only for as long as you want to carry it!" Jez whirled away from her. "Dicken, you've got to *stop* carrying it. You've got to dump it out!"

Dicken's words came in a steely monotone. "Don't you go therapeutic on me, girlfriend!" As she jerked away in frustration, Dicken struck her hand against the wall. She howled, cradling the injury with her other arm and her bent body. Suddenly, her face contorted, and she began sobbing.

Jez watched the big body heave and gasp. Without moving, she extended a broad carecurl. It enveloped the awkward figure, shaping its contours to receive pain and offer ease. Slowly, Jez reached out and drew Dicken down to the pallet.

The stars shifted another inch in the doorway. Still, Jez massaged and chanted. Closing her eyes, she breathed in a measured tempo, trying to feel herself into separate parts of her lover's body, making a scan of the organs and systems.

Immediately, she was assailed by heat, heaviness, and unthinkable pain. Her softself was inside her lover, inside the empty shell of the child that Dicken's softself had abandoned. And Wundu was on her, grunting and puffing as his hardness drove into every sacred corner of her body, retreated and drove in again, deeper and rougher, a relentless ravaging of her softest tissues, her most cloistered secrets, her most shrouded altars.

On the rough pallet in the starlight, Jezebel Stronglaces screamed as she had never done before, a scream of rage and revelation. She hushed it only when she reined in her softself and regained her identity.

Still, Wundu assaulted her. Jez knew now what was happening, knew that she was feeling the cells of Dicken's child-body, living Dicken's memory, while at the same time she had removed herself from from the experience. Unlike the departed Dicken, Jez was still able to feel the pain and rage of the rape. She rode with the feelings and Wundu's defilement, amazed and incredulous.

Beside her, Dicken's uninhabited body lay rigid. Inside Dicken's body, Jez's softself lay rigid. Nowhere could she find a hint that Dicken's softself, too, had made the switch. This was not their usual exchange.

In a haze of disbelief, Jezebel began moving her softself back and forth between Dicken's body and her own. In Dicken's body, she urged the return of Dicken's softself from its detachment. Even as Wundu's plungings continued, she implored Dicken's spirit to come back to her own body—or to Jez's body. "Just come back, Dicken," she sent. "Come back!"

Then her softself was again in her own body, as she held and soothed the forsaken form beside her. When Dicken slowly unclenched her jaw, hope stirred in Jezebel. She kissed the softening countenance, even as it drew itself into an acknowledgement of pain. "Dicken!" she whispered from her hardself. "Dicken, switch to me, switch to my body!" She shifted her softself back into Dicken's body and implored the returning spirit, "Dicken, find the Crystal Gate! Find it! Come to me, to your Jezebel!"

There! Dicken was there! Miraculously, the exchange had happened. With her softself still in Dicken's child body, Jez continued to endure Wundu's thrusts. But now Dicken's softself, barely awake and aware, inhabited Jez's body. It spoke through Jez's lips. "Jez! What gives? What—"

"Love me, Dicken!" Dicken's lips pronounced. "Love me now!"

———◆———

"I didn't forgive him!" Dicken was adamant.

"What, then?" Jez countered.

"I didn't forgive him," she repeated. "It's just . . . I just feel okay." She grinned feebly under a stream of water.

The two women stood in the Single Bucket, Asir-By-The-Sea's version of a shower. Jez alternately dried herself and poured stingy dollops of rinse water into the sieve over Dicken's head.

Dicken opened her mouth to capture and spit out a few drops. She shook herself and reached for the towel. She dried her arms, then collapsed on the wooden bench. "That whole scene's got no charge for me anymore," she said, through streaming tears and a soft smile. "It's like I'll never have to remember all that again. Never."

Jez sank beside her. She wiped beads of water from Dicken's back. "Lover, we changed it. We changed the energy."

She towelled the dark face.

Dicken stared at her.

Jez continued, "From rape into something else."

"No." Dicken was suddenly vehement. "No. No! My body

did not come to sexual climax from rape!"

"I said we *changed* it, love, changed the energy of that memory within you! Your body, even with my softself in it, was healed by the loving of my body, which had your softself in it—and the physical actions of Wundu."

Dicken's anger diffused. She shook her head. "Too much," she whispered, tiredly. She found Jez's eyes. "I just know I feel released. Like I'm getting out of a bailiwick after serving a long sentence." She studied her lover's face. "You're knocked out by it," she breathed. "Aren't you?"

"I am knocked out by it," Jez agreed, "beyond what I'm able to understand." She wrapped the big towel around Dicken's shoulders. "So let's don't try to deal with it now."

Dicken stood and held out her hand. They spoke in whispers as they made their way over the starlit sand back to their quarters. On the narrow pallet, they folded themselves into spoon position, Jezebel behind Dicken, holding her loosely. They spoke the incantation in Arabic and fell at once into sleep.

7
BOMBAY
[2087 C.E.]

> In the words of Mother Monique, "There was a time when
> you were not a slave." In the words of Mother
> Bhodrapona, "There will come a time when you are no
> longer a slave." And in the words of Mother Babette,
> "The reign of men is a no between two yeses,
> a death between two lives, an unfortunate pause
> in the course of Love."
> —*The Mother Right Manifesto,* circa 1978

"Jezebel, I have broken bread with those whose insight is most clear. They offer little hope. They say the Testing and the Protocols are doomed, that neither will ever make the Central Web's consensus." Dhamni Diu Pradesh, Rememorante Afortunada and Central Webster from the Asia Satrapy, was massaging her guest's feet. "The Websters I have heard from feel that their constituencies are against us," she continued, as her strong hands worked their magic, "or at least that they lean toward protofobia. Flossie Yotoma Lutu and your old classmate, Zella Terremoto Adverb, are a formidable pair. They stand as a bulwark against the Protocols and have the staunch support of all the individual rights groups—at least in their two tri-satrapies."

Jez put her hands behind her head, trying to relax into Dhamni's healing pressures. "You'll have more hope after I share some of Dicken's and my information. But," she observed equally, "you're right about Zude, at least. She would never countenance a world that came to peace through violent means."

"*Violent* means," Dhamni mused, shaking her head. "Like the Protocols. Or the Testing."

"Exactly."

There was a long silence. "You know," the older woman said calmly, "we may just have to let it go."

Jez's eyes flew open. "Let it go!" She relaxed once more, still trying for ease. "Dhamni, old friend, you amaze me. How can you talk so blithely about letting it go? After all your work!"

Her host smiled, her strong hands still hard at their task. "Because I make a distinction between *wanting to change things* and *wanting things to change.*" She concentrated on the big toe. "Jezebel, you know I want the Testing and the Protocols to be made into law. But our way of trying to make it happen may not be appropriate. *Wanting to change things,*" she mused, "is also violence. It's just a *little less* violent than persuasion, which is just a *little less* violent than physical force."

"Live and let live," Jez sighed. "You're a purist, Dhamni, a hands-off purist."

"Perhaps," said her host. "I state my case passionately. I earnestly listen to others as they state their cases with equal passion. I admit that they have their truth just as I have mine. I look for a bigger perspective. And without losing my passion or my vision, I stop beating my head against the wall. That's letting go."

"That's giving up!" Jez held up a second foot for its share of Dhamni's ministrations. "Dhamni, I confess that I sometimes find myself trying to persuade people, but you know me and you know that in all these years, in all our work for the Testing and the Protocols, I've tried *always* to find a way that coerces nobody, a way that *hopes for change* without *pushing someone to change.*"

She deliberately breathed deeply, still seeking ease. "But I can't argue passionately in one breath and in the next simply be indifferent about it all."

Dhamni kneaded and rubbed in silence. She shook her head. "It's not about indifference," she mused. Long moments later, she added, "Letting go is more about you yourself being willing to change." She pressed ease into Jez's heel.

"I *am* willing, Dhamni," her guest said quietly. "I am willing to give and give and give, to change and change and change." She sat up straight. "There's only one thing that I think I will never change, one bedrock belief."

"Which is?" She sat very still, holding Jez's foot.

Reluctantly, Jez extricated her foot. She brushed her masseuse's cheek with a kiss, then stood up and stretched, moving slowly toward the courtyard. After a moment, she turned to her host. "The Protocols," she said at last, "and the Testing. In this case, the end does justify the means. Just once, Dhamni, just this one time!"

Dhamni's eyes were closed, and she was frowning. Still, she nodded her head. "The bomb to end all bombing, the war to end all wars, the violence . . ."

"To end all violence," Jez finished. She picked up a hand-sized statue of a nilgai and stroked its blue-grey belly. "Violence drove the animals away and nearly destroyed every inch of the Earth. And it hasn't stopped." She slid her fingers across the tiny antelope horns, then set the statue down again. "Watch any three males, Dhamni—any age, on any street corner, in any country. 'Oh, they're just having fun,' some twitter, or, 'Boys will be boys!' But that tight feeling in your belly tells you that it's not just fun. They're hostile, and they'd like to do something *to* some person or *to* some thing that is weaker than they are. Their very stance suggests the kick they'll get out of blowing it up or torturing it or at least making some kind of mockery of it. They are a danger," she finished, "to all of life."

Before she stood, Dhamni spoke encouragingly to her hips and knees. Then slowly, she rose and stepped behind her guest. "You are forgetting," she whispered, "it's not all men. Not anymore. There has been some improvement."

Jez shrugged, nodding reluctantly.

Dhamni put her arms around Jez and looked over her shoulder into the green-filled courtyard. "I sometimes wonder how the women a century ago survived," she said, her breath brushing Jez's cheek. "Everywhere they turned, it was men. Men's bodies, men's guns, men's wars, men's movies, men's needs, men's property, men's power. There was no escape from it. I cannot imagine having a man in my house, much less one who assumed he owned me, that I was his possession."

Jez sighed. They stood on the high-polish tiles in the morning sun, staring at intricately climbing ferns and mossed rocks. "I learned something in Asir," she said, "from a boy just moving into his manhood. Dhamni, men are terrified they will lose their individuality. They see women as a sameness that will obliterate their individual identity." The women stood, one behind the other, swaying lightly.

Out of the long silence, a tangle bell sounded. And sounded again. The two women did not move. There was a bustle from the street side of the house, voices in formal conversation. A bamboo curtain rattled closed.

Sulankisha found her great-grandmother and the visitor apparently tranced out by the sight of a boontree root. She wiped her hands on her light raineralls and spoke. "Moet." Dhamni turned. "Moet, there was a runner at the door when I came in. She gave me a message for Jezebel Stronglaces."

"I'm Jezebel." She held out her hands. "And you're Sulan. I

met you years ago. On the island."

Sulan stepped back hastily. "I have the wastes of Bombay all over me," she explained. "Garbage rotation. But I remember you. You taught us scrying."

"A version of it," Jez agreed, dropping her hands. "You have become very beautiful."

Sulan did not hide her pleasure or her blush. "Your message is from Bess Dicken. She says you can't reach her until after three. But then you must call her at the Trade Center. At Key 1765-8 L."

Jez frowned. "Did she indicate any urgency?"

"The runner just said to tell you that it is one of Dicken's premonitions." She smiled. "Moet says you will be with us a few days. I look forward to that."

"Thank you, Sulan."

"We are working until late afternoon," Dhamni added, "and I have set a privacy ward. But at dusk, will you eat with us?"

"I wouldn't miss it." Sulan waved as she left for the shower-house.

The older woman picked up her teacup and the pot. She made her way toward the cookery. "Before we get into our work, I have some tell-all for you. Do you want to hear it?"

Jez followed her, relaxed at last. "What do you think?"

"I think you always want to know how you are perceived."

The cookery was an old-fashioned kitchen, with last-century freeze-and-heat units and no transmog. Jez set her cup on a small round table and sank into a pillowed chair. She settled back. "So," she said, "the tell-all."

Dhamni rinsed her cup and spoon, spreading them on the solar tray for drying. "The word here on the streets and in the fields," she said, "is that Jezebel Stronglaces is a dedicated, charismatic witch whose integrity, on the whole, is intact." Jez raised her cup in salute to herself. Dhamni set a plate of snacks on the

table. "And," she continued, "she's very eloquent, highly persuasive."

Jezebel reached for a celery stick filled with cashew nut
spread. "Guilty," she said. "I probably spent too much time as an
Amah cadet, Dhamni. The Kanshou believe in persuasion, you
know, or at least their *Labrys Manual* recommends it as the best
alternative to physical force." She grinned. "Actually, I think some
Kanshou suspect that persuasion is violence and feel guilty about
using it."

"Still, it *is* a lesser evil."

Jez bit into the celery. "And fun," she added, chewing loudly.
"Admit it, Dham. You can get plenty high on a good argument. I
may even have seen that happen . . ." She frowned and looked
into the distance, as if trying to recall an instance.

Dhamni laughed, holding up a cellusponge in protest. "It
must have been a long time ago, Jezebel." She began wiping up
drops of water in the ridges of the splashboard. "The worst that is
said of you," she resumed, "and only a few say it—is that your
protofile stance on the Testing and the Protocols borders on the
fanatic; they insist that you are a Mother Righter."

"That's not true!"

The older woman had her sponge hand on her hip. "Some
think that anyone who supports the Testing and the Protocols
must be a man-hater; ergo she is also a Mother Righter."

Jez laughed and finished off the celery stick. "Oh, my good
friend, I have lived with Mother Righters, and much as I understand *and* respect them, I can't accurately be labelled as one. Real
Mother Righters, Dhamni, think the Testing and Protocols are a
joke! They don't believe men *can* be cured of their violence, not
even by the Protocols! The only way to get rid of violence, they
would say, is to get rid of men completely. From their point of
view, men are evolutionary blunders and must be bred out of exis-

130

tence as soon as possible."

"Ironic, then," Dhamni observed softly, "that anyone should associate them at all with the Testing and Protocols."

"True," Jez agreed. "Anyway, I can't admit to the label. Men, slaves though they are to their unfortunate biology, do add some variety to the world, and heterosexual women should be able to choose them as mates. And the Protocols will take care of their violence." She drained her tea. "I guess the reason I can't be called a Mother Righter is that I have too much hope for men." She paused. "And too much hope in the Testing and Protocols."

Both women were seated now at the worktable. Jez drew the fabric of the noon hour into familiar pleats. "And now, old friend," she sighed loudly, scanning the settings on the compuboard, "is it true that the Big Web itself sometimes acts with less than consensus?"

Dhamni shuffled through comcubes and flatcopies. "Often," she answered. "Consensus is the Central Web's ideal, but if the agenda is full or if the matters are more local than global or if the particular policy will affect only a few, then yes, the Web can resort to majority decisions." She looked at Jez. "This decision will have to be consensus. Nothing more important than this has ever come before the Web."

There was no more to be said. The two women exhaled a common ending breath, activated the humming computer terminal, and adjusted their sights for the work at hand. They shared Dhamni's reports and the news of Jez's travels. Both were heartened by the projections that Jez and Dicken had compiled with women from demesne webs.

They plunged on into the long afternoon, exploring multiple strategies. Most likely, the Web would entertain the proposal for Habitante Testing first, as a matter of prudence. Until research had ascertained that there was indeed an organic, physiological center of violence in the brain for which protocols could be formulated, caution had to be the watchword. The matter of individual freedom was nested deep in the global psyche.

In regard to Adult Protocols, the question of acting against another's will was the issue. To be sure, violent people could choose to change their behaviors, but the point was to *require* the Protocols by global law to assure that *all* violent offenders—who by their very acts of violence had given up their rights as citizens—would be subjected to the procedure. "Violence" itself would have to be defined far more explicitly than at present.

A barrage of doubts assailed Jez. "Dhamni," she whispered. "Dhamni, what if . . ." She inhaled deeply. "What if . . . we don't find it? Any physical cause?"

The activity of subdued hums, clicks, and beeps vibrated from the computer. It sang a plaintive solo for many long seconds. Dhamni took her own deep breath. "Unthinkable, of course," she said. Another short electronic solo of clicks from the terminals. She closed her eyes and pressed her hands together against her chin. A long moment later, her eyes snapped open and her warm laughter broke over their work area. "If no violence center is discovered," she announced, "then we're wrong, Jezebel! We're wrong and relieved of a tremendous burden!"

For a fleeting instant, Jez caught a glimpse of a longer, broader view of their efforts. "Yes," she whispered, joining Dhamni's laughter. "Yes!"

They resumed their work for hours more, late into the afternoon, assessing each tri-satrapy's five Websters—their personalities, their histories, their interactions with each other, their public and private statements regarding the Testing or the Protocols. At last, they called up a wide screen from the large table's center to display the results of their work, and they began to take heart once more.

It was widely acknowledged that, for whatever reasons, the Asia-China-Insula Tri-Satrapy constituted the solid block of Testing and Protocol proponents. The tri-satrapy's only elected member and its at-large Webster was R. Mountainfire Laanolua (Kea, Hawaii). She had actually been swept into office because of her effective advocacy of the Protocols and Habitante Testing. Jez decided that there were five strong advocates for their cause from the Asia-China-Insula Tri-Satrapy.

Laanolua's most powerful adversary, if power and adversaries could be mentioned in regard to the Central Web, was Nueva Tierra Tri-Satrapy's at-large Webster, María Albizú Sotomayor (San Juan, Puerto Rico), who had not actually campaigned against Testing or the Protocols but whose admiration of and loyalty to Zella Terremoto Adverb was well known. She would unquestionably oppose Habitante Testing—and the Protocols as well. Nueva Tierra's two "vigorous" members, Francesca Carolina Love (San Francisco) and Anita Eugenia Mondales (Buenos Aires) had both taken refuge behind a wall of silence on both issues.

Nueva Tierra's two "wise" members, Jacqueline Ortiz (Panama City) and Harriet Woodswoman (Sternville, British Columbia) had also declined public comment. Both had family members who were Kanshou and thus were probably influenced by protofobe ideology, but Jez also reported that Ortiz's Vigilante niece regularly challenged her aunt in loud argument—to the entertainment of their neighbors—about Ortiz's "fascism" on the matter of Habitante Testing. And Woodswoman, Jez told Dhamni, had once announced at a small social gathering that she herself would submit to scientific experimentation if there were a chance that some physical source of violence could be discovered. On the question of Testing, Jez assessed the Nueva Tierra Tri-Satrapy Websters as one "no," one "yes," two "maybes," and one "step aside."

Vigorous Waltha Brentana of New Berlin, for reasons Jez and Dhamni speculated about at length, adamantly opposed any suggestion of Protocols or Habitante Testing. Wise Exikia Sappho Mamadiamtis (Salonika, Greece) was equally as adamant in support of both Protocols and the Testing. At-large Farabi Dasutu (Bissau, Guinea Bissau) was not willing to talk with Jez; Dhamni feared that her refusal bespoke pressure from Tri-Satrapy Magister Lutu, whose rumored support of Dasutu had secured her at-large election to the Central Web. The other two Websters of the Africa-Europe-Mideast Tri-Satrapy could not be counted either protofobe or protofile: Vigorous Thurlanki (Tabora, Tanzania) was reportedly in an agony of moral indecision; and information about Wise Rashida Bekir-Ghazi (Mosul, Iraq) was contradictory. Jez figured for the entire tri-satrapy one "yes," two "nos," and two "maybes."

Dhamni and Jez scanned the screen. No pattern apparent on the Protocols, but on Habitante Testing, there were seven clear yeas and three clear nays, with four unknown and one that would stand aside.

"Not as bad as I thought," murmured Dhamni, deactivating screens and terminals. "Consensus may be possible." She pursed her lips. "I am eased."

Jez leaned back against her cushions and called a glolobe to her. It ignited with her touch. She held it with both hands, letting it warm them. "Dham, we can get the consensus. We have months."

"Months to do what, Jezebel Stronglaces?"

Jez hugged her host. "To inquire, Dhamni, to inquire and to speak our passion. Months to create an atmosphere in which change can occur."

Dhamni let Jez hold her only for a moment. "We actually have more time than that," she said, slowly stirring her long body

134

into action. "Once the Testing is proposed, we will have to move for extended consideration so all parts of Little Blue can be given a hearing. There is so much work to be done! Formal forums and referendums on the satrapy level, on the half-trap and quarter-trap levels, on demesne and sub-demesne levels. Matters this vast and deep require a full year's deliberation. This one could require even more. And as always with that blessed process, the yeas and nays can change. Time may work against us."

"I refuse to believe that."

The cookery was totally quiet now except for one hungry sough from the old drain. "Dhamni," Jez spoke carefully, "shall we go for it? Do we ask the Asia-China-Insula Websters to present the Testing proposal?"

Dhamni tapped her screen-lume against her teeth. "Let us sleep on it. I need another day to ponder." She smiled, holding her hand over her heart. "And to curb my own excitement!"

Jez straightened. "And I need to reach Dicken. Lay out the crunchies, Dham." She stood up. "I'll toss you a wild salad and top it with a sauce straight from the Mayans. You will cry for more when you taste it." She was half-out the door. "Flatfone in the anteroom?"

Dhamni nodded. Jez was gone.

Dhamni gathered the comcubes and readers. She closed her eyes and carefully planned her next series of movements. With a long puff of breath, she rose to her feet and swept the work materials into her arms. She sang softly while she packed them into her portacase.

She was hauling crisp lettuce leaves from the coldcube unit when Jezebel appeared and leaned against the archway.

"Dhamni!"

"What . . . ?"

"Dhamni, three bailiwicks have erupted! Hanoi, Bucharest,

Caracas. One in each tri-satrapy! Simultaneously!"

Dhamni crumpled the lettuce. "No!"

"Vigilantes have the one in Caracas under control, but Bucharest habitantes have escaped into the city. Dicken says no one has heard from Hanoi since Amahs began evacuating free citizens at two, Bombay time. Dicken says she's been fidgety all day. Then when the news broke this afternoon, she . . ." Jez stepped toward her friend. "Dham—" She faltered visibly and reached for a chair. Dhamni rushed to her side.

"Sit down, Jezebel." She put her arm around Jez's shivering body and slid the chair beneath her.

"Dhamni, it's the Testing. The habitantes are protesting the Testing."

"Ah-h-h." Dhamni's voice was low. She closed her eyes and knelt to hold Jez close to her. "Shake, child," she murmured. "It is worth shaking over."

Dicken and Sulankisha found them some time later, still holding each other.

8

> "Habitantes are being punished for crimes against their
> fellow citizens. They belong in cells or at least in
> restraints. To allow them to roam freely is a mockery of
> justice. Who knows what mischief they might conceive
> of under such permissive circumstances? Matrix Major
> Adverb is, frankly, insane."
> —Femmedarme Hedwoman
> Alka Hussein, Mideast Satrapy Commissioner
> —[Proceedings of Global Bailiwick Commission
> August 18, 2076]

*The close-range blast of a shotgun shattered and scattered the face
of Femmedarme Ippolita Kemel. She flew backward just as the bailiwick's sequencing station exploded behind her. Her attacker, thrown
against a deactivated hurtfield, staggered and reloaded for another
assault with his antique weapon.*

*"Stop!" Stone shouted to the man. "Wait!" His voice was a whis-
per against the chaos of alarm coils and phaserfire. "Fucking stop!" he
cried again, scrambling toward the fallen woman. Kemel was one of
his jailers, a hard-driving bitch with a voice like worn brake-shoes.
But she had her decent moments.*

*Two Flying Daggers dropped from the sky. They overpowered
Kemel's attacker. Together, with him and with Kemel, they were
blown skyward again, in pieces this time, by a trinimbric grenade
cluster.*

Screams and howls, klaxons and sirens. Then the rattle of an automatic weapon. Stone saw Ángel, African print boxcap askew, spraying with his uzi the lifeless bodies of two more Femmedarmes. Up and down and up, left to right and left again, bullets in a circle to the left, bullets in a circle to the right, up and down and up again, his wild laughter escalating with the splatter of soft flesh, the sting of fast blood.

Stone's distress turned to anger and began a slow rise from the base of his spine. "Ángel!" he screamed, propelling himself into an arching lunge. He brought the little man down to the dirt and split his grinning face with a single blow. Yes!

Anointed by blood, Stone struck again, harder. His adrenaline surged. There, the cheekbone gave way! He balled up his stinging knuckles and hurled them time and again into Ángel's skullbone, burying them deep into the softness of that fanatic brain. He was omnipotent, invincible. Right fist. Left. Harder! His eyes were glazed, his cadence set for forever.

At last, he peaked and plunged, roaring into a sharp ecstasy. He rode it downward, slowly, deliciously, until he was washed in a peace as vast as the ocean. He rocked gently and let the frenzy leach from his bones. His torso eased. He smiled.

Silence.

Stone lay quiet, aware only of sticky wetness and throbbing fists. The body below him whimpered. He shook it. It was not Ángel's body. It was smaller and far more frail. Stone felt tears mounting the hill behind his eyes. "Petar!" he whispered. Huge sobs rose and fell in his throat. "Petar, I didn't mean it! I didn't mean—"

He could not fill his lungs. He stroked the trembling form in his arms, rocking it, holding it close, resigned to never breathing again, chanting silent words: "Forgive me! Please . . . Petar!"

Petar's lips quivered. Then his small hand reached upward and touched Stone's cheek. Suddenly, and at last, the lock in Stone's wind-

pipe gave way. He gulped precious air, heaving it in and out, laughing and crying together the song of life again.

Lucio "Stone" Baragiali awoke to the squeak of his fold-down bunk bed, with tears and sweat soaking the bedclothes and chilling his bare arms. With a recuperative gasp, he opened his eyes to the solid physical presence of his austere cell. A shaft of sodium light from the window assured him that his habitante fatigues and cap still lay across the chair above his boots, that the books and papers on his otherwise bare table were undisturbed, that his latrine still sparkled with disinfected immaculateness.

Petar was not there. Petar had not been there since that day when Stone struck him. Petar was with his mother in Kragujevac where he belonged. Stone was in the Bucharest Bailiwick where he belonged. And the habitante revolt had not yet taken place.

He snatched a clean undershirt from the cabinet at the end of the bed and pulled off the drenched one to dry the sweat from his bald head. "Eagle," he muttered to one of his tattoos, "mullah, what am I doing wrong?"

The eagle was the proud decoration of his right forearm, while the overlong copperhead on his left arm twined around the tall, bare body of a sensuous black-eyed woman, conveniently covering the three critical points of her erotic triangle. Both drawings were positioned for Stone's eyes, not for those of other admirers. He rubbed the shirt over the tattoos, scrutinizing them in the sodium light.

By damn, they were for sure getting brighter. He thought of his buddy, Gabriel, whose skin was too dark ever to take a tattoo and who razzed him about the animals on his arms. It was the woman, though, who always fascinated Gabe. She looked like Philipa, he said, his step-sister. Gabe would lay a lithe black finger on the woman's navel and whisper, "Beautiful."

"You're just jealous, Monsieur Girardon," Big Stone would

tell him, "because I can have her and you can't!" But even Gabriel Girardon didn't know Stone's secret, that in his peripheral vision all of his tattoos would move and then freeze into new positions.

When Eagle refused to answer him, Stone addressed the snake, looking at his fingertips instead of directly at her. "You got any notions, Vivacious Viper?"

Unmistakably, the snake shivered and shot her tongue in and out. "This woman is a redeemer," Stone heard in his head.

"Who? Tanya? Well, she better be. That's her job." He chuckled. "To redeem me." The female form that Snake encircled, the body that so entranced Gabe, had originally been designed as Stone's ideal woman. Then, when he needed a strong but gentle visage to go with the disembodied computer voice that guided him through his "em-vees," or Miller Violence Exploration Sequences, the tattoo woman had become Tanya, an intimate other self, his mentor, the persona he gave words to in the inner dialogue that now informed his every day. Snake was right. This woman could redeem him.

He wiped sweat from his chest. Cooler now, he lay on his back and resolutely resisted the demanding behavior of his penis. Instead, he placed his arms loosely at his sides and began a clearing ritual. He relaxed and summoned the dark-eyed Tanya's smiling countenance. "Come here, Puss."

"Not a good start, habitante," the image countered.

"Sorry. Hello Tanya, my sweet, my beloved friend. How's that?"

"Better. Now," she seemed to say, "let's take it slow. The bailiwick is exploding, right? It's D-day, when you and Ángel and the rest will be blowing the place sky-high to protest the Testing and Protocols."

"Right."

"And it's blowing sky-high?"

"Yeah. Too high."

"You hate it. You hate the violence."

"I hate it," Stone responded. "Kanshou don't have to die. Nobody has to die. The take-over ought to be bloodless."

Stone formed with his lips the words he was assigning to Tanya. "Like you beating up on Ángel."

"Foul, Tanya! Foul!"

"You bastard," he made her say. "Nothing made you happier than smashing in Ángel's face. You loved it."

Stone paused in his script. "I loved it."

"Now we're getting somewhere."

"We're getting nowhere!" He clenched and unclenched his fists. "So I love it, and I hate it. So what's new, Tanya?" He shifted his body. "I dream the frigging dreams, I do the frigging exercises, and I still love it! I love the ooze and the crunch of that head busting apart! It's a high. It's a pure burn! I can't help it, do you hear?" He was striking the bunk beside him. "I love mashing faces!"

"Even Petar's."

Something moved in his gut.

He gave Tanya her voice again. "Tell me about the Crossover, habitante."

For the thousandth time, Stone described the Crossover, how his sly psyche secretly plotted it for hours or days before it happened. The cycle always began with mounting irritation at small occurrences: a friend's innocent gesture, an insignificant word from Aleska. Then, like a donation from the gods, some unsuspecting person would step into his pathway and make a casual remark. Sometimes, just before the Crossover clicked into place, Stone teased himself: "If his mouth starts even a little trip toward a smile, I'll lay it on him," or "If he moves one inch closer . . ." or "If he blinks . . . ." Step by tiny relentless step, he would drive the person to make the ultimate move. So he could cross over. And strike.

"And then comes the exhilaration and the letting go," Tanya prompted. Stone nodded. "Now, tell how you crossed over with Petar." He had cued himself almost before he was ready. "Do it now!" Tanya ordered.

Stone swallowed. His buddy Vasi had recognized the symptoms. "You are cruising for a bruising, Stone, man." Stone had almost crossed over with Vasi that morning, but he'd resisted, escalating through three more incidents that day, until, in the kitchen after supper, Petar had dared to toss his headful of brown hair. Stone saw his own hand rise. "I told you to get a haircut!"

"I swatted him hard!" he blurted. He moved his hand with the words. "He made me do it! His hair—"

Tanya stepped in. "But you stopped, Baragiali. Yes, you crossed over and you hit him, but you stopped before you got that surge of pleasure. Remember that."

"I stopped."

"Say how you stopped the surge."

"Because it was Petar," he recited. "And he forgave me." The tears again.

"Where is all that exhilaration now?"

"Waiting."

"Acknowledge it."

"I acknowledge it."

"Bless it."

Stone hesitated.

"Bless it, Baragiali! It's yours."

"I bless it."

"Feel it now."

"I fucking feel it!" he roared.

"And now get beside yourself!"

Immediately Stone lay in his softself, next to and outside of his supine physical body, watching that body tighten, its mouth curving upward.

"Breathe!"

"I'm breathing!"

"And what do you see, breathing?"

Stone watched his tensing body, watched the fury and the rapture rising there. He felt the whole sequence in his softer self, like a shadow.

He caught the exhilaration just before it crested, and held it there in a holy conversation for which he had no words. Childhood scenes played themselves out with savageness, outrage, and uproar; other scenes passed in montage, each carrying its payload of pain.

Through the waves of anguish, Stone spoke the litany he had formulated for this moment, and for every moment like it. "This is my violence," he said, "and this is my hurt. This is what I did to Petar. This is what I have given my Spirit over to." He spoke louder. "But now I reclaim my Spirit! Come home, Spirit."

"Good!" Tanya said. "Stay with your softself! Call Spirit home again!"

"Home, Spirit, home! Come home . . . ."

"Spirit loves that violence, Baragiali. Spirit loves it from its different place. And you love it now, from Spirit. Love that violence, love that ecstasy!" When Stone hesitated, the voice came again: "Love it like a father!"

Stone's softself reached out, cradling the vicious joy, talking to it, loving it tenderly. The images flared and faded. Then there was only breath and the easy ebbing of the joy. He was back in his body. And he was calm.

Eagle and Snake were calm too, both of them glowing, both of them vibrating with well-being. Stone held them against his chest.

Tanya's voice was soft: "You think you can live without that

143

exhilaration, Habitante Baragiali? Without that high, that pure burn?"

Snake and Eagle hummed with affirmation. "Sure," Stone answered, "sure, I can handle it." Big tears bathed his temples. "Tanya, when I'm in this place I can handle anything."

"Let it come."

Stone choked and swallowed and cried. Eagle and Snake sang praises in his head. "What a place, what a place," he blubbered. "Why can't I stay here?"

Tanya's voice soothed him. "You can. You can stay right here in this place. And let Ángel and Gabe pull off their bailiwick revolt without you."

Stone froze.

"You don't have to be a part of it, Baragiali," Tanya added.

Habitante Lucio Baragiali clasped his tattoos tighter. Snake and Eagle danced with joy, threatening to fly off his arms and wake the whole bailiwick with celebration. Stone's tears flooded his cot; his chest heaved. "Tanya, I . . . I might, I might . . . if . . . ."

"If what, Baragiali?"

"If only . . . they'll stay with me!"

"Who? If only who—"

"The animals," he sobbed. "If they'll help me, if . . . ." He held his arms close, rocking left and right.

"Where are they, Baragiali, where are the animals?"

He eased a little. "Sometimes . . . I feel like they're here—all of them. Well, not here, but close." He eased his grip on his forearms, letting them tingle without restriction. "Like maybe just on the other side of my skin."

"What would bring them through, Stone?"

Stone shook his head. "They'll come when it's safe," he whispered, tears still streaming.

"Safe."

He nodded. "They'll come when there's no more violence. Anywhere." He listened for her response. "Tanya?" Silence. He thought he could hear her smile. He shouted aloud. "Tanya!"

His reverie broken, Stone lurched to his feet and held his arms wide from his body. He could feel Eagle and Snake dancing—and probably Tanya, too. He moved toward the small window, not daring to look at his arms. In the black night, the bailiwick was peaceful, the sodium light a misty glow.

"No more violence, anywhere," he repeated. He rubbed his bald pate, then thrust his arms up in front of his face, focusing directly on his tattoos. "Okay," he said aloud, "okay! I'll tell Ángel!" Eagle's wings lapsed into composure. "And I'll tell Gabe, too," he said, watching Snake ease into a languorous stretch. He felt lighter, like he'd lost a burden.

He was turning back to his bunk when his cell door clicked and swung ajar. Simultaneously, the call box keyed to his cell came to life. "Baragiali, Habitante Baragiali! Report to cushcar ops now!" Stone swore and seized the squawk box. "It's not even daylight!" he howled into it.

"Hot foot it, mister," rasped the Femmedarme's voice. "We're on to dispatch thirty cushcars downriver before seven, all at peak operation status. You get to clean them up, Baragiali! Sun-bus leaves in five. Move!"

Four hours later, Habitante Baragiali was flat on his back under two tons of suspended cushcar, patiently manipulating the last one of the craft's forty-eight air jets into a full circle, assuring himself of its mobility. He grunted with satisfaction and flipped up his goggles so he could survey the whole range of his work. "Done!" he exclaimed.

"Baldy!" Gabriel Girardon was flat on his belly shouting at his

145

friend. "You wanted to talk to me, Baldy?"

Stone touched the hydraulic and shot out from under the cushcar. "Gabe, I got passes to walk, all the way back to the mess. You okay to come with me?"

"Si bon vous semble!" Gabe took Stone's tool sheath and goggles as both men stood. He set them in front of the uniformed woman at the workstation.

Stone handed Gabe one of the white caps that would identify them to any Femmedarme as habitantes-en-route. He pulled the other cap onto the back of his own head, then signed a magnopad for the Kanshou. She glanced at him, at the pad, and at Girardon, then nodded and waved them on their way.

Still in her earshot, Stone slapped Gabe's shoulder. "Let's go, monsieur!"

"Good to see you, Baldy."

The two men emerged from the maintenance berths and set out toward the food rotunda. The narrow road wound through tracts of grain, resting fields of sweet crimson clover, and groves of trees.

Stone felt at ease, almost happy. He'd liked and trusted Gabriel Giradon from the moment he'd met him a few months ago. They walked together now, two big men casually scanning the early morning sky as if their only concern was getting to the coffee at the mess hall. "Anytime soon?" Stone asked lightly, setting their pace.

"Got to be," Gabe answered, equally casually. They walked ten steps without speaking. Then Gabe peeled a gnawstalk and stuck the end of it in his mouth. "So what's up, Big Stone?"

Eagle and Snake lay at ready on Stone's swinging arms, eager for his announcement. "Easy," he told them mentally. "This is Gabe, my buddy. I get to approach him gradual-like." A grudging response from each arm. "Well, Monsieur Girardon," he said aloud, "the violence re-training exercises, the em-vees—I think they may be working for me." Snake's head swayed with contentment. "I had this dream—"

"And a session with your doxy, huh? Hey, let me see her, can I?" Gabe halted their walking.

Stone grinned and pulled up his left sleeve. Snake lay quietly around Tanya's body.

Gabe studied the tattoo. He shook his head. "Stone, man, I don't understand how your Tanya can be my Philipa. Two women in one!" He stroked the tattoo, then dropped Stone's arm. He chewed happily on his gnawstalk as they resumed their progress. "So, the re-training," he said, "sure it works. It's the only thing that does."

"Hold on, Gabe," Stone frowned. "I just said the re-conditioning is working for me. It may not work for others. Maybe some people out there would rather get their brains adjusted—"

"Now you hold on," Gabe countered mildly. "There's nothing there to get adjusted. Nobody's found it yet, Big Stone, that so-called violence center in the brain. They probably never will." He let out a long breath. "They'd have to use thousands of habitantes to find it. They'd have to use you and me, Stone, 'violent offenders against society.'" Three steps later, he added a grim certitude. "And we are not playing in that game." He looked at the gnawstalk and returned it to his pocket.

Eagle and Snake were uneasy. Stone's gut echoed their agitation.

"Baldy," Girardon went on, "when it comes down to dust, it doesn't matter what causes all us 'violent offenders.' Could be conditioning, could be genes. Doesn't matter. Even that so-called violence center in the brain—it doesn't matter. They might find it, they might not. The point is, they're willing to make guinea pigs out of us to look for it. Without our say-so. That's the real violence, Big Stone."

He hauled them to a stop and studied Stone's face. "That's why right this minute, twelve thousand habitantes in three separate tri-satrapies are ready and waiting to blow their bailiwicks to kingdom-come. They know it's an outrage." He paused. "And so do you, Baldy."

Stone looked back at him steadily. "I know it, Gabe," he replied earnestly. "What they're willing to do without our consent, that's the outrage." He held Gabe's eyes.

From the west, Stone heard the purr of a surveillance cushcar moving toward them. In a smooth unhurried motion, he eased Gabe forward with a head signal, adding to his behavior an expansive laugh and a nod for the benefit of the approaching Femmedarme. The two men started walking again—casually, conversationally, as the cushcar slowed above them. "Keep it sweet and light, monsieur," Stone warned, at the same time lifting his cap and wiping his bald head. His mouth was shielded by his handkerchief.

Girardon's voice was suddenly fierce. "Motherfucking rubbernecks!" he muttered, head down and his lips barely moving. Then his dark face became animated again. "So let me tell you, Big Stone, about the beautiful Philipa, about my Wicked Step-Sister." Gabriel launched into his story-telling mode, playing not just to Stone but to the Femmedarme above who was certainly monitoring the loudest portions of their conversation by remote audio sensors.

"Philipa," Stone prompted. "You loved her." He could feel to his right some of the pressure of the air jets that held the hovercraft aloft.

"I worshipped her," Gabe said wistfully. He stared straight ahead as he walked. "After my father died, my mother fell in love with Dame Pola van der Weyden of Brussels. She had three daughters, and when I was eight, my mother, my real sister, and I moved into their big house in Algiers. That's six females I got to live with, Stone. Cheek by jaw. Six." Gabe's sarcasm was masked by an enthusiastic smile.

Stone nodded and chuckled. The cushcar purred overhead.

"Philipa was the oldest girl, fourteen, pure white and very pretty. But she paid me no mind at all. I used to follow her around like a puppy dog, begging for a smile, a nod, anything that would tell me she knew I existed. One day, she turned on me and said, 'Gabriel, what will you give me for a smile?' So I said, 'Anything, Philipa, I'll give you anything!' 'Be my slave,' she said. 'Do whatever I say.'" Gabe did not disguise his disgust. "Then she showed me off to to her sisters and her friends, me grovelling, kissing her feet, me fetching and carrying for her while they all laughed. So when we were alone again I said, 'My smile, Philipa. Now I get my smile!' She just raised her eyebrow. No smile. Then she walked away."

The hovercraft continued to drift forward with their progress, at their same pace. Gabe ostensibly ignored the overhead intrusion. "I was crazy," he continued. "I ran after her, crying, and for months, I bowed and scraped for her, loving it even when she belittled me or made a fool of me in front of others. One day when she had been especially cruel and I was snivelling hard, she shook me and said, 'Gabriel, you will always be my slave!'" Gabe stopped his walking. Stone stopped, too.

"Bald Man, it hit me right then what I was letting her do to me. I shut up. I looked at her. And I ran out. She never got to me after that." They walked again.

The cushcar had drifted ahead of the two men. It stopped abruptly, clearly waiting for them. As if only now discovering her presence, Gabriel Girardon looked up at the Femmedarme, discernible through the windows of the hovercraft. With a dazzling innocent smile, he pointed to his white hat and waved. The driver offered no acknowledgement, she merely pressed the air jets to lift the car to a slightly higher altitude.

"Cuntlicker!" Gabriel whispered through motionless lips.

Stone had glanced at the cushcar as Gabe was doing his act. He pulled his buddy back to the story. "So did the girl ever smile?"

"Never." Gabe shook his head. "She's head of a big convent in Canada now, bossing other nuns. Still not smiling, at least from what I hear lately." He paused. "Well, Philipa managed to isolate me from the whole family. Lied to my mother and Pola, made sure everybody thought I was some kind of freak." Gabe punched Stone's arm with his elbow. "Get this. When I was eleven, she showed my mother a complete list of the war flicks I'd been borrowing every day from the flatfilm library, even some of the restricted ones I'd gotten under an assumed name. My mother completely lost it. She sided with Philipa and cut off my privileges." He glanced up at the cushcar.

"That's when I split, lied about my age, signed onto a old freighter that took me to sea and then down to Central Africa where I found my mother's people. I ceremonially took back my tribal name and claimed my old man's name as well. And I learned to handle weapons. That's where my 'life of crime' began. Anti-Kanshou pressure groups, secession movements." Gabriel walked in silence for a moment. "Yes," he finally said, pointing to Stone's sleeve, "I certainly do hate that woman." He looked upward and hissed through a frozen smile, "And same to you, sweetheart!"

"Cut it out, Gabe." Stone covered a grin with a finger swiped across his nose. The hovercraft still hung above them.

Girardon put his gnawstalk back in his mouth and continued, conversationally. "She likes our company, Big Stone. So on with the parlor talk. How come you got yourself on the wrong side of the holy Kanshoubu? You hit your kid. You told me that."

Stone picked up Gabe's mood, lock-stepping with his friend as he told his story. "I been cited . . . oh, maybe twenty times for picking fights . . . scrapping, you know. But then I got slammed into bailiwicks for major offenses. Three times." He shoved his hands into the pockets of his fatigues. "The first time I'd been pissed for days, and a traffic 'Darme ordered me to wait at a corner. I told her she was arrogant. She looked at me like I was some scumbag, so I laid into her."

"You hit a Kanshou, Big Stone?" Gabe's voice was full of admiration.

"I tried. She decked me, right in the middle of the street, and hauled me up before the sub-demesne tribunal. Since it was a first offense, they modified my term to only three months." The hovercraft still purred above them. "When I got out, Aleska and Petar and I lived six happy years. Good years they were, until one night at a bar, I got loaded and tore up a Ruskie who gave me some disrespectful lip. Two years in a bailiwick for that."

Gabe was sucking on his gnawstalk. "The last time, you weren't drunk when you hit your boy."

"No. Just irritable. Soon as I did it, I was sorry. I grabbed him and tried to apologize. Scared him half to death. Then I ran all the way to the the Kragujevac Femmedarmery and committed myself to the nonviolence program here at Bucharest Bailiwick." They walked in silence for a few paces. "This last training has been the hardest. But," he added, "the best." He felt Snake shimmy and Eagle's wings flutter. Stone grinned, his spirits high. "So now I got a better handle on what happens, on how I cross over and go for the kill."

The hovercraft had dropped behind them now, but still tracked them. They rounded a stand of trees and looked out on the flamboyant public buildings of Bucharest Proper in the far distance. Below them in the valley lay the bailiwick's sediment fields, miles of rectangular beds of crushed coke, which transformed the human wastes of the Balkans into fertilizer for the tri-satrapy's farms.

"And here we are, Baldy," Gabriel chuckled, "you running your em-vees and re-route sequences, me re-framing and trying to forgive a bitch of a step-sister." Gabe's walk had a bounce to it. "But my stuff is a little different from yours."

"How do you mean?"

"See, at heart, my friend, I am not really violent."

Stone searched for the joke. "Come on, Gabe. You wasted six people, for chrissake—"

"By accident, man! The building was supposed to be empty! It was just a little demolition demonstration to let the bureaucrats know we were serious." Gabriel shifted the gnawstalk to the other side of his mouth, noting the cushcar's distance and talking more easily now. "See, I get no kick out of hurting or killing." He chewed thoughtfully. "Well, maybe a buzz out of accuracy sometimes . . . ." He grinned. "But what worries the girls at the Miller Center is that I don't get off on it. 'Dissociated,' they call me. But actually, I'm not into beating up on anybody. I'm just a good old-fashioned woman-hater."

Stone guffawed. "Can it, Girardon! You've filled every cunt in two satrapies!"

"Sure I have!" Gabe swaggered a little. "It's my way of fucking the government. I just fuck their Femmedarmes, tell them I'm crazy about them, and when they're in good and deep, I split. Never lay an angry hand on them. Just leave them crying for more." He stopped and looked over his shoulder toward the retreating cushcar. "But my dear," he called out earnestly, hands over his heart and walking backward, "I never loved you! You just misunderstood!"

Stone slapped Gabe's shoulder, laughing. The hovercraft

veered to the west and become a large dot against the clouds.

In his head, Stone heard a patient voice. "Now," said Eagle.

"Baldy," Gabe said, "what is it? You got something in your craw."

"I do," Stone confessed. He drew Gabe back into walking again. He was cool-headed and easy now, supported by a well of endorsement flooding from his arms. Snake and Eagle were alert, and Tanya's presence brushed the edge of his awareness. He spoke evenly, his eyes on the horizon, his voice focused toward his friend. "I want out, Gabe. I can't do the action."

Snake and Eagle were poised just short of exhilaration. "Go, Baragiali!" Tanya whispered.

Gabriel Girardon's eyes were also on the horizon. His boots, in sync with Stone's, hit the pavement nine times before he spoke. "That's a tidy little bombshell." Two more steps. "Why?"

"I could tell you that I want out because it won't work, and that's true: it won't work."

"Or you could say you've decided it's okay for them to tinker with our heads."

Stone exploded. "Gabe, I just got through telling you I think that's an outrage! I just got through telling you there's no way I want them using any of us without our say-so! I just got through telling you that I've got good feelings about my own re-training now, that I got some hope now that I'll never have to consider getting 'adjusted'!"

Stone caught a movement from behind them. He drew Gabe aside so a suntruck full of Femmedarmes could pass them. The driver nodded brief thanks. He felt Gabe's eyes on him as they resumed their walking. He waited until the suncart had cleared the far patch of trees. "Here it is," he said. "I just can't be a part of that violence."

Girardon flared. "'That violence'! Who's doing the violence,

Stone? Not me or you or Ángel or any habitante! The violence is the Testing. We are simply resisting it!"

"Resisting it is the same as the violence." Stone's arms tingled with delight.

"The same—!" Gabe sputtered. "So, Baldy, are you going to let them cut on you?"

"I didn't say that!"

"That's what you mean!"

"No!"

Girardon snapped to a halt. "What else can you mean?" he roared.

"They won't do it!" Stone roared back.

"They won't . . . ! Man—"

Stone overrode him. "Gabe, I know it! I know they won't do the Testing! I don't know how I know it, but I promise you, it's true!" From his arms surged an ongoing explosion of yeses; he rubbed them gently.

Girardon stared at him, incredulous. "Man, you have lost it," he said gently. He pointed to Stone's arms. "Your animal buddies, are they telling you that?"

Stone smiled. "Maybe," he said. He tried to urge Girardon forward again.

"Wait." Gabriel was earnest. "Baldy, I hear you saying you don't want to be part of it." As Stone nodded, Gabe nodded, too. "But I do not hear you saying you'll try to stop us."

Stone sent Eagle and Snake an assurance. "I can't stop you," he said. "I may keep yelling at you, trying to make you see it my way. But I can't stop you." He paused. "Look, Gabe, you know I got no reason to snitch or tip off anybody. You can trust me on that."

"I trust you, Baldy. But listen up," Gabriel went on, still holding Stone's eyes, "don't say anything to Ángel yet."

"Why not?"

"Just lay off telling him. A day. Two days. This is between you and me. Okay?"

"I got to tell him, Gabe."

"I know, I know. Just not right now. Okay?"

Stone quieted the objections on his arms. "I can wait until tomorrow, Gabe," he said. "No more than that. He's got to know."

Both men scanned the open valley to see who might possibly have heard their altercation. They were alone, and the bailiwick's buildings lay just below them now. The two men sealed their habitante fatigues chin-high against a rising wind and set out walking again, now in silence, down to the mess hall.

As they approached the common buildings, Gabe slowed their progress. "Baldy, you want to know a secret?" He smiled toward the dawning day as he spoke.

"Sure."

"I've never said this to anybody, man." Girardon cut his eyes toward Stone. "So repeat it, and you're dead."

Stone pointed to his chest with his thumb. "It stops here."

"Baldy, the happiest I ever been in my life is in a bailiwick."

Stone slowed to a stop, looking at him.

Gabe held up both hands. "No. Rock-bottom truth. I realized it when I finished my term up at Oslo. Stone, I been looking for men all my life. Strong men, interesting men. Looking for men in a world of girls. And what's mostly in a bailiwick?"

"Come on, monsieur, you're not—"

"No, I don't mean gay. I tried that, but no cigar. I don't need bedfellows, just buddies." They walked again, encountering two Femmedarmes. The women greeted them and passed on. Gabe continued. "So I guess what I'm trying to say is that I've found good men in bailiwicks, Stone. You're one of them."

Eagle and Snake were swelling with pride and appreciation.

Stone flushed. "Well, I'm glad, monsieur," he said.

They were in the midst of 'Darmes and habitantes now, coming and going with the start of the bailiwick day. Gabe stopped them at the door of the food rotunda, speaking in his habitual hearty voice. "I hope you'll change your mind, Big Stone, and stay on the team."

"I don't think I'll change on this one, Monsieur Girardon. Your no-rest rugby is too much for me."

"At least think about it," Girardon urged.

Stone smiled. "Sure, Gabe. I'll do that. I'll think about it."

They went into the mess hall, slapping each other's shoulders.

———◆———

Five hours later, Habitante Lucio Baragiali left early from his regular morning shift at the bailiwick's Weather Monitoring Comcenter and rode in a humming suncart along a raised roadway through the sediment fields. His head was spinning, his heart was thundering, and the tattooed friends on his arms unceasingly broadcast their presence with surges of alert attention and concern.

The weather was changing rapidly, with the high-noon sun disappearing behind a bank of dark clouds. The coming rain had been unpredicted.

As the suncart sped along, Stone looked south, deliberately seeking out the sludge dam in the distance. Its massive headwork loomed over the valley, above the ranks of conduits fanning out over the hillsides. There, tons of preliminarily treated wastes rested against a grandly structured poratac bulwark. Poratac, Stone thought, the cement that breathes! The entire sewage enterprise depended on poratac's strength and efficiency, its unique permeable and nonpermeable properties.

Stone's grinning companion, Habitante Victor Cuza,

drummed on the suncart, barely controlling a wild excitement. They were headed toward their culvert assignment deep in the bailiwick's filterlands. Behind them rolled a batchbarrow of gelatinous poratac cement. For the third time in almost as many minutes, Stone pulled out a handkerchief and wiped the sweat from the headband of his light green broad-billed cap.

Femmedarme Nyosa d'Soninke's loose black pants, draped at midcalf by knee elastic, covered the tops of her plastiped boots. She drove with vigilant eyes and minimum conversation. When she leaned in their progress around one corner, her large breasts moved visibly under the green cotton of her tabard.

Cuza punched Stone with his elbow, his mouth a leer and his eyes glued to the breasts. Stone ignored the gesture and wiped his headband free of sweat. Then he wiped his smooth head. And his hands. The weight of the cement behind them seemed like a feather compared to the load of information he had been carrying for the past half-hour. He folded his forearms together and held his elbows steady against the jogging suncart. He watched the leaden clouds, more certain than anyone, even Cuza, of the storm that was coming.

9
[2087 C.E.]

> The careful Kanshou
> tastes danger's spark before it
> crosses into flame.
> —*The Labrys Manual*

Femmedarme d'Soninke deposited Stone and Cuza at the culvert where Habitante Ángel Espartero was already at work squaring the forms. She briefly discussed with the three men the capacity of the poratac to quick-set before the storm descended, gave them the go-ahead for making the pour, and then hastily departed.

"Ángel, it's on! From Caracas!" Stone called out, quickly positioning the batchbarrow. He cast his eyes to the threatening sky.

"Another false alarm," Ángel muttered. He pushed his African print boxcap more firmly to his head.

"No," Cuza joined in. He pushed on his black beret in emulation of Ángel's motion. "Stone says this time, it's all three of the code words!"

Ángel involuntarily paused in his adjusting of the chute. He

159

looked at Stone, then swung the chute over the largest of the forms. "'Sidewinder' and 'Lush'?"

Stone nodded. "Yes."

The poratac rolled. Cuza punched up and down in the filling forms with a long pole. "And 'Burnt Ground,'" said Stone, diminishing the flow. "All three."

"Show me!" Ángel moved the chute to the next set of forms. Stone handed him a magnopad.

Ángel frowned as he studied the message. "Update at 0416 hours," it said. "High pressure system stabilizing over Burnt Ground in the Bahamas with monox readings at 8.9, well into the green but should be monitored, particularly if sidewinder winds replace lush fogs over Himalayan concourses."

The frown faded. "Ande, ande! It happens!" Ángel whispered fiercely, his dancing eyes on the sky. "And the rain! It comes right now, from God!" As if in confirmation, a sharp thunderclap sounded.

Stone began, "Ángel—" The hardest edge of a wind gust stopped him.

Cuza struggled to smooth the poratac on the filled form. "More here," he intoned. "It sets up fast." The wind was becoming a gale.

Stone filled a floater from the batchbarrow and handed it to Cuza. "We can finish," he said. He maneuvered the batchbarrow for the second run of cement, adjusting the balance as Ángel steered the flow down the chute.

"Rolling Brown. Operation Rolling Brown," Ángel asked urgently. "Did you initiate it?"

"No," Stone answered. He shut off the pour, directing Cuza and his tools toward the center form.

Ángel exploded. "I told you, I ordered you—"

"I didn't," Stone repeated. "But Hejaz did." He jockeyed the batchbarrow toward the last of the forms.

"You're sure?"

"Watch. Any minute."

Ángel shot a look southward toward the sludge dam. "Any minute!" he intoned ecstatically.

It was actually five minutes before an accelerating excitement began to break over the filtration field, plenty of time for the men to complete the pours and clean the batchbarrow, to cover the freshly-filled forms with heavy plastic, and to park the tools and the batchbarrow at a safe location. Ángel ordered Stone to duck out of the emergency action as soon as possible and to meet him and Cuza at the Depot. They would hole up there until all contacts reported in.

"Ángel," Big Stone blurted, "I got to talk to you."

"Later," Ángel answered, "when we've—"

Suddenly, two Flying Daggers hovered in gert above them, directing them toward an approaching suntruck. "The dam," one of them shouted, "it's about to break!" The gert soared again, joining the hasty relocation of cushcars toward the south. Another gust of wind scooped Stone's cap from his head. Simultaneously, the squawk of the general alarm burst upon his ears.

The valley and hillsides came alive. Green-and-black-clad Femmedarmes suddenly swarmed everywhere—in cushcars and suncarts, on foot and dropping from the sky in pairs, shouting over wind gusts and occasional thunder. They gathered habitantes into suntrucks and deployed them at silos where sandbag teams and terreforming equipment had swung into desperate action. Every eye strained southward, drawn by the magnet of the sludge dam, and below it, the conduits that would soon be too full too fast.

Stone barely retrieved his cap in time to protect his exposed head from the splatter of plump drops of rain. He saw Ángel and

Cuza turning up their coverall collars. Another roll of thunder. More raindrops, this time on his neck.

The Kanshou Captain who was driving the suntruck ordered them into it without coming to a full halt. The rain had begun a hard steady tapping now as she gathered work parties onto the vehicle and deposited them at different sites. She did not see Ángel and Cuza drop off with a large group and head by a circuitous route for one of the old water pumping units.

"Take it, Big Stone!" Without warning, the Captain turned the truck controls over to him. She stood on the suntruck's seat and braced herself on the tiny dash, spilling out orders to all sides, directing Stone's driving, calling habitantes by name as she herded them on and off the truck. The comunit around her head blared reports from cushcars and dispatch centers.

Stone never knew when the sludge dam broke. Its rumble coincided with a roll of thunder. He was aware only of an endless succession of stops and starts, turns and swerves. He drove in heavy rain for the better part of an hour, merging with the chaos, with the urgent redirection of huge accumulations of sludge into diversion ditches. With a curious mix of dismay and satisfaction, he watched the overflowing conduits as they began to cover the pristine filtration berths with a massive counterpane of excrement, inches in thickness, acres in breadth.

At a change of assignments, he disappeared into a quartermaster station, fortunately deserted by its occasionally presiding Femmedarme, and hauled double armfuls of light green jumpsuits, caps, and underduds from the shelf. In the adjoining toilet, ,he loosened the rear floor panel in one stall and dropped into the blackness beneath, pulling the clothes after him, the panels back into place.

Stone stood for a moment, leaning on the dirt wall. "So fast," he said to his inner companions. Snake and Eagle filled his head, slowing his heart, soothing his breathing. "It's okay, guys," he whispered. "I'm okay."

He checked his direction by touch, then hurried in total darkness through the tunnel. Just beyond a cross-passageway juncture, a dim shaft of light shone from above, delineating the trapdoor of the Depot. Stone emerged upward into the candlelit activity of Ángel, Cuza, and Gabe, together lifting and opening long boxes. Along the sides of the room, they unpacked an assortment of personal weaponry: old issue M-16's, pistols, knives, and garottes; grenades, disrupter snares, and even a phaser-rod, unfortunately useless for its lack of matrix enabler.

"Stone here," he sang out as the men turned toward him, Gabriel with a bright white smile.

"Bravissimo!" Ángel hissed, taking warm dry clothes from Stone's upthrust arms.

It was Ángel who, on salvage detail almost a year ago, had studied the strange architecture of the old water plant pumping post. He later discovered this hidden Depot in the center of the building, storage place of cast-off accumulators, valves, winches, and other equipment. The room was sealed away from the plant's larger areas and from the storage ports that had been added on around them. Generations of unsuspecting Femmedarmes had forgotten or had never known of it; nor did they suspect the existence of the utility tunnel through which the room was exclusively accessed. Guarded only in regular nightwatch, this secret Depot served as headquarters for Ángel's grand plan and as a resting place now while the last pieces of that plan fell into place throughout the bailiwick.

Most immediately, the Depot served as a change room for three men who stripped and dried themselves, spreading their drenched habitante coveralls and underduds on crates and an upturned trough. They picked over and chose whatever soft dry cotton fit them best. Only Gabriel declined the clothes.

"What's up, Monsieur Girardon?" Stone asked, trying to catch Gabe's eye. "You too good for these dry threads?"

"Naw, Baldy. I'll just drench them again. I got to go back to watch." Gabe's short-cropped black hair still held beads of water. He paused at the trapdoor by Stone. "You okay?"

"Fine," Stone held his eyes evenly. "You going to be back here soon?"

Gabe glanced around the room. "When Dobruja relieves me," he said. He nodded imperceptibly. "Count on it, Baldy. I'll be back."

Stone returned the nod and watched the broad figure drop down the trapdoor without a sound.

Ángel was pulling on dry fatigues, Cuza rolling up the sleeves of an oversized jumpsuit. Stone stood in his T-shirt and dry boxers, hauling his own coveralls on only waist-high. He lit another candle and set a dry cap on the back of his head as he sank his long frame onto a crate by the table. With extra undershirts, he began carefully wiping his arms—wiping dry Eagle, Snake, and Tanya. They fidgeted for him, then lapsed into being normal, well-behaved—and expectant—tattoos. Stone drew in a determined breath.

"Ángel—"

"Ángel!" Hejaz's voice came from the trapdoor.

"Hejaz, brother!" Ángel paused in his dressing to help Hejaz into the room. "This is it! It's a go, Hejaz, a veritable go!"

Stone balled up an undershirt and threw it at Hejaz's boots. He swung off the crate and began a controlled pacing of the small room.

"You pulled off the dam, Hejaz!" Cuza slapped the table with his black beret.

Ángel added, admiringly, "The perfect distraction!"

164

"Yeah! They're still trying to contain it." Hejaz picked up the shirt and began drying his neck.

Cuza leaned toward Hejaz. "Blew the Green Pussies right off their feet, didn't it?"

Hejaz grinned. "They're brown pussies now."

Cuza's laugh was a bark. "Hey, Big Stone! They're brown pussies now," he repeated, still laughing.

"I saw our beloved Brenenz standing in malodorous feces up to her waist," Ángel announced. He reached into a large sack and painstakingly began unwrapping the padding from an automatic weapon.

"You talking about the Adjutant?" Hejaz asked, rubbing his wet hair.

"Cuntface Adjutant Brenenz, herself." Ángel admired the uzi. "What is it, Hejaz? You have business about her?"

"Bet he does." Cuza stood now like an altar boy by Ángel, assisting in the unveiling of the sacred weapon. "I saw him scoping her pot at laundry detail, getting boney as a—"

"Like hell!" Hejaz grinned and threw a damp shirt at Cuza. "I wouldn't piss up her butt if her guts was on fire!"

Suddenly, Cuza shrieked his laughter, pounding the table in a drum roll. "Liquid shit rolling down the valley," he chanted, "like a volcano busting! Wow-eeeee!"

Hejaz topped him with his own voice, pounding on Cuza's shoulder. "And they'll never know why it broke!" he chanted.

Stone found his breath. "They'll suspect," he muttered under the din.

Hejaz sobered. "Stone, you are such a goddam crape-hanger. Lighten up! The girls will spin their tight little asses into molly screws before they'll ever find any evidence." He addressed Ángel. "Smythe is on lookout here with Girardon. Dobruja will relieve Girardon any time now."

Ángel nodded. He spread wide the fingers of his right hand, then drew them into a fist. He closed and extended them again and again, worshiping his hand with his eyes. He smiled into the glow of the candle, then returned his attention to the long-barrelled uzi. Beside him, Cuza sank onto one of the room's two chairs. Earnestly, he began laying out the parts of a big-barrelled shotgun.

Stone ran his hands over his smooth head, calling on support from his tattoos. He cleared his throat and moved toward the table. "Ángel, Hejaz—"

Ángel's voice overrode him. "Your Barracudas, Hejaz. Are they ready?"

"Ready. Have been for a week."

Stone closed his eyes. Tanya's voice whispered, "*Easy.*" Snake and Eagle were an echo. "*Easy,*" they chimed in.

Hejaz continued. "We're passing in and out of the emergency crews, all of us in raineralls so it's hard to tell one from another. We heft a sandbag now and again, making sure the 'Darmes recognize us, know we're there. Then we disappear and nobody notices. We're mostly at the south central cyclery now. Dispensing ammo clips and closing the information circuit."

Suddenly, Cuza leapt to his feet and pounded the table again. "Man, did you see that shit bounce and fly?"

Stone steadied a bushing that threatened to leap off the table, then he sank onto the crate again. Eagle's wing-flutter cooled his brain. And slowed his racing heart.

Ángel gently pressed Cuza back into his seat and, with his eyes closed, began a meditative massaging of Cuza's shoulders. "The 'Darmes will double their surveillance tonight, so be certain, Hejaz, that all is ready by evening mess. Everyone is to show up there. We shall all report normally to evening classes and meetings or stay in our units reading, being accommodating prisoners." He smoothed the hair back from Cuza's forehead. Cuza sat rigid under that touch. "Tell them, Brother Hejaz," Ángel continued, "to sleep tonight if they can."

Hejaz wiped his forehead. "O-eight-hundred hours, Ángel. The cuntlickers won't ever see a check-in like tomorrow's will be!" He moved to the trapdoor. "I'm taking the tunnel to the north sediment fields. I can daylight there."

"Watch your back, Hejaz," Stone said.

"I will." Hejaz smiled at Stone. Then he clapped Cuza on the shoulder. "For freedom, brothers!" He slipped down the floor passage and was gone.

Ángel withdrew his hand from Cuza and sat in the empty chair by the table. He began saturating a small rag with oil. "Brother Stone," he said, "did you confirm receipt of the coded message? Anything from Hanoi?"

"Yes. And no, nothing yet." Stone jockeyed his arms into the top half of his coveralls.

"Get back to Comcentral. Stay on the board to get Hanoi's acknowledgement."

"Can't," Stone replied, sealing his coveralls. "My shift is long over." He fitted his cap to his head. "Eftimiu has the board. He will notify you when Hanoi confirms." He rolled up his sleeve just to the edge of Snake's poised head.

"Ah. Then, good." Ángel turned to Cuza. "Victor." Cuza's head snapped up. "Get to Maimonides. He's to alert all the messes in every quadrant that it's time for the Djelfa ginger in tonight's kaskasa. Then those who are with us will know by nightfall that tomorrow is the day."

Cuza set his beret at a rakish angle, grinning. "Djelfa ginger!" He lunged toward the trapdoor.

"Cuza!" Cuza froze. "Slowly, Cuza, slowly!" Ángel reached up casually and touched the man's cheek with his forefinger. "There's no rush, Brother Victor." He looked steadily into Cuza's wide eyes. "Is there, now?" Cuza shook his head. "Good," Ángel whispered. Cuza shuddered. "Walk with dignity, Victor Cuza. A strong man always walks with dignity."

"Yes, Ángel," Cuza croaked.

Ángel nodded slowly, smiling. He dropped his finger and spread both hands wide in the movement of release. "Good, Brother Victor!"

Cuza swallowed visibly, then moved carefully past Ángel, his eyes fixed on the trapdoor. In an instant, he was gone.

Stone turned away from the interaction, his innards quieting a sudden nausea. Pounding rain drove its clamor against the distant outer walls of the building. He could hear it gust and recede. I'm riding the storm, he thought, and there's no stopping it now. As if in response, the blustering wind rose again, deafening him with the authority of its destiny, the tumult of its urgency. "Now it comes," murmured Snake and Eagle. "Trust yourself," Tanya whispered.

Stone leaned toward Ángel and started to speak.

Ángel preempted him. "So, Brother Stone," he said, still watching Cuza's exit, "what did you mean by your pronoun?"

"My—"

"You said, 'Eftimiu will notify you when Hanoi confirms.'" Ángel began removing the uzi's long barrel. "Did you mean he will notify 'us'?"

Stone met Ángel's eyes. "No," he said steadily. "I meant he would notify you."

Ángel waited.

Stone spoke slowly. "Count me out, Ángel." His tattoos started dancing.

Still Ángel waited.

Stone leaned further over the table, his eyes level with those of the shorter man. "Out, Ángel, out!" he rasped. "I want no part of it!"

Languidly, Ángel tested the fit of a nine millimeter barrel into the uzi, removed it, and sighted against one of the candles down the short bore.

In the next instant, Stone half rose from the crate, his hand fisted and drawn back. "*Baragiali*!" Tanya shouted. For a moment, he stood outside his body in his softself. "*Breathe*!" said Tanya. He dropped his fist and clasped his left forearm, his shoulders hunched.

Ángel blew into the barrel and held it up to the candle again. "There's no getting out, Brother Stone. You are already in too deep."

Stone leaned on the table. "Then lock me up," he whispered tightly, "so I can't rat on you until the whole thing's over."

Ángel laid down the uzi part and examined his thumb. He frowned, then scooped free a curl of dirt from under a fingernail. "You know I wouldn't do that, Brother Stone." He rolled the dirt between his thumb and forefinger, then wiped it carefully on the rag.

Stone was on him in an instant, his hands seizing the front panels of Ángel's fatigues. He dragged the chunky man to his feet, setting the candles aflicker and sending the boxcap bouncing to the floor. "Look at me, Ángel!" he roared. "I am talking to you!"

"And I am listening, Brother Stone." Ángel's face radiated hurt astonishment.

Stone shook him. "You will not ignore me!" His fist grew ready.

"Of course not, Brother Stone. I made a mistake. I apologize." He spoke earnestly.

Stone searched the guileless face, then held his eyes closed a second. He listened to the echo in his head. "*No more violence.*

169

Anywhere." Roughly, he shoved Ángel back onto the chair and
retrieved the boxcap from the floor. He threw it in the man's lap
and paced the length of the table. For a moment, he halted, distinctly aware of his tattoos applauding him. He cleared his mind
and ran a hand over his bald head.

"Ángel," he said evenly, grasping for calm, "this is all crazy.
The 'Darmes have too many response options and too many rein-
forcements, and even if we succeeded and took our hostages, who
says Highcrotch Magister Lutu would ever listen to our demands?
Hell, we don't even agree on what we're demanding!"

"Sure we do." The voice came from below his knees. Stone
looked down to see the shining face of Gabriel Girardon and,
behind it, the big physique pushing up through the trapdoor.
Gabe went on, smoothly. "We agree that the bodies of habitantes—like free citizens' bodies—have to be guaranteed safety
from involuntary medical experiments." He drew himself onto
the edge of the opening and sat, looking for a drying cloth.

Stone threw him a shirt. "Gabe, I want out of the action. I
just told Ángel."

"So I heard." Gabriel wiped his face, said something in
French to a figure below, and in an easy motion, spun himself out
of the trapdoor to stand up. Runnels of water coursed down the
leg of his raineralls, making a puddle on the floor. "Ángel," he said
as he began stripping, "we can't budge now until we hear from all
the wards. You want me to prod them?"

"No, Brother Gabriel. They will report in a timely fashion."
Ángel straightened in his chair. He picked up a tiny flask of oil
and saturated the rag again. "You've no optimism, Brother Stone,"
he said conversationally. "Don't you see how God is protecting us
in our venture?"

Stone's head snapped toward him.

Ángel held his hands wide. "Did He not send the storm at

170

precisely the moment we needed it? Does He not continue to protect us with the chaos of the rain? The foolish Femmedarmes don't suspect a thing. Or even if they do, let them come! All that needs to be done is being done right now. By the time they get organized, we will be model habitantes again, obeying orders." Ángel leaned forward, pointing to the ceiling. "Until our moment arrives!"

Stone folded his arms across his chest. He articulated each word carefully. "Ángel, your bloody revolt will only prove how violent we really are. It'll make the world stand up and cheer for the Protocols."

"*Right!*" announced Eagle. "*Yes!*" sang Snake.

Ángel's voice was cloying. "*We*, judged as violent, Brother Stone? We are only fighting for our rights!"

Stone kept himself from advancing on the little man. "You don't give a rip-shit about the Testing or the Protocols, Ángel! This whole revolt is nothing but an excuse for you to play with your toys!" His arms were burning. He rubbed them.

"Hey, Baldy!" Girardon sealed the opening of his dry coveralls and laid his arm around Stone's neck. "I been thinking," he said. "You ought to tell Ángel the real reason you want out."

Deliberately, Ángel abandoned his uzi parts. Carefully, he wiped excess oil from his hands. "Brother Gabriel," his silken voice said, "you and Brother Stone have been discussing this matter?"

Stone stopped Girardon's answer with an upraised hand. "I told Gabe about it this morning, Ángel. And now I'm telling you." He moved behind the empty chair. "Are you listening, Ángel?"

"Of course, Brother Stone." Ángel folded his hands in his lap, leaning back in his chair. "I will always listen to a comrade." Gabriel stood behind him.

Stone glanced at Gabriel, then braced himself on the chairback. "Then here's the real reason: I'm not going to help blow up this bailiwick, Ángel, because I don't want to be a part of that violence." He paused. "And I'm not going to have my head adjusted!" His arms were singing praises now, so loud he was sure the other men must hear them. He leaned forward urgently. "*Nobody's* going to be tested, Ángel! *Nobody's* going to have his head dinked with! We don't have to do this lunatic revolt! It is *unnecessary!*"

Ángel's eyes widened.

"So call it off, Ángel!" he shouted. "Call it off!"

Snake and Eagle sang Stone's refrain: "*Call it off!*"

"Stone!"

"Shut up, Gabe!" Gabe was crowding him, cutting off his space. Stone gestured him away.

Girardon ignored him. "Baldy, you don't understand these girls! They're not about to back off from the Testing! They want to know what causes people like us, what makes us tick!"

"Get out of my face, Gabe!" Stone swept by him and escaped to sit on the trough by the wall. Inside his head, he yelled, "Get him away from me, Tanya! Don't let me go after my buddy!" Elbows on his knees, he held onto his arms.

Gabe whirled toward Stone. "No, listen up! They're obsessed with us! We're what they talk about nonstop! You think they're going to quit now? Now, when they think they've got an answer to it all?" He bent over Stone, inches from his ear. "I guarantee you, they are going to mess with our heads!"

Stone stared at the floor and spoke to his tattoos. "One centimeter closer and I'll break his neck!"

Snake was coiling and hissing, Eagle dangerously shaking his wings. Tanya's voice: "*Careful, Baragiali, careful!*"

Stone pressed his arms tight against his legs, breathing hard. Aloud, he said evenly, "Shut up, Gabe."

Gabe leaned half a centimeter closer. "Baldy, you know what they want? They want to make us into zombies. Quiet, empty, docile men without two braincells to rub together!" Gabriel dropped to one knee by his friend, trying to look up into his face. "Man, we can't let them do that to us!" He shook Stone's shoulder. "You got to help us stop them! These cuntlickers want to take away our souls!"

Stone closed his eyes. Sweat dripped from his temple. With one last effort of restraint, he spoke without looking at Gabriel. "Take your hand off me, Gabe."

Gabriel drew back, suddenly alert to the menace in Stone's voice.

Snake and Eagle released a small mutual sigh. Stone sighed with them.

"My brothers!" exclaimed Ángel into the silence. He surveyed the disassembled shotgun parts that Cuza had left on the table. "You neglect the truth." He stood and raised his hands over the gun parts. "They cannot take away our souls!" In a sequence of lightning moves, he set barrel to action, threw the mid-mounted locking bolt, keyed in the buttstock, and slid the sideplates into a fully-assembled weapon. In three more swift motions, he broke the breech, slipped a shell toward the bore, and snapped the shotgun closed again. He arched his handiwork into an arm's length exhibit for their approval. "Our souls belong to God!"

"Angel, lay off—" Gabriel began.

"And God will protect our venture!" Ángel hissed fiercely. He snapped the shotgun's breech open and closed again.

In that instant, a landscape shifted in Habitante Stone Baragiali. He found his deepest conviction, his purest rage, and the truest object of his loathing. They all mounted together into a single purpose. Stone felt his face widening into his best Crossover leer.

Slowly, he began to get to his feet.

In the distance, he heard Tanya's pained protest, Eagle and Snake warning, "*No!*" He sealed off the voices and turned to relish the bright-eyed countenance of Ángel Espartero.

"Hey!" Gabriel stepped briskly between the two men. "Hey!" he shouted louder, holding his flat hand up toward Ángel, then toward Stone. Stone bent his head and halted. From under his brow, he looked patiently at his friend, humoring him, if only for the moment.

Ángel smiled at Gabriel. Carefully, he placed the gun on the table and made his gesture of release, his face a background of composure for his shining eyes.

Gabriel turned to Stone. "Stone," he said.

Stone watched Ángel.

"Stone!" Gabriel said again, moving toward him.

Even as he let Gabriel ease him back onto the trough, Stone kept his eyes riveted on Ángel.

"Come on, man, pull it together now," Gabe insisted. He tightened his arm around Stone's shoulder. Stone's eyes narrowed, still on Ángel.

"Brother Stone cannot pull it together," Ángel said calmly, lowering his hands to the table.

That voice cut through Stone's focus with a purifying asperity, laying open the vision of Ángel's slaughter of the Femmedarmes, that chilling laughter escalating with the splatter of soft flesh, the sting of fast blood. The words started low in his gut and rose by tiny increments until they exploded into slow pellets of rage. "Ángel, you fucker!" He shot to his feet and lunged toward the man beyond the table.

Suddenly, he stopped and listened intently. His tattoos vibrated on his arms, singing the truth in his brain: "*No, don't, Big Stone! He is our brother!*"

Across the stream, Little Lucio Baragiali saw the other little boy in a funny African print hat running desperately down a long road after a disappearing figure and crying like his heart would break. The little boy fell, howled, and got up to run again, only to fall once more, this time lying in the dust, exhausted and sobbing. Lucio crossed over the stream, reaching out his hand to the child to help him up.

Ángel Espartero saw the big man's sudden stop and the subsequent softening of his features. When Stone extended his hand in peace, Ángel studied his face, holding Stone's eyes with his own. Then he picked up the shotgun and fired it point-blank into Stone's chest, rocking the closed little room with the sound and force of the explosion.

Stone's body hung motionless for an instant before it pivoted backwards. He fell against Gabriel, who had stood up to stop him.

During the instant of Stone's mid-air suspension, Gabriel covered his eyes, rubbed his ears, and shouted, "Ángel, you fucking fool!" Then he fell under Stone, heaving him to the side just before their two bodies hit the floor. "Stone! Stone, man!" His elbow dropped into the viscid cavern that had been Stone's chest. He pulled himself over the blood and sticky flesh toward his friend's face.

Remarkably, Habitante Baragiali still breathed.

Gabriel embraced the exploded chest and pushed his mouth toward Stone's ear. "Stone, man! I got you, I got you!"

The whisper was faint. "Gabe?"

"I'm right here, man, right here."

"They didn't leave us, Gabe," Stone panted lightly. "The animals," he rasped. "They didn't leave us." He tried to move.

"Stay still, man, stay—"

"They're all right here, Gabe!" Stone's eyes were bright. He was smiling.

Gabe laid his head against Stone's shoulder, listening for the next breath.

Stone shuddered and was still.

Gabe held him tight. A huge pain began filling him up and flooding the room around him.

A dispassionate voice reached him from across the room. "He was a dangerous man, Brother Gabriel."

Gabe winced. In his gut, the pain turned to fury. Carefully, he draped cool wraps around the anger and pushed himself away from Stone's body. Bile washed over his tongue. He resisted spitting it full in Ángel's face.

With ritual calm, Gabriel folded Stone's arms over his body. On impulse, he lifted the left sleeve to look once more upon the woman entwined by the snake.

The white skin of Stone's forearm was smooth. And completely free of tattoos.

Girardon turned the arm over, shoved the sleeve higher. Quickly, he pushed up Stone's other sleeve and beheld there no eagle, nothing at all. Just smooth, undecorated skin. Gabe closed his eyes tight and shook them open again. "Jesus!" he whispered, looking from one arm to the other.

He shivered, bunched his shoulders, and rotated his neck full circle, letting his eyes close and his head hang limp. After many moments, he wiped his face and peered at the figure beyond the table. Ángel cradled the shotgun and caressed its wooden stock.

Girardon's eyes narrowed. Deliberately, he made his fists open and fall casually by his sides. Then he made his face into a mask, and said evenly, "You didn't have to do that, Ángel."

"Think a moment, Brother Gabriel," Ángel responded. "What else could we have done? All our lives are at stake here."

Gabe stared at the little man before him.

Ángel waited politely for some reply.

Slowly, reluctantly, Giradon closed his eyes and nodded.

"Good," said Ángel. "Cuza will report that Habitante Baragiali never returned from sandbag transport at the levee. Until they can search, the 'Darmes will assume that, alas, the Great Dambovita River must have swallowed up Brother Stone." When Gabe did not answer, he continued, "You are right to mourn. We shall all mourn our brother."

Gabe smoothed Stone's sleeves so that the tattoo-less arms could rest on the shattered chest. He retrieved Stone's cap from the corner and set it at a jaunty angle on the bald head. His face still a mask, he rose to face Ángel and the affairs of the coming day.

10
[2087 C.E.]

> As Kanshou, I am guardian of each individual person's
> physical safety. For an individual's safety or assurance of
> continued existence is the most important element in
> her life and, ultimately, in the life of her species. I pro-
> tect first the safety of any person threatened by violence.
> I protect second the safety of my Kanshoumates. I pro-
> tect third the safety of the person doing the harm.
> —*The Labrys Manual*

On a bright Bucharest morning, outside a modest building of
stone and wood, citizens gathered to greet and embrace each other
with smiles and a suppressed anticipation. Most were women,
wearing long cotton dresses or skirts of varying tints and shades of
purple and appointed with black, violet, or white sashes and belts.
Petite bows of lavender ribbon dotted the tresses of girl children
and every adult woman wore a purple or lavender scarf, wrapped
or pinned so as to cover at least part of her head.

The men wore black suits, shirts of white or lavender, and black
yarmulkes, sometimes covered by plain black hats. Each man's face
was framed by two long single curls of his otherwise short hair, and
his beard more often than not covered all but the ends of his bright
purple neckpiece. Invariably, from the waist of each man hung the
zizit, the short strings of his four-cornered undergarment.

179

Every person—women, men, girls, boys—carried a tallit, or prayer shawl. Most were unfolding them and preparing to place them over their shoulders when two purple-skirted women dropped foot-first from the sky, landing like feathers on the pavement amidst embraces and laughter. They freed their skirt hooks, and, along with their friends, moved hand-in-hand toward the place of prayer.

Rebbe Sarah Bas Miriam was in great spirits. It was a splendid day, one of those testifying to the harmony of all life. There was sunshine, there was freshness from yesterday's rain, there was a tune in her heart, and there was the Torah. The new roof on the shul was near to completion, and Batya Aranoff, she should lighten her purse, had finally withdrawn her resistance to the plans for the library.

Sarah stood in the foyer of the shul, collecting her energies and preparing to join the community that was in her keeping. Breathing deeply, she listened to the hum of the congregants socializing inside the large prayer hall. Avrom stood near the door, nervously fingering his tallit. She caught his eye and sent him a "you'll-do-fine" wink. He grinned his thanks. We should all have such sons, she thought. This was indeed a special Shabbos.

She looked down the aisle formed by rows of stiff benches, full of chattering adults and barely restrained children. If today had been a century ago, the women and men would have been separated by the mehitza, the wall that used to grace old shuls and synagogues. Now, congregants stood together.

Before Rebbe Sarah moved an inch, she felt the hush that gradually overtook the worshippers as they became aware of her presence. Nearly a hundred pairs of eyes turned to her. All breath seemed to halt. Small children raised bright expectant faces in her direction. A precious moment, thought Rebbe Sarah.

She stepped into the gathering hall, and chaos erupted. Every body went into its own motion, every voice into its own song or prayer, every heart into its own self-examination and rejoicing. She moved down the narrow aisle toward the distant bimah, flanked by davening and spinning people. As she reached the front of the hall, she vocally added her prayers to the cacophony, and when the rhythm was exactly right, she let her voice reach out above all others. "Blessed art Thou, O Lord, who blesseth Thy people, Israel, with peace."

The room fell silent. The service had begun.

Daniel the Baker led the praise and blessing of the Besht, the Baal Shem Tov, and then of the Hasidim, the first to teach its daughters the study of the Torah. Livia Radishchev broke into a familiar wordless tune that was taken up for several minutes by the gathering. Suzanne Bas Katrina danced a blessing to the Holy One, and Barbara of the Woods prayed for the return of non-human animals.

The high point of the service was coming into focus. All eyes turned to the eastern wall of the shul, to the Ark, wherein lay the Torah, the wellspring of joy. Two women brought the sacred scrolls from the Ark and raised them high, accompanied by an exhilarated and intensifying hubbub. As they carried the Torah among the congregation, praying people crowded around it, blessing it with kisses and smiles and light touchings. The shul was a tumult of expanding voices.

Then the sacred writing was brought to the bimah and spread open to the Portion of the Week. The time of the rising up had come, the time of the encounter with history, the time of the speaking of that which bound their hearts together in a community of love, study, and service. The texture of the sounds in the room changed, as if all those present had flooded their spirits into the young man who would read on this day.

Amid interweaving voices, Avrom moved up to the bimah,

stepped upon the raised platform, and stood before his people. He placed his hands to the sides of the Torah and bent his head, then lifted an extraordinary countenance to the faces below him. The fervor of the voices rose up and then hushed, awaiting the familiar sounds and rhythms that only the Torah could provide.

Avrom picked up the silver pointer, set it upon the text, and opened his mouth to read.

His words were lost in a burst of gunfire from an automatic weapon just outside the shul. The noise split the air and shook the building.

The front door of the building flew open and, immediately thereafter, the door to the big room itself. In the doorway loomed the figure of a large caucasian man wearing a heavy, brightly-figured caftan, its hood flung back. He took one look at the astonished gathering and then turned upward toward the roof a ponderous automatic weapon, vintage 1988. With a long continuous burst of fire, he riddled the ceiling in a zigzag pattern.

Single gunfire shots, phaser zings, and spatters of more automatic weapons were coming from the street beyond the foyer of the building. Shouts and whistles and the sound of running feet stood out from a background of crowd noises and the hum of flex-cars. Three men flung themselves into the room, one of them firing a modified uzi toward the front doors and the street. He pushed his African print boxcap hard onto his head and kicked the outer doors closed. He broke a stained glass window in the foyer, thrusting the nose of his weapon through the opening and shouting into the street, clearly marking the limits of his retreat.

The big intruder who had fired at the ceiling took up guard duty, swinging his big gun back and forth over the crowd. The third man, in a black beret and who seemed almost swallowed up in his jumpsuit, waved a shotgun as he moved swiftly down the western wall and opened doors beyond the bimah, quickly searching the back rooms. When he returned, he mounted the bimah and swung his weapon back and forth over the gathering. The hatless black man was walking up and down the eastern wall shouting, "Stay where you are! Stay right where you are!" He pushed back with his rifle barrel any individual who started to break for an exit.

To the people gathered in the shul, the sounds of ballistic weapons were recognizable but distinctly foreign, reminiscent only of occasional incidents reported from newscenters or of the bloody flatfilms some had viewed from a century ago. The immediate response of the gathering to the first shots was almost uniform: they fell upon children and loved ones, dragging each other to the floor or beneath benches.

Avrom was one of those who did not drop to the floor. Instead, he flung himself upon the Torah, hastily gathering it into his arms. He headed for the Ark and the tall doors that protected it on the eastern wall. When the shots broke out, Livia Radishchev expelled a shout and reached the Ark in time to help Avrom enclose the Torah within it and push closed the doors. The two of them stood like statues in front of the small closet, guarding it with their bodies.

"Brother Gabriel! Pick it off!" The figure in the boxcap with the uzi had returned. Snatching a yarmulke from the head of a young man, he propped it on the back of a bench. Instantly, the black man across the room lifted the yarmulke again with a bullet from his rifle. "Now kill this!" shouted the man with the uzi. He flung a scrap of stained glass into the air. The black man shattered it. "And this!" Another scrap of glass, another shattering. "Ace Shot Gabriel Girardon," bellowed the man in the boxcap, pointing grandly at the marksman, "pride of the Congolese Resistance! He will at all times have one of you in the sights of his rifle!"

The four militants surrounded the gathering now, one on each side of the room, the menace of their weapons claiming every eye. Neither the intruders nor their captives had observed a small form, which, at the sound of the first shots, had broken from the front bench and slid like greased lightning to the door behind the bimah.

Yukana Asachi had dashed immediately for the back bathroom and the narrow window above its organic waste toilet. She was squeezing through the window when the shots that riddled the ceiling ceased. She was contemplating the eight-foot drop into the backstreet when she heard doors slamming. There was no cover in the alleyway, but to her left, a large shutter flapped. Yukana uttered a fervent prayer and swung onto the narrow molding behind the shutter, pulling the hinged wooden slats over her body.

She had no time to tremble. The man in the black beret thrust his head and his shotgun out the window and looked up and down the alley. Satisfied that no one was around, he slammed out of the bathroom, leaving Yukana with a renewed faith in God.

She released a long breath. She didn't know why she had run. She'd simply found herself doing it. Did she intend to flank the building and tackle the intruders? Find the Femmedarmes and storm the shul? Too many *Kanshou Comix*, she told herself, like Marguerite always said. Too much immersion in those glorious stories of the Kanshou, of Captain Aru Boko and her Fighting Sisterband of the Lowland Foot-Shrieves.

Yukana could hear shouts and alarm bells from the front street, and from inside came shufflings and loud excited voices, one of them shouting, "Stay down, all of you! Down, and you won't get hurt!" Immediately, she was struck with remorse. Rebbe Sarah was in danger and so were her mothers and friends. She had to go back! But what good would that do? What would Captain

Aru Boko do if she were here? Then, in that instant, Yukana was struck with a high resolve. She knew exactly what she had to do.

She had spent the last two weeks being tote-and-go for the construction crew that was renovating the shul's roof. The shul had once been a theatre, and above its big room, there was a false ceiling that made a kind of loft or crawlspace between the roof and the ceiling. Yukana knew from her many explorations that if you found the right crack in the loft, you could watch everything that went on in the gathering hall below. She knew these parts of the building like the stitches of her hand-sewn head scarf. She must get to the loft!

She remembered that there was scaffolding just beyond the corner of this outside wall. She could scoot to it along the molding. Holding onto the windowsill, she unhooked her cumbersome skirt and let it drop to the ground, leaving her legs chilly in their purple cotton tights. Then she pushed off her Shabbos shoes and socks, and set her bare feet on the narrow molding. The shiplap that covered the wall was old and uneven enough to provide holding points for her hands. She clung with her fingertips until she could let go with one hand and reach for the next fingerhold. Then she moved her feet to the point under her forward hand.

She looked neither down at the ground nor forward to her goal, concentrating instead on the how to's: how to pray, how to fold the shawl, how to bake challah, how to find the next fingerhold. Then, there was the scaffolding, one of its planks extending beyond the corner, just at the height of her shoulder. Less than a foot distant.

But the scaffolding might as well have been a mile away. Between it and her hand the boards met exactly with no convenient overlap and no holding point. Yukana wanted to cry. "So close and yet so far," she reported to Captain Aru Boko. "Sorry Ma'am, I just can't reach it."

*"Can't reach it! Nonsense. Since when did a Femmedarme Foot-
Shrieve give up?"* Captain Aru Boko's strong deep voice chided her.
"You have to try, Tyrotrooper. For the Sisterband, you have to try!"

Suddenly infused with determination, Yukana replied, "I can
do it, Captain!" Without giving herself time to doubt, she gathered her strength and launched her whole body toward the scaffold board, reaching out with both hands, reaching for the glory
of the Sisterband, for the rescue of her people! To her amazement,
she grasped the extended plank, and it held! She swung from it,
victorious!

The imaginary Sisterband cheered. Yukana heaved with all
the strength of her eleven-year-old biceps, bracing her feet against
the building and vaulting onto the scaffold. She returned Captain
Aru Boko's salute.

She could hear more shouting now and crowd noises in the
distance. The alleyway was still deserted, and the scaffolding rose
above her, right to the top of the shul. She was climbing now, just
as she had done dozens of times over these last weeks, may
Marguerite never look this way, scrambling up one level after the
other until she reached the roof. Quietly now, she moved up the
steeply pitched roof section, just over the prayer hall itself. She
headed for the raised portion of the building, toward the flat roof
of the old fly space over the area that had once been a stage. The
opening she sought was just below its eaves.

As she topped the ridgepole, a loud part of the street beyond
came into view. Red lights blinked, shouts filled the air, bells and
buzzers tapped out constant coded messages to bright-green-and-
black-clad Femmedarmes who were urging citizens off the streets,
back into buildings. Two Kanshou flex-cars hovered at second-
story level, humming quietly. Other flex-cars blocked off the
street while 'Darmes in twos and threes deployed themselves to
the sides of the shul, probably surrounding it. Sure enough,

Yukana could hear them now: noises from the back alley.

She knelt there, caught up in the activity. She had never seen so many Femmedarmes in one place, and with so many weapons! Usually, she had seen 'Darmes in pairs, walking up and down the neighborhood, talking to citizens. Many of them didn't even wear their dart guns or stunners. But always she knew that, in spite of their smiles and the casual way they moved, they were ready for instant action! They were wonderful, highly trained and—

Suddenly, behind her and from the scaffold, bullets whizzed and ricocheted again. Yukana plastered herself to the pitched roof, genuinely terrified. A man's voice shouted from inside the shul, followed by another burst of automatic gunfire. She heard women's voices. One said, "Back, Band! Back!"

"*Hurry, Tyrotrooper!*"

Yukana pulled herself over the top of the roof and then began scrambling toward the safety of the loft.

At that moment, the most extraordinary experience of her young life took place: someone grabbed her and lifted her up. She saw the roof of the shul drop from under her. She started to cry out.

"Hush, kit!" The voice enfolded her. And so did the arms of two women who were carrying her between them. Flying Daggers! The Flying Daggers of the Femmedarmery! She was flying!

Yukana looked down and again almost bellowed her fear. Instead, she clinched her eyes shut and offered to God the most fervent prayer she had ever uttered. As if in answer, her fear drained from her, and she found herself laughing and looking all around and sailing high over Bunch Park on a sun-warmed Shabbos morning with two green-and-black-garbed women holding her securely between them.

One of the Daggers, the larger one, was talking into the

comunit on her wrist. "—out of range now. Let's take—"

"There," interrupted the smaller woman, pointing to the park's bell tower just beyond and below them. They began dropping fast.

"Hold on," said the larger woman.

They swooped around the top of the tower and landed on the far side of its high observation platform. Yukana hardly felt the impact.

"Now," said the smaller Kanshou. "How are you? Are you hurt?" She was bending so as to be on Yukana's level.

"No. I'm fine."

"And your name?"

"Yukana."

"Yukana," said the smaller 'Darme, "I'm Bukhari, and this is Absod. Tell us, what were you doing on the roof?" She brushed Yukana's hair from her brow.

"I was trying to get in the loft so I could see."

Absod knelt. "The loft of the shul?"

"Yes." Yukana thought Absod was probably the most beautiful woman in the world.

The two women looked at each other. Then Absod said, "Is it easy to get into the loft?"

"Well, yes. But it's hard to find the door."

"Could I get in?" Bukhari asked. "Could Absod? Could we all three?"

"Sure. But they'd hear us if we were loud."

Bukhari took a deep breath. "We would be very quiet, Yukana. We need your help. Will you take us there?"

Yukana grinned. "We get to fly back?"

Absod smiled an assent, then said to her partner, "I'll report." She stepped aside, pressed the back of her wrist to her mouth, and began whispering rapidly into the subvocal sound field.

Bukhari sat on the platform and pulled Yukana to her lap. She shook open a green-lined cape and wrapped Yukana in it, then began rubbing her cold feet. "Were you in the shul, Yukana?"

Yukana nodded. "I got out when the shooting started. Please tell me what's happening."

"Well, you're the only one who got out, kit. Four habitantes invaded your Shabbos service. They have escaped from the bailiwick, and they're holding as hostages all the people in the shul."

"Hostages?"

"They're going to keep your friends there, threatening them with their guns until they get what they want."

"They're going to kill them?"

"I hope not. No one has been hurt, at least so far."

Yukana released her breath. "What do they want?"

"That's complicated. Mostly, they want the government to promise that they will never be surgically operated on without their consent."

"But why——?"

"Yukana, this is no time to explain. I'll tell you later. Right now, you and Absod and I have work to do. Are you strong?"

"She got up to that roof, Buke." Absod had finished her report. "And we've got the okay to take our position in the loft. Flex-cars will back off, and the fogging unit will hold, too. But they'll both cover the scaffold, keep the habitantes from coming up onto the roof in case they get that notion. The men know now that the scaffold is there." She looked at Yukana. "How big is the hole you can see through from the loft?"

"Not very big. Nobody can see it unless they're really looking hard. But we could take out another panel. Are we going to jump them from up there?" Yukana's Sisterband identity began to re-emerge.

"No, but we might want to use tanglestick. That's——"

"That's a net that drops down over a criminal and captures and freezes him, like a spider's web," finished Yukana. "It doesn't hurt them, though."

"Right," smiled Absod. "Well, we'll have to see when we get there. Will you help us get your folks out of this?"

"Yes, Ma'am, Captain!" She held up her hand in the half-womb salute.

Absod grinned, fitting her own thumb and forefinger to Yukana's to make the full-womb salute. "Good, Tyrotrooper! Let's go!" She nodded to Bukhari, and the two Daggers stepped into their spooning position, placing Yukana in front of them. They uttered an incantation barely audible to Yukana, and then the three of them pushed upward into the sky and swooped down toward the shul.

And thus it was that Tyrotrooper Yukana Asachi secured a leave from Captain Aru Boko's Lowland Foot-Shrieves and the Fighting Sisterband in order to carry out a high priority mission with the Flying Daggers.

———◆———

Sub-Aga Dimitria Iorga laid open the flatscreen for Marshal Alexa Litulescu, miles away at Bucharest's western dispatch center, where she faced her transmitted image of Iorga's flatscreen diagram. The projection showed not only the exact location and capability of all flex-cars and Foot-Shrieves, but also a plot of the shul itself, including the two Flying Daggers, who crouched with their young guide above the gathering room of the building. A dotted line circumscribed the area occupied by the hundred or so hostages, and depth swipes demonstrated the relative layout of benches, steps, bimah, and lighting fixtures. Four red triangles blinked at points approximately equidistant from each other on the perimeter of the dotted line. As Iorga made her report, brief whistles accompanied the occasional shifting of the squares that represented Femmedarmes or flex-cars outside the building.

"What you see," Iorga told her superior, "is projections from sonar-Kurlian units combined with sub-vocal descriptions from Bukhari-Gert-Absod as they observe from above." The Femmedarme's voice faded momentarily as she leaned back to check the elevation and location of her own parked flex-car. "The two 'Darmes are in constant verbal flow, reporting everything said or done in the room below. Their guide is able to identify every one of the hostages. We are recording all we get from them for reference. And we're working to define the positions of individual hostages inside the dotted line."

Iorga paused. "The habitantes are taking their orders from Ángel Espartero. Ángel stands here now," she said, pointing to the triangle on the west side of the hall, "still with the short-barrel uzi in the rebbe's back." She highlighted the blue circle by the triangle. "Here's the sharpshooter, Gabriel Girardon, across from him in front of the Ark on the east wall. Gabriel's nervous, keeps wiping sweat, rubbing his arms.

"Every now and then, Ángel raves," the Sub-Aga continued. "He apparently had Girardon make a little show of his marksmanship, then he and Cuza appeared at the street door holding the rebbe in front of them as they repeated their demands."

Marshal Litulescu pointed with her own lumerod to the shul's street door. "That was here?" she asked.

"Right," Iorga said, following the light, "south side."

"No chance to stun them?"

"Not with the rebbe in front of them." Iorga then drew her own lumerod to another pairing of a triangle and a circle, this time at the building's north side. "When Victor Cuza came back into the hall, he took up a position here at the bimah. He has his gun in the neck of one of the women . . . ah, they say her name's

Hasora, Hasora Nelavrancea. Bukhari reports that it is not an automatic weapon as we first thought, but probably a single barrel shotgun, as best she can determine from right above him there at the bimah." She moved her lumerod toward the foyer across from Cuza.

"Lucas Dobruja carries the big M-60. He's guarding the street entrance. Bukhari and Absod report that he ripped up the ceiling with that thing." She paused. "Both Dobruja and Ángel are mass killers," she added. "Either one of them could take a notion at any time to wipe out all of the hostages."

The Marshal drew in a long breath. "No accident that they are the ones with the automatic firepower." Another pause. "Looks like all four are fairly close to the big group."

"Yes," answered the Sub-Aga, "all four of them are approximately ten feet from the crowd."

"Close enough to scare everybody out of their pants," muttered Marshal Litulescu.

"Bukhari says they're plainly scared but very calm. They've got a regular conversation going on, with lots of people from the group speaking up. Every now and then, Girardon or Dobruja will yell at them to shut up, or Ángel or Cuza will threaten to waste the rebbe or Hasora. Then they do get quiet, but only for a little while. They're trying now, if you can believe it, to reason with the habitantes." Iorga paused. "Ma'am, Ángel gave us half an hour. That was . . . seventeen minutes ago. We're holding for your orders."

"And you keep on holding. I'll have Magister Lutu's go-ahead for negotiations as soon as she and Hedwoman Miaorescu complete their conference."

There was silence from the Sub-Aga. Then, "Ma'am, with respect, I don't think they'll negotiate. They aren't just trying to escape. And they're not just demanding that they'll be protected from Habitante Testing. They say that the whole proposal for the Testing and the Protocols is unconstitutional and inhumane. They want assurance that no habitante will ever have to be subjected to such dictates."

"Sub-Aga Iorga," came the Marshal's chilly reply, "I am acquainted with those demands. You yourself referred them to me, very clearly and efficiently. But nobody, not I, not Hedwoman Miaorescu, not the Kitchen Table or the Central Web, not all three of the Magisters or the whole of the Kanshoubu, can guarantee those things." Litulescu's voice was tinged with despair. "The most they could do is grant these four men immunity to any future use of the Testing or the Protocols, and even that would encourage others to riot for the same favor."

The Marshal was brisk again. "But yes we negotiate. We try everything and anything that might insure the well-being of the people in that building. Is that understood?"

"'Stood, Marshal."

"Other questions or comments?"

"No, Ma'am."

"Good. I'm out." She broke the connection.

Sub-Aga Dimitria Iorga had seen Cuza's eager face as he held the shotgun to the rebbe's temple. She'd heard the arrogance in Ángel's voice as he shouted out the nonnegotiable demands. She shook her head, looked at her chronometer, and returned to her monitoring duties.

In the gathering room, small groups sat on the benches or stood holding each other, watching their four captors, encouraging each other with glances and barely perceptible nods. No longer focusing on the bimah, they faced in every direction, variously drawn or repelled by the threat that met them on all sides.

Girardon had forced Avrom and Livia from their protection of the Ark to seats on a bench. Widow Sandvei sat fanning herself. Vabili Tatosbuc stood with his arm around a taller man, his life partner, Eleazer Ben Asher. The eyes of both of Yukana Asachi's mothers constantly roamed the room, in search of their offspring. Other children were holding close to adults or sitting with puzzled faces in conspicuous inactivity.

Up in the loft, Femmedarme Bukhari lay with a stunner poised at a small concealed opening in the ceiling. Absod and Yukana lay a few inches away by another hole, a second stunner resting beside them. When someone spoke aloud down in the gathering room, Absod would repeat the words a split-second later into the sub-vocal transmitter on her wrist, even as she continued to listen. When there was no one speaking in the room below, Yukana would take up her soundless whispering into Absod's ear, and Absod would repeat those words into the transmitter.

"The one with the prayer book is Naomi Isachs," Yukana breathed. "She's a postal worker. And a writer. Nicolai is beside her, her daughter. Bela is her husband. He's with their other daughter, Silvie, over there, in front of the man at the street door."

Absod moved her lips against Yukana's ear. "That's Dobruja."

Yukana watched Dobruja with his big gun, striding stolidly back and forth across the entranceway, covering both the front doors and the gathered people. His boots marked a sharp rhythm on the wooden floor. Occasionally, a slap to the side of his weapon coincided with one of his steps, escalating the room's uneasiness.

Across from him on the bimah and almost under the Femmedarmes in the loft, Cuza was shifting from one foot to the other, watching the crowd, occasionally glancing at the end of the shotgun which nestled behind Hasora Nelavrancea's ear.

"What's your name?" Hasora's voice was even, almost conversational.

He looked at her. "Cuza. I'm Cuza," he stammered.

"Cuza. My name is Hasora." She held her shawl easily around her shoulders.

Cuza nodded sharply. Hasora nodded back. Mild panic crossed Cuza's countenance. He pushed the gun tighter against the woman's neck, placed a deliberate scowl on his face, and looked out over the crowd.

Rebbe Sarah Bas Miriam was imbued with cool intention. She stood calmly against the muzzle of Ángel's uzi. Ángel leaned a little upon the west wall, breathing shallowly. At every opportunity, Rebbe Sarah spoke. She spoke to give strength to her people, she spoke to disturb her captor. Each time she spoke, Ángel would jerk to attention and command her silence, pushing the uzi harder under her ribs.

When Rebbe Sarah was not speaking, others were—to each other and to the habitantes. They quoted Moshe, the Talmud, obscure and even spurious texts. They told stories. They questioned, challenged, cajoled, admonished, and in every possible way agitated politely, testing and pushing the limits of their captors' endurance until one or another of the four men exploded again into invectives and threats. After a lull, someone else in the assemblage would dare to speak.

Gabriel Girardon was not in good shape. His big body sweated and ached and itched. He had replaced the Weatherby rifle's four-shot magazine and stood now, letting it drift from one figure to another in the crowd, sometimes drawing a careful bead over the iron sights, more often simply pointing the weapon and watching his targets shift nervously. He risked letting go of the trigger long enough to rub his arm. Jesus, his flesh crawled.

We're all on the edge, he thought to himself. No sleep in the last eighteen hours, and then pulling off a number like that, a prison revolt unparalleled in history. He had to hand it to Ángel.

Their plan had gone like clockwork, right up to the big hitch, when they lost their chance for Femmedarme hostages and had to improvise.

He figured civilian hostages were even better. And this bunch was fascinating—for all their curls and costumes, they were high-spirited and downright brazen. He shouldered the Weatherby and settled the sights on the older woman fanning herself and hugging a small boy. Then on two men with their arms around each other. Everybody, in fact, was holding somebody. He played the rifle in a slow figure-eight over the crowd.

His mind flashed back to the Depot, to Big Stone lying in his own blood, smiling and talking about the animals with his last breath. Gabe pursed his lips and pushed down the pressure that rose behind his eyes. Such a good man. Baldy, you were such a good man. Then there was Ángel with his thin little smile, Ángel stroking the hot shotgun. Fucking fool.

Well, Ángel was having his problems today, across the room there with the rebbe. Now that was a piece of work, he thought, the rebbe. She was faintly familiar, like maybe he'd seen her on space westerns or holofests. He relaxed his vigilance a moment to work his neck in a circular stretch and wipe his face on his sleeve.

She had acted up again, that woman, calling out to the other people and reassuring them of their ultimate safety. She was giving Ángel too much lip. He'd blow her into the middle of next week without batting an eye. This time, he noticed, Ángel had responded by seizing the rebbe's sash, jerking it from her body with his free hand and slipping it under both of her upper arms so he could hold her arms behind her. Gabe scratched his wrist against the rifle stock.

In the loft, Yukana whispered, "Bela is talking now." She leaned down to hear.

Bela Isachs had turned between two benches, directing his

words to the whole group and to each of the habitantes.

". . . that many of us here, perhaps most of us, are in absolute sympathy with your demands. We hold that no one has the right to tamper with the body of another, and that includes habitantes. But what you ask for no one is able to grant at this time." Bela started to walk with Silvie toward the rest of their family several yards away.

"Hold it!" shouted Gabriel, waving his rifle. "You don't move!"

Bela protested gently, "I am simply trying to—"

Gabriel fired a shot into the ceiling. "Stop, I said!"

Bela froze in his steps.

The shot pinged off a light fixture near the watchers in the loft. Momentarily, Absod paused in her transmission. Then she and her companions touched each other in reassurance that they were safe.

Cuza exploded at Ángel. "Balls, Ángel! Let's blast out of here! These—"

"Shut up, Cuza!" Ángel left off his attempt to immobilize the rebbe's hands behind her back. He dug the gun under her ribs and scanned the room. "Time, Lucas!"

Dobruja stopped his pacing and consulted his wristwatch. "They got seven minutes." He stood spread-legged and dropped the M-60 to his hip, waving it back and forth in a belligerent promise.

Ángel snatched at one of the rebbe's rebellious arms. "What's happening in the street?"

Dobruja stepped back into the foyer and crouched, peering out the broken window. "Flex-cars haven't moved. Nothing's moving."

"Then we don't move. Not yet." Ángel scanned the room.

The wait went on. Dobruja punctuated the silence with his

resumed pacing. Cuza swallowed. And swallowed again. Gabriel swiped his face with his sleeve and panned the rifle over the crowd. Ángel tightened his one-handed hold on the rebbe's sash.

In the loft, Absod began transmitting again. "Only a warning shot. We are holding stunfire, as ordered, unless they fire on one of the hostages. Our range is doubtful anyway, except for Cuza directly below us." She continued describing the scene, concentrating on Ángel now, who was fretting visibly because the rebbe's arms kept resisting his binding of them behind her back.

"Brother Gabriel!" Ángel boomed suddenly "Focus on this target!" He pointed to the rebbe's forehead. As Gabe shifted his rifle, Ángel very deliberately laid his uzi on the floor beside him and wrenched Rebbe Sarah's arms behind her. He began securing them with a jerk that drew her body into an erect and strained posture.

The ambience of the gathering room had begun to shift. Breaths got shorter. Bodies grew rigid. Eyes moved in quick glances and met other eyes. Livia Radischev's hand found Avrom's and wrapped it in a slow strong squeeze. Hasora, pushed against the podium on the platform, stretched her head to the side, as if to slip away from the muzzle at her neck. Cuza responded to her gesture by expelling a rough expletive and pushing the barrel deeper under her jaw.

Widow Sandvei, no longer fanning herself, was drawing her nephew's small body closer to her on the bench and filling her other arm with two girlchildren. She closed her eyes and listened to the rhythms in her head. Then she let the rhythms touch her vocal cords and began gently to hum a little tune, a niggun. One of her neighbors began humming softly with her and then brought the wordless melody into a full sound.

Livia and Avrom, across the room from Widow Sandvei, picked up the melody with their voices. Others in different parts of the shul began to join in the open-mouthed humming, tentatively at first, and then more pointedly.

Dobruja stopped his pacing and looked around the shul, trying to locate the singers in a mass of slightly open-mouthed people. "Shuddup!" he shouted. "Shuddup!"

Throughout the shul, the volume rose.

"Shuddup, shuddup!" Dobruja yelled again. "Stop the ya-ya-ing!"

The ya-ya-ing grew perceptibly louder.

The instant after Ángel's command, Gabriel Girardon raised his rifle and found himself in a distorted world. At the end of his aim stood Rebbe Sarah Bas Miriam. Her face seemed huge, completely covering his field of vision. The crosshairs of a telescopic sight rested on her brow, just as if he were sighting through a high-powered Leupold 1-4X. He blinked both eyes and lowered the rifle.

The whole scene was normal size again—the rebbe resisting Ángel, Ángel behind her affixing her bondage, the scattered energies in the room beginning to coalesce into some dangerous pattern, the rifle sporting no scope at all but only its ordinary iron sights. Gabe fought off a fuzziness in his head. He wiped a wet hand on his thigh and re-shouldered the weapon.

There was her head again, like on a huge screen, and the crosshairs, too, quivering on her temple. As she yielded finally to Ángel's successful capture of both her arms, Rebbe Sarah tilted her chin further upward in defiance. Gabriel began shaking. He did know her! He'd seen this woman before, the translucent skin, the strong jaw . . . Stone's doxy! The vixen tattooed on Big Stone's arm! At that moment, the rebbe turned her full face toward the rifle barrel and fixed Gabriel with flashing black eyes. Philipa, his Wicked Step-Sister!

Gabriel uttered a low cry and stepped backward, struggling to keep the rifle on target. And still her face filled his vision. He blinked both eyes open again and looked around, drinking in with glad relief the reality of normal-sized people nodding their heads and singing, the truth of Dobruja's shaking the M-60 as he railed at the louder intonations, the sight of Ángel drawing the rebbe into a rigid stance as he tightened the sash into a knot at her back. Thus heartened, Gabriel took his aim again . . . and stood galvanized, staring incredulous at the magnified target, at the black eyes that probed his own.

Across from him, he heard Ángel's attempt to override the room's swelling sound by the sheer volume of his voice. "You will be quiet! You will stop the noise!" He knew without looking that Ángel was trying to reach his uzi and hold the rebbe immobile at the same time.

"He will kill her!" Ángel shouted. "You will stop or he will kill your leader!" Gabe knew that Ángel was pointing at him.

The enlarged visage of his target shimmered. Her eyes —Philipa's eyes!—still blazed at him. Beautiful! And treacherous. An intoxicated vengeance rose in his gut. He took his marksman's breath and settled the crosshairs in the precise center of the woman's forehead. A triumphant shout was being born in his throat.

Abruptly, the rebbe ceased her singing of the niggun. Her countenance rested in composure for an instant, the black eyes warm and soft upon her executioner. Then her lips began the unfolding of a gift that Gabriel did not dare to receive.

Rebbe Sarah Bas Miriam turned on Gabriel Girardon the complete and magnificent glory of her smile!

A torrent of gratitude engulfed Gabe. He wanted to cry, to fling down his rifle and run to her, throwing himself at her feet! He wanted to laugh and sing and dance. And still, she smiled at him. Across the gathering of her people, the rebbe's black eyes commanded her assassin.

Gabe's vision split. One part trembled on his target beneath the crosshairs. The other beheld the whole gathering room, a scene that was about to shift from hesitation to action.

Cuza ignited it. "I said shuddup!" he bellowed at the rising chant, swinging his weapon toward the hostages, at last committed to firing into their midst. "Shuddup!"

Hasora, freed from the shotgun muzzle, leapt at Cuza and seized him by the neck. She pulled him backward toward the side railing of the platform. He faltered, then braced himself and pushed the stock of the gun hard into Hasora's stomach. She fell from the platform, and immediately he raised the gun again. With a howl, he drove its butt hard into her face.

At that instant, the congregation's song became a roar.

From every part of the room, like an enormously mounting tide, the people began to move. As one body, they heaved upward from their center and surged outward in every direction toward their captors, gaining momentum as they rose. An irresistible resolve drove them forward, and with them, from their collective throat, rolled the thunder of a profound justice.

Ángel shrieked. "Kill her, Brother Gabriel! Kill her now!"

The sights of the rifle centered on the forehead of Rebbe Sarah Bas Miriam. Gabe's finger automatically tightened on the trigger. Then, with deliberate unimpassioned purpose, he shifted the rifle several inches to the right, capturing there the enhanced countenance of Ángel Espartero, his one arm barely controlling the rebbe, his other still straining toward his precious uzi on the floor.

Calmly, Gabe fixed the crosshairs at the top of the bridge of Ángel's nose, on the spot just above and equidistant from each of the eyes.

He fired.

Ángel's head wrenched backward, and a round spot appeared

between his eyebrows. In frozen, wide-eyed astonishment, he sagged out of the range of the crosshairs and onto the floor by the bound rebbe.

Gabe lost his telescopic vision. The rebbe was at a normal distance now and so was the eruption of the congregants. As he watched Ángel sinking to the floor, Gabe marvelled at the pattern unfolding before him: women, men, and children, with their arms upraised, their voices afire, their wild purples flying, were rolling outward, relentlessly and irrevocably.

Simultaneously, he watched the crazed Cuza raise his shotgun again and fire into the midst of those who advanced upon him. Several figures staggered or dropped. Others stepped over them to smother the raging Cuza with their bodies.

At the same time, Gabriel watched Lucas Dobruja, his posture set for an orgy of annihilation, laying open a full spray of death from his M-60. Eleazer Ben Asher, arms outflung, hurled himself from the top of a bench into the line of Dobruja's fire. In midair, he jerked into stillness. Simultaneously, an invisible blow stiffened Dobruja into a grotesque mimicry of Eleazer. Both figures toppled and were enveloped by the waves of a black and purple sea.

And Gabriel himself was being overpowered by the throng of people surging toward him. He offered no resistance. Thinking only of the rebbe's smile, he dropped his rifle and yielded to the bodies that covered him.

———◆———

Chaos and pain filled the gathering room. An unbelieving congregation, so recently an unlikely army, reached for its wounded and held each other in comfort or relief. Children clung to adults or to each other, watching with big eyes as Ángel's body was rolled onto an anti-grav gurney and gently steered out of the shul and into a hovercraft.

Eleazer Ben Asher, who had blocked Dobruja's barrage, was also dead. He lay in the gathering room in the arms of his weeping lover, Vabili Tatosbuc, while the rebbe and the people surrounded them in song and ritual invocations.

The shul swarmed with Femmedarmes. They moved quickly but quietly around the mourning group as they secured the building and its periphery. They dispatched all the wounded congregants, including Hasora, to healing centers—none of them, fortunately, in danger of death. Seven people, some hurt worse than others, had caught the pellets of Cuza's shotgun, and two women had been struck by Dobruja's fire before Kanshou Bukhari's stun blast from the loft had immobilized him.

Gabriel Girardon sat, flanked by Femmedarmes, in the foyer of the shul. He was bound in a forcefield wrap that allowed only his head to move. Cuza and Dobruja, each in similar custody, had just been hustled out to flex-cars. Gabe waited his turn.

Tyrotrooper Yukana Asachi stood in the door of the gathering room, watching Gabriel. Her eyes were red and puffy, suggesting that she was learning early the cost of courage and glory. She drew a long breath and then approached one of the Femmedarmes. "With respect, Adjutant, please let me talk to him." She indicated Gabriel.

The 'Darmes exchanged glances. Then the Adjutant answered, "You can. He's secured." She smiled. "And we'll protect you."

Yukana smiled back. She turned to the black man and met his eyes. "Tell me something, Mister—?"

"Girardon. Call me Gabriel."

"Gabriel," she said. "My name is Yukana."

"Yukana."

"Yes." She shuffled and stood firm again. "People are saying it was an accident. An accident that you missed the rebbe."

Gabe's eyes narrowed. "That so?"

"It wasn't an accident, was it?"

Gabe did not smile. "I'm a pretty good shot."

Yukana nodded. She started to turn away.

Gabriel stopped her. "Wait . . . Yukana. Would you do me a favor?"

Yukana looked at the Femmedarmes and back to Gabriel.

"I need to scratch my arms mighty bad," he went on. "And I can't. You see?" He tried in vain to move his arms. "I figure a law-abiding citizen like you could convince these officers—"

"Girardon, are you pulling a fast one?" The Femmedarme moved in front of Gabriel.

"Word of honor, Adjutant. I just need to scratch. That too much to ask? Do the Rwanda Accords say a prisoner can't scratch?"

The Adjutant's voice was impatient. "If it's something painful, then all you need to do is ask." She gestured to Yukana. "Step back some." She crossed a button on her subvention belt that deactivated the forcefield. "Scratch away, Habitante Girardon."

Gabe did so, gratefully pushing up his sleeves and raking his nails up and down the insides of his forearms. "You are a considerate officer . . . ." He froze.

The Femmedarme's eyes followed his. "What you got there?"

Yukana drew close again, frowning. Gabe's forearms were covered with thin white lines. "That looks like . . . ."

"Girardon, how the hell did you get tattoos?" Both Kanshou were examining the figures on Gabriel's arms.

"Are they tattoos?" Yukana asked.

Gabriel sat galvanized. They were all there, Eagle on the right arm, Snake and the doxy on his left. They were outlined as if with the superfine point of a piece of chalk. Plain as day if you knew what you were looking for. His hands shook as he drew his sleeves over his arms again. His eyes were big, and his breathing was uneven. "Just a . . . rash, Adjutant." He tried to smile. "I'm fine."

Any retort from his guardians or Yukana was lost in a low murmuring from the gathering room. People poured out the door and stood aside, making way for a sheet-covered gurney being floated by Avrom and Bela Isachs. Vabili Tatosbuc followed the body of his lover out into the street. Then scores of people came after him, among them Yukana's mothers toward the end of the group. One of the women beckoned Yukana to her as she went out the door.

"Wait," Gabriel said, again clad in the forcefield wrap. Yukana paused. "Will you give a message to that man's . . .to his friend?"

"Sure."

"Tell him that I'm really sorry." Gabe held her eyes for a long moment. He was sweating.

"I will," Yukana nodded. "I will." She turned and ran after the crowd.

"On your feet, Girardon. We can go now." The Adjutant had deactivated the lower portion of his forcefield.

Gabriel stood up and moved slowly with the Femmedarmes toward the street. At the door, he stopped, turned back, and got to look one last time into the black eyes of Rebbe Sarah Bas Miriam as she stood at the door of the gathering room. She was clearly herself now, not his Philipa at all.

She gave to him the shadow of a nod. He returned it with a slight nod of his own. Then he held his head high and stepped out into the bright morning of Bucharest.

11
PEACE ROOM
[2087 C.E.]

> The seasoned Kanshou knows that yes and no
> are but two of three answers.
> —*The Labrys Manual*

Zude barely thanked the Vigilante gert that deposited her by the wind chute on the Shrievalty roof. As she dropped the seven floors to the Peace Room, she learned by audio from her staff the state of the tri-satrapies in the aftermath of the multiple habitante revolts. The Caracas Bailiwick was quiet and in Vigilante hands. Damage to Caracas City water lines was substantial and required immediate shunts from neighboring cities if panic and deaths were to be avoided. Magister Lin-ci Win was ready to join Zude on inter-tri-satrapy holohookup, and Magister Flossie Yotoma Lutu had not yet been reached for the three-way conference.

Captain Edge emerged from the glow of tocsin lights at the door of the Peace Room and escorted the Vigilante Magister through the soft beeps and bells, the hum of low voices, and the maze of screens, to a contour chair in near-recline position. Before she plugged herself into the full-spread commuflow of a companion chair, Edge directed the swift construction around herself and the Magister of an electronic enclosure that brought all of Little Blue to their fingertips even as it assured them of a measure of privacy. Maps and flatfield reproductions swung into place above and to every side of them; key plates lifted and cocked to eye-activation marks. Zude allowed herself to be instructed in the use of new access orbs and turned her attention to the ceiling, where the actions of Kanshou in Caracas, Bucharest, and Hanoi were projected in flatcast.

In Caracas, Sea and Foot-Shrieves hung with hoses from bridges and buildings, directing water to cottage-size holding bags; other Vigilantes molded crowds, moved traffic, and interviewed bailiwick habitantes; Sea-Shrieves rode the Caribbean in old oil tankers, now filled with precious drinking water from Río Chico. In Bucharest, Femmedarmes on foot and in flex-cars surrounded a public meeting house at several elevations, and pairs of green-clad Flying Daggers approached it at staggered intervals, dropping to neighboring rooftops and waiting.

In Hanoi, red-garbed Amahs moved between and atop buildings, stalking lone habitantes, firing darts and stun-guns at culprits armed with far more dangerous weapons. Zude watched with a critical eye as Foot-Shrieves diverted and held the fire of a large group of habitantes barricaded behind cushcars and touring carts. Overhead, pairs of Flying Daggers hovered without being discovered, and on signal, released strand after strand of the benign tanglestick that fell like threads upon the habitantes below. Some of the culprits managed to fire at the Sky-Shrieves before the threads stuck to them and immobilized them under neurological bonds, ultimately rendering them unconscious; others simply shouted and fought the descending blanket of entanglement, tripping and falling, flailing wildly in vain until they passed out. "Reggie would love this," Zude muttered, recalling her chosen daughter's affinity for action flatfilms about Kanshou.

"Magister Lin-ci Win, Ma'am." Edge's voice in discreet reminder at her elbow was formal, yet warm. Zude pulled herself away from the dramas above her and set her attention to her Kanshoumate and companion in Magistership.

"Magister," Zude said directly to the figure in the air before her. Lin-ci Win sat cowelled and cloaked in a setting of quiet activity similar to Zude's own. As she returned Zude's greeting, her holo-techs phased out the background bustle and brought Lin-ci's head and shoulders to Zude's level and size. The corners of her Greatchair—the wheelchair in which the Amah Magister always sat—were visible behind the red-clad figure.

"It is good to see you again, Magister Adverb," said Lin-ci Win, "though we could wish for happier circumstances."

"To be sure, Magister Win," said Zude, matching her own level of formality to the other woman's. "Still, your Amahs just presented us with a textbook demonstration of the tanglestick's proper use. That was quite a coup."

Lin-ci Win smiled. "Only an Amah could have appreciated it so fully. Our colleague is not with us yet?"

"If I know Yotoma, she's rocketed to Bucharest—"

"Wrong, Adverb." Flossie Yotoma Lutu's long-waisted holofigure materialized at a sixty degree angle to each of them. "I'm right here in Tripoli." Her dark face barely stood out against the blackness of the holoroom. "I've been brain-to-brain for an hour with my Hedwoman in Bucharest. We're moving toward negotiation now unless something blows first." She scanned her consoles and analysis boards. "Are you getting flatcasts of the bailiwick? Or of the shul?"

Zude looked at the ceiling for confirmation as she spoke. "We've got the 'Darmes surrounding a city building. Nothing

209

from the bailiwick."

"That's because the bailiwick is no longer a problem. Leadership of the uprising is right there in the building you're looking at. Four habitantes holding about a hundred people hostage. Here." Yotoma waved her hand to bring an electronic flatmap across her chest, a diagram of the shul with lume points that moved as the voice of the Femmedarme Sub-Aga in Bucharest described the drama unfolding there.

Zude and Lin-ci Win focused attentively on the description of the Bucharest standoff. Then Lin-ci interrupted. "Pardon. Here's news from our observers." The Amah Magister re-directed to Los Angeles and Tripoli the audio report of the cessation of all fighting in Hanoi. The report ended with the request of the surrendering habitante leaders for a meeting with Magister Lin-ci Win to discuss their demands.

Zude glanced at the ceiling. The Hanoi flatfield there displayed a group of subdued men speaking in turns to attending Amahs, their voices over the holotransmissions resigned but still filled with frustration and anger.

Zude let go of a pound of tension. "That's two in control, one still to go," she sighed as the three women turned again to each other. "We know all this is no accident. I'd like to understand how long this particular conspiracy has been brewing. Lin-ci—"

Lin-ci Win drew her considerable bulk into the posture of gigantic affront.

"Magister," Zude corrected herself immediately, "when you speak with those habitantes, I hope you can determine when the collaboration with the other two bailiwicks began."

"Of course. That is, if I speak with the habitantes."

Zude's hackles rose. "What do you mean, 'if,' Magister?"

"I mean I may not choose to grant them an audience."

Zude moved as close as she could to Lin-ci Win's holo-image.

"With respect, Magister," she said softly, "this isn't just the baili-wicks' bi-monthly complaint about food and the trusties' privi-leges. This is an explosion of violence, carefully planned and remarkably timed, in three discrete containment ranges separated by vast distances. It is a concerted and highly visible effort on the part of three bailiwicks, one in each tri-satrapy on this globe, to gain the attention of the public and the Kanshoubu. They have unquestionably succeeded. You *must* talk to the habitantes, Magister. Not only do they have the right to demand your audi-ence, and not only do we need to honor their concerns about a matter growing daily more critical, but we also need any infor-mation they can provide about how the plans for this uprising escaped us."

Lin-ci Win closed her eyes. When she re-focused, it was first on Yotoma, then on Zude. "You are right, of course, Magister Adverb. But I remind you that our Asia-China-Insula Tri-Satrapy has suffered far more uprisings recently than Africa-Europe-Mideast has. Or your own Nueva Tierra. I've talked personally with far too many habitantes lately, with too little effect, to rejoice in the prospect of more such verbal contention."

Flossie Yotoma Lutu unclasped her black and green Magister's cloak and addressed Lin-ci-Win. "I'm with Adverb on this one, Magister. How come we didn't have any hint of this global cooperation? Is our security that faulty? I'll be talking to the habitantes in Bucharest, and you can be sure I'll press them for that informa—"

The figure of the Femmedarme Magister faded and then returned, together with an escalation of background voices and electronic activity. Yotoma explained that the habitantes inside the Bucharest shul had begun firing upon the hostages. Zude looked at the ceiling to see the surge of green-clad Femmedarmes pouring into the building through doors and windows and rappelling from the roof. The Sub-Aga's voice was announcing that three of the habitantes had been apprehended and the fourth was dead. The toll of free citizens: one dead, ten wounded and under healing care.

Flossie shook her head. When she leaned back into her contour chair, she did so with a masked pain. I've never seen her look so weary, Zude observed silently. She blinked and tightened her lips.

The Magisters watched as Kanshou in all three tri-satrapies went about the task of restoring order in three of Little Blue's large cities. Now's the hard part, thought Zude. The glory's over. And who does the cleaning up, the salving of hurts, the calming of fears? The Amahs. And the Femmedarmes and the Vigilantes. That's who does it. She let herself feel a burst of pride at the way the Kanshou had conducted themselves, at the obvious gratitude and respect that the people showed to them. Just plain decent, she thought. Decent.

Lin-ci's voice broke her reverie. "Kanshoumates, we have fortunately not needed this meeting. If you will excuse me, I will get back to my duties."

Yotoma held up her hand. "I'd like to get back, too. But we need to confer on another matter. Just before everything broke loose this morning, I was about to call us together in emergency session."

Lin-ci Win sighed patiently. "I can think of no duty so compelling right now as that of re-establishing a secure and orderly daily life in each of our respective precincts."

"I also have a matter of concern," Zude said. "To all of us. If we don't talk now, we'll have to do it before another day passes."

Lin-ci Win studied her Co-Magisters with a mild curiosity. "Very well." She twisted from the waist in her Greatchair and spoke to her staff in Hong Kong. "Send my congratulations to every Amah who participated in quelling the Hanoi riot and indicate that I shall be speaking with them shortly. We are shifting our conference to confidential priority status."

She continued to delegate and refer tasks to her aides even as Zude spoke to Captain Edge. "Slip us into a restricted subchannel, Edge, but stand by. You coming, Magister Lutu?"

"Lo, I am with you," responded Yotoma. She spoke briefly to the Femmedarmes below and behind her before she joined her Co-Magisters.

Lights lowered, the ceiling paqued out, and the Peace Room dropped away. As invisible walls rose around her, Zude felt her contour chair physically elevated to another dimension. The figures of Yotoma and Lin-ci Win were raised with her. Zude smiled, knowing that each of the Magisters was perceiving herself as inflesh and the other two full figures as holoprojections.

Yotoma spoke to the air behind and below her. "Are we secure, Maggie?" She turned back to the others. "We are alone but on confidential record. Satisfactory?" Both her colleagues nodded.

"Let me begin, Magister Lutu." Zude removed her cloak and withdrew from her tunic a small cloth bag. She shook its contents into her hand for the other women to see.

Yotoma shed her cloak entirely and leaned forward as if to pick up the tiny objects. "The ballbakers?"

"Yes." Zude looked at Lin-ci Win.

Magister Win nodded. "Crystals used to destroy testicles. They must be tuned electronically, but since they are contraband, that is not often done."

"Then how are they tuned?" Yotoma asked.

"By a witch who can contain and direct the energy. The crystals themselves are not rare, but the women who can make them into weapons are." The Amah Magister looked at Zude. "They are common in our provinces. Uprisings there, perhaps even the one in Hanoi today, are a clear protest against their increasing use by independent groups of women."

"So your Amahs told me," replied Zude thoughtfully. "But surely the riots protest Habitante Testing and the Anti-Violence Protocols?"

"That too," shrugged Lin-ci Win.

Zude reached again into her tunic. She pulled out another cotton bag and emptied into her hand an identical set of the crystals. "This first set came to me by way of your Amahs, Magister Win. This second was thrown out the window of an abandoned building here in Los Angeles night before last. The woman who had been carrying them is called Noyoko Oraki, presently released from custody. We're tracking her. We think she is distributing the crystals in this country. Or perhaps she's an itinerant tuner of such crystals."

Yotoma looked at the Amah Magister. "Zude and I talked earlier today, Magister Win, and I immediately made some cursory investigations. There's no indication as yet of the use of these ball-bakers in my Africa-Europe-Mideast satrapies." Then she looked at Adverb. "It's time to get it all on the table, Zude."

Lin-ci Win's eyes moved from Yotoma to Zude.

Zude cleared her throat. "It's only hearsay, but among the three of us, we've got to be clear. Magister Win, the tale-tellers and undercover populace sources from your tri-satrapy insist that Mother Righters are inciting the bailiwick riots in order to demonstrate the need for research and, ultimately, for the Anti-Violence Protocols. They escalate rumors in the bailiwicks that habitantes will be the first victims—non-consenting adults—of Habitante Testing. And later of the Protocols. Then the response of the bailiwicks becomes in itself a demonstration of the violence that the Protocols would prevent.

"Moreover, these crystals are apparently being produced in

large quantities and distributed there not just to take vengeance on men, but to create an atmosphere of threat as well. Their very existence stirs up sentiment for the Testing and the Protocols. Along with their use goes the message, 'If you had your head properly fixed, we would not have to castrate you.'"

Zude took a deep breath, then continued. "Magister, the word on the street, at least in Gorakhpur and Shandong Province, is that some Amahs are complicit in this agitation. And even in the distribution of the ballbakers."

Beneath her red head covering, Lin-ci Win's immobile face began to flush. She held Zude's eyes for a long moment. "That is a very serious charge, Magister Adverb."

Zude counted a heartbeat before replying. "These are very serious times, Magister Win."

The Amah Magister waited. When Zude said no more, Lin-ci Win's eyes narrowed almost imperceptibly. "Do you imply," she inquired in a velvet-over-steel voice, "that along with the Amahs I myself am alleged to be involved in the agitation of the bailiwicks and the distribution of the crystals?"

Zude's response was immediate and fierce. "No! I—"

Yotoma interrupted, addressing Lin-ci Win. "Magister, you have made no secret of your strong support of the Testing and the Protocols. Citizens all over Little Blue are aware of your efforts to right the wrongs that men have committed against women—citizens not just in your own Asia, China, and Island satrapies, but in Nueva Tierra as well—Sur, Central, and Norte. Certainly citizens throughout my own jurisdiction are aware of your position. The answer to your question is 'yes.' The rumors we refer to do in fact, suggest that in your heart you might actually want to praise the women who castrate violent men and to thank them for taking the law into their own hands. The most vehement of them have even labelled you a Mother Righter."

Zude's heart sank. In the profound silence that surrounded the three of them, she mentally replayed all that she knew of Magister Win: her sterling record at the Amah Academy; the bullet in her spine, which had only temporarily halted her brilliant career rise but which had, nevertheless, consigned her everafter to a wheelchair. Lin-ci Win had then moved to the civilian sector, where she transformed the China Satrapy's Size Bureau into an efficient mega-organization that had become the model for commerce, agriculture, and population limits over the whole of Little Blue. She had made a determined comeback to the Amahrery as an active Kanshou, a Vice-Magister, and ultimately Magister. She had early on taken a thoughtful and public stand as a protofile, one of those in favor of Habitante Testing and the Protocols. She had been personally committed for thirty years to the woman whose tiger sculptures guarded public buildings all over China, and even Kanshou in other tri-satrapies had heard of her skill at 3-D Go and all-dimension chess. She had a predilection for smoothies and ancient silks. The rumor of a certain tattoo called a blush to many cheeks.

Once in Buenos Aires at a light weapons policy revision conference, when Zude was only a Matrix Major, she had worked in person with the visiting Magister Lin-ci Win. Their mutual esteem had been immediate. Their exchanges, now that Zude was her ranking equal, had always been cordial, if more formal than Zude would have wished. Recently, with the escalation of the Protocols controversy, Lin-ci had become more taciturn, her demeanor often formal and impenetrable, her emotional antennae more sensitive to potential insult. And now, Flossie Yotoma Lutu's expression of candor had brought them all to the brink of diplomatic peril by landing squarely in the middle of Lin-ci Win's sense of personal integrity.

Lutu and Lin-ci Win sat deathly still, regarding each other on a level that Zude could not fathom. She had no doubt that a whole internal drama surged now in the silence between them. They were the planet's most sophisticated diplomats, two old hands seasoned to the operation of vast bureaucracies and to the bargaining for what each understood to be justice and peace. Each had been tempered by fires that Zude could only imagine in her own future, and not for the first time, she felt like a seedling sprouting between two sequoias.

It was not Lin-ci Win but Magister Lutu who broke the silence. "I say these things only to answer you truthfully and to remind you that it would be strange if such rumors did not attempt to malign and indict you, given your strong and courageous stand in favor of the Protocols." She caught Zude's eye, then addressed Lin-ci Win again. "The suggestion that you could be complicit in such intrigue is, of course, too absurd to be entertained by any who know your history. Never, not even for the sake of one of her bedrock beliefs, would Magister Lin-ci Win misuse the power of her office or fail to protect the rights of any person in her tri-satrapy. I believe Magister Adverb agrees with me in this." She paused, looking at Zude, who nodded emphatically.

Lin-ci Win sat perilously still. Then her eyes fastened on Zude's. "Magister Adverb, you have told me that Amahs are rumored to be actively agitating for the Protocols and even distributing the crystals. You did that simply to inform me of the rumors?"

"Precisely that," answered Zude.

"And you in no way suggest that I might be involved in their actions, or that, knowing of their behavior, I might look aside and neglect to discipline them?"

"Never," Zude said. "I expected, and still expect, that you will meticulously and extensively investigate the rumors and that you will discipline with earnestness and dispatch any Amahs found responsible for any such behavior."

Lin-ci Win turned to Yotoma and waited.

"Magister, I repeat," said Yotoma, "you would never allow wrongdoing to go unpunished. Not even if you were in sympathy with the wrongdoer."

Lin-ci Win looked at Yotoma. "Your candor is actually refreshing, Magister Lutu, and my present concern is not so much with the sullying of my name by the slander of the streets as with the intentions of my Co-Magisters." With the bare shadow of a nod, the Amah Magister addressed them both. "I consider your words to be of good intent, if perhaps indiscreet. I take no offense."

Zude's sigh was audible. Yotoma's shoulders relaxed by a barely perceptible centimeter. Lin-ci Win sat silent.

None of the three women stirred.

Then, the Amah Magister moved her torso slightly back. "We have just negotiated a very narrow strait," she announced. She looked at her colleagues. "I am eager to sail again on the open sea."

Zude felt at last easy in her chair. "Sail on, Magister," she said.

"Thank you, Magister Win," said Yotoma.

Another silence, blessedly softer in texture.

Then Yotoma spoke once more, her voice taking on an oratorical timbre. "Today, the three of us and the Kanshou who work with us have quelled some extensive riots. We have returned Little Blue to a state of peace—uneasy peace it may be, but peace."

Lin-ci Win cast a glance at Zude, who at that moment was casting a glance at her.

The Femmedarme Magister held up a hand. "Hear me out," she said, still in her most formal mode. "Yet nothing in what we have accomplished today as chief executive officers has been more important than what we have just done together in negotiating what you, Magister Win, call our very narrow strait. I am genuinely grateful for that process."

Zude resisted an impulse to reach out and place the back of an inquiring hand on her friend's brow. "Floss," she said slowly, never taking her eyes off Yotoma, "Floss, this sudden homage to process—you sound like the worst kind of purist." Her smile was a question.

"She sounds like a wise woman," Lin-ci Win observed. Then she breached her own formality with a rich laugh.

Suddenly, Yotoma and Zude broke through their own tensions, eager to join Lin-ci's altered mood. The three world leaders sat in a vibrating holofield, laughing together, laughing loud and long, into the universe, into some country that no one of them could have named but in which they stood together, clasping each other's hands.

The Femmedarme Magister was the first to sober herself into speech. "Thank you again, Lin-ci. This makes it easier for me to bring up the matter that has obsessed me for some days now. Can we continue?"

"The Lakota say that after laughter, all is lighter," Zude observed. "I suspect there could be no better time, Magister Lutu, for us to continue."

"It *is* a kind of lightness of being, Zella," Lin-ci Win agreed. "All political conferences should be conducted in this state. Please continue, Flossie." She waved her hand lightly. "The Amahs and the bailiwicks can wait."

Yotoma concealed her relief at Lin-ci's manner of address and spoke to staff members outside the holofield. Her holosize was reduced by a fraction so as to accommodate screens of scrolling statistics on each side of her for the attention of her Co-Magisters. "How often do you two check population statistics?" she asked.

"Twice daily," said Lin-ci, "like cleaning my teeth."

219

"I guessed as much, and I feel a bit presumptuous in bringing up the matter. Lin-ci, you're one of the world's experts on population, and I hear that in Asia and China, population-watching is an entrenched ritual."

Lin-ci nodded acceptance of the compliment. "Sometimes," she noted, "the eye closest to the microscope misses the larger landscape. To answer your question: we are holding, overall, at some 558,000,000. No meaningful increase."

"Total over Nueva Tierra Sur, Central, and Norte," Zude offered, "is 285,000,000. Just under normal on the Sablove Percentage Scales. No alarming increases anywhere, not even in new cities."

"My own tri-satrapy also maintains safety status," Yotoma added. She activated a series of cartograms. "But our analysis teams have picked up a change that worries me in figures on the quarter-trap and demesne levels." The continent of Africa bloomed out of the Africa-Europe-Mideast Tri-Satrapy, only to be replaced by a magnification of its southern half, then by a further cut to its lowest tip, and a freeze on New Cape Province with its lakes and rivers. Statistics in accompanying insets announced the total number of female, male, and doublesexed births and deaths. Another displayed the infant mortality rates; still another, the breakdown of the statistics for each major historical community—Zulu, Xhosa, Sesotho, Afrikaan, South Asian, White. Further insets available for magnification cross-referenced current changes in food production, housing, water tables, employment, education, literacy, manufacture, health services, and familial patterning.

Yotoma talked as she pulled up statistics on school populations. "You both have in mind the upper danger zone figures, and Size Central itself is alert only for population increases."

Zude lit a cigarillo. "What are you saying, Flossie?"

220

"Just that you get what you look for. When you look for assurances that we're not overpopulating, you usually get assurances that we're not overpopulating. Or you see us increasing into the danger zone, and you respond accordingly with investigation. But watch." She split the screen to compare current schoolroom statistics in New Cape Province with those of a year ago, then with those of five years ago. She read aloud the stats as they appeared on the monitor. "Schooling citizens in Pretoria at present 19,640, a year ago 19,986, five years ago, 20,517. In Johannesburg at present 47,262 in school, a year ago 47,743, five years ago 49,924. Benon at present 5,556, a year ago 5,627, five years ago 5,764."

Lin-ci Win sat up straight. Zude doused her cigarillo.

Yotoma wiped New Cape Province and flooded the screen with data from Western Africa. "Bobo Dioulasso, more subtle but still creeping downward: 7,866 today, 7,936 a year ago, 8,249 five years ago. Dakar today 26,606, last year 26,717, five years ago 27,457. Bissau 3,686 today, last year 3,728, five—"

Zude stopped her. "Wait. Can we voice activate?" When Yotoma nodded, Zude commanded the computer, "Harriet, give us Size Central, population, Rio De Janeiro, school population now, a year ago, five years ago."

The flatfield to Yotoma's other side came alive with Nueva Tierra Sur's hump and split-screen data: at present 304,077 schooling citizens in Rio De Janeiro, the year before 307,006, five years before 318,769. "Harriet, give us Houston!" Zude fairly shouted. The flatscreen obliged with the Texas coast: at present 96,845 students, the year before 97,813, five years before 100,875.

Lin-ci Win studied the field. "That is almost a full percent decrease each year. Harriet, Shanghai please, same path."

Yotoma activated the computer voice to reinforce the

information on the visual field, which now revealed the China coast. "At present, 366,000 schooling in Shanghai," said Harriet. "In 2086 C.E., 369,571. In 2081, 384,593."

As Yotoma knew they would, her colleagues called up several more cities. As she knew it would be, the same pattern was borne out time and again. Yotoma watched patiently. Then, as she knew they would, her Co-Magisters called up full global population figures, found some hint of overall decline, and sought percentages.

"There is a drop," Zude said. "Significant. From 1,240,000,000 to 1,237,000,000."

Lin-ci Win differed. "Not that significant. When we failed to contain the Fourth Virus seventy years ago, the drop was over a third of a percent. This one represents less than a quarter of a percent. Not that significant."

"But global schooling figures," Zude protested, "are down close to a full percent, as you pointed out. That's the population still largely under twenty, even with universal adult education. Deaths? Among the young and the strong? Floss, what's going on? Why haven't we discovered this drop?"

The Femmedarme Magister allowed herself a rueful smile. "Let me point out that we *have* discovered it. We've just discovered it late. Shall I name you four factors that contributed to our ignorance?" Hardly pausing for permission, she continued.

"First, we haven't been looking for *declines* in population or even in birth rates. And we've been busy focusing on the Testing and the Protocols to the exclusion of almost everything else. Second, Lin-ci is right. Even if we had noted the declines, we wouldn't be worried. We've had more extreme global dips before, several times, and no serious consequences. Third, like you've started to understand just this evening, the most marked decline is within a discrete population, with no corollaries that I can find with any other group.

"Finally, and most important," said Magister Lutu, "there was a shake-up three years ago in the programming of the education sector of the Size Bureau. If you'll remember, half-trap web decisions in at least seven satrapies drove statistical teams crazy and put whole blocks of information in limbo for months. The dispute was, I believe, over the definition of the word, 'student.' It's clarified now, and the bureaucracy has resumed its intrepid operation. But I suspect that the figures we presently see attached to schooling citizens may not, until recently, have been made official. Over the years, we may well have been looking at other figures entirely, figures that did not reflect a decline. We can probably make a more accurate assessment if we measure specific age-groups instead of 'schooling citizens.' That's a calculation that, believe it or not, has never been a part of Size Center's population program. I've got my staff at work on that now."

Lin-ci Win was leaning forward. "Harriet," she said, "let us see the global figures for population since the year 2000 of the Common Era." She pushed back her cowl to reveal close-shaven ebony hair, then looked at her Kanshoumates. "We need to determine if any particular decrease occurred among school children over those years. As opposed to overall population."

They studied the turn-of-the-millennium figures from large cities and small hamlets, for pre-adolescents and trade-school enrollees, all cross-referenced and compared internally by sex, ethnic background, age, and Nurturance Quotient. Set against the decline of overall population during those years, the school figures were boringly consistent. Inquiries into manner-of-death statistics for the present decline yielded no reported increase, much less any pattern, in the incidence of illness, accident, or suicide among children or youth. The Magisters worked on—digging, speculating, searching for some key to a nagging puzzle. More than two hours later, Yotoma closed down the flatfields, and Zude lit another cigarillo.

"We need more information," Lin-ci Win muttered, rubbing the stubble on her head. "Flossie, your analysis team there in Tripoli needs to lead the way with what it's already uncovered. Then we can model your paths. I'll send you the best we've got in systems design to help spark the process."

Zude risked an earlier familiarity. "Lin-ci," she said, "we could also use some of your trained clairsentients, operators who can read others' feelings. I'll bet my pension that our best leads will come from schoolchildren themselves—that is, if some significant number of such children are curling up to die."

"Curling up to—that's not what's happening, Zella," Lin-ci began. Then, in an uncharacteristic display of doubt, she looked at Yotoma and back to Zude. "That's not what's happening. Is it?"

Zude prematurely smothered her cigarillo. "What else can it be? Do three million school kids just disappear from the face of the Earth? Or, allowing for older schoolers and normal deaths among our youngest age group, even two million? Or a million?"

Yotoma maintained an enigmatic silence. Lin-ci Win stared at Zude. "You're right, of course. Whatever is happening, children and adolescents themselves will best be able to identify it." She scratched her head and then drew her neck cowl up, resuming her nun-like appearance. "I am, unfortunately, distant from any small ones except the three in our household. They seem fine . . . ." The Magister subsided into a reverie. Then, suddenly, she uttered an oath from an obscure language and leaned toward Flossie. "My chosen grandaughter. She's six. She told me the other day of a little friend who had died. When I asked her how that had happened she said, 'I don't know. She just decided to die.'"

The three Magisters looked at each other. Then Zude stood up in her holopocket. She stretched her arms above her head.

224

"Well, we may be making a mountain out of the proverbial mole-hill. Like as not, we'll discover tomorrow some rational explanation for it all." She looked at the other two and they looked back at her in silence.

Zude sank into her chair again. "It's no good, is it?" she admitted. "I can't talk myself out of this. Can't shake this feeling, this crazy feeling. . . ."

Yotoma did not speak. She shook her head.

As if by common consent, and without another word, all three women nodded in courteous farewell to one another. Then their respective Peace Rooms redeemed their holo-images from the ether, and each was left alone, staring at the emptiness that had held her colleagues.

———————◆———————

As each Magister returned to the duties of her own tri-satrapy, Jezebel Stronglaces in Bombay had just learned of the bailiwick outbreaks. In the dying sunlight of Dhamni's courtyard, she sat in open trance.

"Jez!" Dicken's voice prodded her gently. "Are you back?"

Jezebel moved her body in small but deliberate stretches. "Just visiting, with some snakes and eagles," she said with a sigh. "And," she added with a slight frown, "with . . . a calico cat, I think . . . ." Her eyes were fixed on the garden wall beyond the boontree root, even as she spoke to the woman on the bench beside her. "Can you hear the singing, Dicken?"

"Singing?"

"Yes." Jez's eyes were soft. "Lots of children . . . singing."

Dicken closed her eyes. "I'm not hearing them." Then she whispered, "Love, Dhamni and I are on flatfone with some women in Hanoi. Do you want to join us?"

Jez shook her head. "Later," she said. "There's something

here, something I must do . . . ." She felt Dicken slip away from her, back into the house.

The song called to her, its cadences distant and strange, but like the chantings of her ancestors, also hauntingly familiar. She sank again into her expanded awareness.

She could not explain to Dicken just yet the summons of the sounds and images that flooded her mind . . . the tiny flashes of incandescent light, this song, the calico cat, and the image half a world away of the figure in a Vigilante uniform, who could only be one woman . . . .

◆

In her darkened office, Zude stood with her hand on the back of the taxidermed calico cat. "If you were here," she said softly, "I'd ask you to sleep on my bed tonight, and walk with me in my dreams." The yellow eyes flickered, and Zude cocked her head, urging her ears toward words just a shiver beyond their grasp. She listened in vain.

Reluctantly, she withdrew her hand from the crouching cat's body and stepped to the depaqued window that framed her city. Below her, the lights lay like jewels strewn by a bountiful god, each sparkling its separate story, each rich with life. She followed the illuminated paths of cushcars and the city's Rolling Beltway. In the urban glow she could make out a Vigilante gert descending from the Shrievalty's roof, dipping lightly toward the streets. Were the two women called to some small crisis, some domestic strife, perhaps? At least the Los Angeles Bailiwick had not erupted into violence today . . . the gert was not headed for clean-up or incident inquiry. Maybe, she thought, the two Kanshou were simply going off-duty, home to their private lives.

Zude remembered painfully her first assignment as a newly graduated Kanshou: Amah Lieutenant Adverb and two companion Foot-Shrieves of Calcutta's Maiden Precinct were dispatched to a rapidly escalating barroom brawl in which several of the combatants slashed at each other with switchblades. The Kanshou quelled the row but could not save the life of one of the men. Zude had almost disarmed one assailant, only to feel him break free of her hold at the last moment. She watched helplessly as he drove his knife deep into his adversary's solar plexus. She was a full-fledged peacekeeper; but what peace, she asked herself now, had she brought to those two men who so fiercely *wanted* to kill each other? Would their lives have been different if they had had some magical surgery, some medical protocols that might have divested them of their violence?

She leaned against the window's edge. What if all those sordid human urges *could* be physiologically controlled? If the protofiles were right, and if they had their way, men like those in the bar might never strike at each other in the first place.

"It's still too big a price to pay," she muttered aloud. "Let them die in their own blood, if necessary, but let them die untampered with and free."

At that moment, a ripple of light caught her eye. The crystal ballbakers lying uncovered on her desk were pulsing, perhaps stirred to life by the ambient light of the city—or perhaps roused by a sinister resistance to her own thoughts. She moved toward them and bent close in order to observe their palpitation. "You beauties," she told them with reluctant admiration, "between you and the Protocols, men are righteously scared these days."

Carefully, she picked up the crystals by their tiny wooden handles and held them high at arm's length. They continued to quiver, forming a glowing vortex that encased her hands and drew her seductively toward a less substantial realm. She stood fascinated, watching their rhythm. "Somewhere on Little Blue," she murmured hazily, "there's a boy who sooner or later could turn your power to a far better use than burning off men's balls." She spoke as in a dream. "But we may never see his genius because we'll cripple him before he's able to grow up. He may be out there right now," she added, looking toward the sprawling city, "somewhere in Los Angeles—"

"He's out there, all right," came a familiar voice, as if from her gleaming hands, *"but not in Los Angeles. He's in Arabia."*

"Jezebel!" Zude called frantically, "Where are you?" She responded not so much to the strange words as to the voice that spoke them.

"I just found him day before yesterday," the voice continued calmly, *"and I must still believe, Zude, that he will discover his creative genius <u>only because</u> he will no longer be violent. He will have had the surgery."*

Zude was speechless. Unwittingly, she dropped the crystals onto her desk—and broke their thrall.

"Jezebel!" she whispered. When Jez's voice spoke no more, Zude snatched up the crystals again, willing the return of her past lover's presence. Yet the ballbakers, too, were dark and inert. Ruefully, she thought of Bosca—if she had some of the training that Bosca promised her, she might be able to reignite the ballbakers and retrieve the sound of Jezebel's voice.

Zude lowered herself into her chair, pushing the crystals aside, trying hard to recall the words that Jezebel had said in those surreal moments. "Where are you tonight," she cried, "Jezebel, my witch?"

Still no answer.

Zude's fingers clasped the unpartnered unicorn earring. Unbidden tears rolled down her cheeks. The love and anger, the kinship and the betrayal—all the buried memories welled up from years past and rained their desolation upon her.

In that moment, she opened the gates to more than her longing for Jezebel, letting a sea of conflicts and crises flood into her awareness. She burned with rage against habitantes willing to take worshipping citizens hostage in a shul, raged equally against protofiles who would deliberately cripple such habitantes. She despised any women who would use the ballbakers to wreak vengeance upon men. She despaired anew of any answer to the violence from both sexes that assailed her world.

She rose and paced, clutching fistsful of her hair tight against her scalp, attempting to relieve the growing pressures there. She tried to invoke a thing that would lift her heart, her chosen family: "Ria, Kayita, Regina, Enrique!" But their names as she spoke them fell lifeless upon the air. Her pride in the Kanshoubu, her respect for her Kanshoumates—all burst into fleeting flame and fell to Earth in ashes. Her anguish drained the joy from every corner of her life.

And now, she noted wryly, even the lights of her city's homes were going out . . . steadily . . . one-by-one, leaving dark places especially deep and ominous tonight.

Zella Terremoto Adverb stood, cynical and immobile, inwardly spiralling down into a place she had rarely allowed to overtake her sensibilities, into deepening desolation, into barren plains devoid of meaning where no hope could dawn. She sank again into her chair. She had never before uttered the words that crossed her lips.

"I give up," she whispered and stared into space.

The ballbakers began pulsing again. Listlessly, Zude picked them up, then held them as before. She wondered, wretchedly, if those tiny crystals could kill. Her hands began glowing again in that vortex of flickering brightness. She swallowed hard.

"That's good," she heard in the light that enfolded her hands. The voice was high and lilting, almost frivolous. This was not Jezebel.

Zude's fingers, holding the ballbakers tightly, began to tremble.

"Who are you?" she rasped, belligerently.

"You will name me 'Swallower.'"

"Swallower?"

"Bosca will explain."

The voice had a tinkle to it. Groping for some assurance of control, Zude raised the crystals higher.

"Magister Adverb," the Swallower lilted, *"I am here to guide you in your coming changes. Or am I too early? Do you prefer to wallow further in your pain?"*

Zude's whole body broke into a prickly sweat. "Whoever you are, I don't want—"

"What do you want? That's the only question."

Zude let the sudden tears fall without inhibition. "I want . . . I want so much," she whispered helplessly. "I want to see animals every day . . . horses and dogs and snakes and birds and mosquitos! I want a solution to the Protocols, one that won't trample anybody's rights, but . . ." her voice broke, " . . . but one that *does* give us a more peaceful world!" She rested her elbows on the desk, balancing the glowing crystals. "And," she added softly, "I want to see her again . . . Jezebel."

The illumination around her hands intensified.

"Then your work," said the Swallower, *"is to move toward joy. Your work is to visualize more peace with no one's rights denied. Your work is to live as if any day now you will see all the animals again . . . and Jezebel, too."*

"My *work*, you genie," Zude snapped, trying to hold the ballbakers steady, "or whatever you are . . . my *work* is to protect this planet and its people, my *work* is to put my body in harm's way if necessary to stop anything that could hurt them! My *work* is to fight for justice and freedom—"

"Your work is far more difficult than fighting," interrupted the Swallower.

Zude felt on the verge of throwing the ballbakers to the floor. "I'm too busy," she roared, "to spend time in fantasies!"

"*Then you are too busy to learn your true destiny!*"

Zude froze.

The sphere of light that encased her hands burned with a low incandescent heat. "*Here is your path of change, Zella Terremoto Adverb!*" the Swallower announced. "*You have been a woman of action. Now you will become a woman of vision.*"

Barely breathing, Zude waited for the Swallower to say more. Instead, she heard again from the dimming light of the crystals the one voice that would always lift her heart.

Jezebel's words were filled with truth and adoration. Zude took them with her into the night: "*To this, my love,*" Jez commanded, "*you must surrender.*"

THE MAGISTER

Book Two of the *Earthkeep Trilogy*

by Sally Miller Gearhart

A Preview

NUEVA TIERRA NORTE, LITTLE BLUE ———

[2088 C.E. St. Paul, Minnesota]

In the director's office of the Dolly Ruark Athletic Center Jezebel Stronglaces and her lover, Bess Dicken, sat watching a flatfilm with the Ruark Center's director, Beabenet.

On the screen, a dark-skinned child stood in her bedroom, rubbing her cheek against a fuzzy tiger. She kissed the toy and started to set it back on its stool. She stopped, held it at arm's length, and cocked her head as if listening. Then she clasped the tiger to her. She walked toward the mikcam and into the arms of the bewildered woman who sat on the bed.

"Jula," she told her mother, "we're just going to play with our friends." The round little face was earnest. "They're waiting for us." She looked at the tiger and gave it a squeeze. She curled up in the woman's lap and laid her hand on the woman's bosom. "You can come too, you know." Then, flashing a brilliant smile,

235

Mary Frances Safful closed her eyes, and slipped into an apparently blissful sleep.

Beabenet cleared the flatfield. "And . . ."

"And she never woke up," finished Dicken.

"That's right." Bea closed down the flatfilm casing and activated a tab on her chairarm panel. Skylights and windows came alive again with light. "That's the only film we've got," she said. "And we wouldn't have had that if Franny's big sister, Lyn, hadn't had the instincts of a historian. As you saw, she made it almost a daily game with Franny, getting her to talk on camera about sleeping so much. Lyn let me borrow the flatfilm chip. She said Jula couldn't stand to look at it anyway."

She picked up a strip of audio chipnests and a flatcopy report. "Here." She set them on the desk. "You can hear or read about the other three. Pretty much the same story. All in good health except that, according to two of the families, their hair changed color. Only one of them had been sleeping more than usual. The others died completely unexpectedly, yet apparently very peacefully. Just didn't wake up one morning. Only one of them had any history of disease or injury—an anti-grav tumble nearly four years before."

Bea sighed. She pressed two fingers against her temple. "One of the mothers went wild. Swore her daughter was just comatose, but still alive. She kept her lying in state for over a week, refusing to embalm, bury, or cremate her." Bea looked from Dicken to Jez, then continued. "We have this information only because staff members here knew and loved those children. We have no authority to carry out any kind of investigation. And Demesne Service apparently sees nothing out of the ordinary in the deaths. 'Nothing to be concerned about,' they say."

"Jez, am I crazy?" she blurted. "Is this all just coincidence?" She looked at Dicken. "The death of one child in one of our programs, okay. Not unusual. Might happen even once a year. Two? Well, maybe even two. But four? Four children in the last six months? All between the ages of three and eleven? Like I told you on the flatfone, that's more than coincidence."

Dicken moved to a sculptured fountain in the corner where trickling water dropped into a small rock-bottomed pool. "You're not crazy," she said. "Just waking up." She pulled herself away from the soothing water sounds. "And if you want to get wide awake, then start watching Size Central's population trends. Not much public attention to exactly what's happening yet, but give it another month—maybe just a week—and the gathering energy of this mysterious tidal wave will sweep the Testing and the Protocols right off the front page." Bea's eyes narrowed. "You're telling me children are dying in other places?"

"Yes. Little girls and boys just tipping their hats and leaving." Dicken reached out to let the water course over her long fingers.

"Why?" Beabenet was frowning.

Dicken shrugged. "No reason. No consistency. All arbitrary."

Jez's voice startled them both. "That's not totally true. There is one common factor that stands out." They looked at her. "All of these children go willingly, even happily. Nowhere is there any hint that they resist. Or that they were victims of any illness or injury. They simply decide to die."

Bea stared at her. Slowly her eyes widened and her lips parted. Her head moved up and then down. "Like the animals," she whispered.

Jez watched realization sinking into Beabenet's cells. "Like the animals," she whispered back.

NUEVA TIERRA NORTE, LITTLE BLUE ⸻
[2088 C.E. New Nagasaki, New Mexico]

Jezebel Stronglaces watched the setting sun from the roofgar-
den of the Give Away Casino.

"Pardon, Señora." The voice was close behind her. "But have
you perchance lost a unicorn?"

Jez made herself turn slowly.

Nothing in all the annals of alchemy or the Craft could have
kept down the swift sharp tears that rose at the sight before her:
the proud Kanshou bearing, the uniform, the warm brown eyes,
the long slightly-turned nose, the waves of salt-and-pepper hair.
Handsome. Compelling.

"Zudie." She held out her hands.

Zude took them, smoothly, with none of her old characteris-
tic awkwardness, holding them firmly, with all of her old charac-
teristic gentleness.

238

"Jezebel," she said, matching the brightness of Jez's eyes with a fullness in her own. The presence that faced her pulsed with vigor, from the crown of the shoulder-length hair to the high cheeks and long hands, from the strong easy shoulders down the lean body's flow to the brown sandaled feet.

Both women were blanketed by keen memories and barely contained longings, pervaded by such sudden intimacy that neither could speak further. They stood transfixed, daring neither breath nor movement.

"The unicorn is yours, Vigilante Magister," Jezebel said at last, with a small formal bow. "In pair with its proper mate, it celebrates the rebirth of magic."

Zude took one of the earrings from her ear and held it up. "But the magic is not yet fully born, Señora." She pressed the tiny unicorn into Jez's hand and held it with both her own. "And you may have need of it again."

"Then I shall take it, Vigilante Magister." Jez placed her other hand on Zude's.

Zude searched for words but found only her tight throat and stinging eyes. She opened her mouth, closed it, cleared her throat, and swallowed. "Jez—" She drew a deep breath. "I don't have to tell you, do I?"

Jez shook her head. "No." She smiled.

Zude laughed softly. She lingered for just a moment, holding Jez's eyes with her own. Then she drew Jezebel to one of the chair circles. They sat, more at ease now, making way for the closing in of the desert night. Carefully but lightly, they spoke of the events of their lives since the Amah Academy, each acknowledging with ironic smiles the increasing distance that had separated their diverging paths.

The threat of full nightfall prompted Zude to reach out for Jez's hand.

239

"Just let me look at you, Bella-Belle. I feel so thirsty for the sight of you."

"I've had the advantage," Jez replied. "I've seen you on public flat-transmissions many times." She pressed Zude's hand. "My Magister."

"And," Zude paused, "your adversary."

Earthkeep CHRONOLOGY _____

Common Era Date

2003   World Health Organization announces that alternative and complementary health practices lend hope for long life to persons of HIV-positive status. Deaths from Virus I (HIV) balloon in Indonesia, Bengal Bay, and Hong Kong as a result of contaminated blood supplies from the 1990's.

2004   Pan-European medical establishment announces first truly effective vaccine (Vaccine I) against Virus I, to be available immediately.

2005   *Flossie Yotoma Lutu* is born in the Sudan, fifty miles from the White Nile River.

2006   Precipitous emergence of mutant virus (Virus II) from the Virus I vaccine.

2007   Beginning of decade of escalating natural cataclysms, such as spikes in global warming, earthquakes, hurricanes, tornadoes, floods, droughts, famine, malaria, rivers poisoned by acid rain. China, India, and southeast Asia are especially stricken.

2008   Effective vaccine (Vaccine II) against Virus II is announced.

2010   Emergence from Vaccine II of a new strain of drug resistant virus (Virus III).

2012   Vaccine III against Virus III is announced.

2014   Emergence of new viral mutation (Virus IV) from Vaccine III.

2015   Global riots against medical establishment take hundreds of lives.

2018   Global crusade to inoculate every citizen against Virus IV with Vaccine IV, "the vaccine to end all vaccines," which has been tested extensively on cloned animals.

2019   Widespread drought resulting from ecocide and global warming sends masses of starving people northward from Central and South America into southwestern United States. The defensive response of the U.S. military includes releasing upon the invading people swarms of Culex tarsalis mosquitoes carrying an influenza virus against which its own troops are inoculated. Tens of thousands die.

2020   The international outcry against the U.S.' use of biological weaponry deals the deathblow to the global power of the United States as it had existed and assures the inclusion within North American borders of the newly formed Reclaimed Territory of Aztlán, extending from Los Angeles to the Mississippi River.

2021   "Empty Monday," April 12, the day of the Animal Exodus from Little Blue. The death or disappearance of all multi-cellular animals except Homo sapiens. All subsequent attempts fail to clone stored animal DNA.

2022   Beginning of a decade of upward spiralling global unrest, exhibited in street wars, food riots, homeless rebellions, increased martial law, worldwide disruptions of power, communication, and transportation services.

2023   International Disarmament Accords end the possibility of biological, chemical, or nuclear war worldwide.

2024   Announcement that Vaccine IV has irrevocably suppressed the Y chromosome in men and reduced fertility in women by 80%. Estimates concur that by mid-century, global population will be just over one billion and that the ratio of women to men will be 12-to-1.

2026   *Lin-ci Win* is born in Hong Kong.

2027   Worldwide secession from their parent nations of religious fundamentalist sects whose precepts include enslavement of women and individualized strains of racist theology. Their staunch defense of their sovereign communities initiates the bloodiest decade of Little Blue's 21st century.

Formation of International Congress, representing nearly 75% of the nations of the world.

2029   Founding of the Amahrery's Kanshou Academy in Hong Kong, ushering in the era of women's peace-keeping principles and practices.

2033   Founding of the Femmedarmery's Kanshou Academy in Tripoli.

2034   Founding of the Vigilancia's Kanshou Academy in Los Angeles.

2035   Worldwide legal reforms begin the conversion of prison facilities into containment areas called *baili-wicks*, whose inmates become *habitantes*. Local police forces formally adopt Kanshou peacekeeping principles, practices, and ranks.

2036   Inchoate governance model based on values and practices familiar to women begins to emerge for Middle East geo-political territory, spearheaded by *Presiding Sifter of the Syrian Kitchen Table, Flossie Yotoma Lutu* and called a "satrapy."

2038   Transmogrifier technology is tentatively approved for worldwide distribution by International Congress. The profusion of world credit systems is standardized to accommodate the rapidly changing economy. (See TERMINOLOGY.)

2039   Beginning of worldwide efforts to integrate and codify among nations economic and governmental relationships based upon values and practices familiar to women. Hearings, forums, and convocations in every major city explore the requirements of world government, delineating legislative, judicial, and implemental functions.

2041   *Jezebel Stronglaces* is born in Lakemir, near Lake Michigan, North America.

2042   *Zella Terremoto Adverb (Zude)* is born in Barranquilla, Colombia, South America.

2043   The Kitchen Table, international judicial body, is formed, initially with five sitting Sifters. Half-trap, quarter-trap, and demesne tribunals are established upon the Kitchen Table Model.
(See GLOBAL GOVERNANCE.)

2044   "Earthclasp," April 12, the day that citizens all over the world celebrate Earthkeep priorities, including the hoped-for return of the animals.

2046   Centralizing of global peacekeeping policy by the formal merging of Amahrery, Femmedarmery, and Vigilancia into the Kanshoubu. First convening of the Heart of All Kanshou, composed of Amahs, Femmedarmes, Vigilantes of all ranks and charged with determining policies of the Kanshoubu. (See GLOBAL GOVERNANCE—PEACEKEEPING.)

2049   Central Web, with 15 sitting Websters, is officially established to replace International Congress as world legislative body. Half-trap, quarter-trap, and demesne webs begin forming on the Central Web model. (See

GLOBAL GOVERNANCE.)

2050   International census for the first time categorizes "satrapies" and "tri-satrapies" as geo-political entities. The global population is reported to be 1,242,000,000, of which female citizens are 92.3%, male citizens 7.7%. "Little Blue" is officially acknowledged as the most common popular reference to the planet Earth.

2053   The Year-Long Plenum in Tokyo formulates precepts of new global governance. The Plenary Constitution, a planet-wide governing document, takes shape. "Global" begins to replace "international" in the daily parlance of citizens. Newly formed bureaus and boards take up the regulation of economic affairs and the implementation of legislative decisions.

2057   Nueva Tierra Norte Satrapy, after long negotiation with its southeastern precincts, finally confirms both the spirit and letter of the Plenary Constitution, thus completing the ratification of that global document.

2062   *Amah Captain Lin-ci Win* is wounded and paralyzed at a cotton mill looting skirmish in Wuchang (Hupeh Province).

2066   *Flossie Yotoma Lutu* becomes Magister of the Africa-Europe-Mideast Tri-Satrapy.

2067   *Zella Terremoto Adverb (Zude)* enters the Amah Academy in Hong Kong.

2078 *Lin-ci Win* becomes Magister of the Asia-China-Insula Tri-Satrapy.

2080 *Zella Terremoto Adverb (Zude)* becomes Vice-Magister of Nueva Tierra Norte Satrapy.

2084 *Jezebel Stronglaces* becomes the unofficial leader of a global movement to eradicate violence.

2085 *Zella Terremoto Adverb (Zude)* becomes Magister of Nueva Tierra Tri-Satrapy.

2086 Global Consorority of Neurosurgeons reveals proposal to use bailiwick habitantes in "the search for a physiological violence center in the brain" (Habitante Testing) and the possible institution of Anti-Violence Protocols, surgeries to eliminate any such physiological center.

bailiwicks Containment areas for offenders against society, similar in function to 20th century prisons.

"ballbakers" Contraband crystals, tuned electronically or by a witch, which are being illegally distributed and sometimes used to castrate violent men, particularly rapists.

breathshine Creation by breathfriction and focused intent of an independent and "totable" source of light, as in the creation or rejuvenation of a glolobe.

breeks A Kanshou's loose-fitting black pants of light cotton.

cape, cloak A Kanshou's black cape of tekla, hanging to mid-thigh and kept folded in her subvention belt, except when used for warmth, balance, or protection. Magisters wear the near ankle-length cloak instead of the cape.

Central Web Little Blue's global legislative body of fifteen Websters, the highest level of the planet's Legislative branch of government. (See GLOBAL GOVERNANCE.)

chela A beginning Kanshou cadet.

com-, commu- Referring to "communication," as in comcube, comunit, comline, or commuflow.

comfortsuit A Kanshou's skintight bodystocking of rhyndon.

compu- Referring to "computer," as in compucode, compufile, compukiosk, compupost, compusite.

cowl A Kanshou's tubular neckpiece of tekla that can be spread and extended upward to cover her head for protection from weather.

credit system Little Blue's primary method of value exchange, used in all metropolitan districts and in most rural areas, except where citizens have opted to be a barter or gift society. Generally replaces currency used in former eras.

cushcar A hovercraft used primarily for personal transport, such as the "solocush" (borne on only four air jets) or the "standard 24" which can seat four passengers and is sustained by 24 jets. In contrast to the cushcar, a "cargocush" is the transportation of choice for freight and is borne on 48 jets. Cushcars have replaced vehicles powered by a four-stage gasoline combustion engine in popularity.

Daily Voice The ongoing global opinion poll, offering citizens of Little Blue the opportunity to voice their opinions regarding proposals being heard by the Central Web and lower webs or cases being heard by the Kitchen Table and lower tables. One vote allowed per citizen per day.

dartsleeve A close range personal weapon through which a Kanshou may blow darts laden with "sodoze." The sodoze is a neurological inhibitor that temporarily disables the person targeted within seconds.

demesne (duh-<u>mane</u>) The governmental sub-division of a quarter-trap, whose size and shape are determined by discussion (and if necessary, by referendum) among the citizens who are involved.

dreamwork The mutual exploration undertaken by two women who are physically touching while sleeping, and in which they inhabit the same dreams, as in dreamwalking, dreamweaving, dreamwatching.

Earthclasp April 12, 2044, the day that citizens first celebrated the highest of Earthkeep priorities: the rehabilitation, preservation, veneration, and appropriate "use" of the Earth for citizens and for the hoped-for Return of the Animals. Pundits and cultural analysts have since marked the day of this celebration as the turning point in the global economy from scarcity to "No Hunger, No Poverty." The day is also commonly regarded as the time at which women were acknowledged to be the uncontested leaders of socio-political affairs on Little Blue.

Earthkeep The prevailing mass consciousness on Little Blue, derived in response to the disastrous events of the first half of the 21st century. The values attendant upon the Earthkeep consciousness are: a reverence for the planet and its biosphere as a living organism, an awareness of the interconnectedness of all beings, and a celebration of diversity and self-determination within Nature and among the human family.

Empty Monday The day of the Animal Exodus, the 48-hour period inclusive of April 12, 2021, when every non-human animal on Little Blue mysteriously died or disappeared.

Exodus The Animal Exodus from Little Blue in which all multicellular animals, including insects, gave up their lives. No bacterial, fungiform, or plant life was affected. Phytoplankton survived.

flat Used to distinguish "regular" objects or processes from holographic reproduction, as in flatfilm, flatcopy, flatcast, flatfone, flatmap.

flex-car The Kanshoubu's multi-purpose and variously-powered vehicle capable of movement on land, in air, and on or through water, usually combining only two of these capacities in the ability to operate both vertically and laterally.

forcefield wraps Spheres of energy established by set nodes and used by Kanshou in the detention or transfer of violent offenders. Different areas of the harmer's body can be quickly immobilized or released.

free enterprise The encouragement of private industry or commerce under open competitive conditions, a part of Little Blue's mixed economy but strictly within the boundaries of Earthkeep priorities. A Board of Use must deliberately grant to a commercial or industrial enterprise its use of any land, water, and/or airspace, however large or small, that is under the Board's jurisdiction. Boards of Use may revoke any grant at any time for violation of the conditions of use.

gert To fly together as Kanshou, designated as, for instance,

Rhoda-Gert-Longleaf. Or a "spoon" of two Kanshou women who are able to fly together because they are or have been lovers. Applied specifically to the Flying Daggers of the Amahrery, the Femmedarmery, and the Vigilancia.

gift society A community committed to the development of an economy based upon the gifts that its residents offer and receive. Central to such a society's philosophy is the individual's subsistence solely upon the largesse of her/his neighbors.

glolobe A source of light generated by breathshine and sustained by a pattern of ambient influx. Glolobes may be suspended in the air or carried to other locations by mindtote.

habitante A person remanded to a bailiwick because of his/her violent behavior.

hempbrew A tea-like hot drink made from processed hempstalks.

holo Designating some feature of holotechnology (e.g., holotech, holosize, holoscene, holoroom, holofest).

hovercraft Any air conveyance, usually a cushcar or cargocush, used for public transportation or personal short-distance travel. It is powered by fusion thrust or hydrogen-enhanced photovoltaic units but kept aloft by air suspension in the form of multiple jets of air in constant pressure against the ground (or water).

hurtfield Invisible electrical "fences" which surround most bailiwicks to prevent the escape of habitantes.

Kanshoubu (kahn-show-boo) The global peacekeeping body, composed of Amahs, Femmedarmes, and Vigilantes. A part of the Implemental branch of Little Blue's government.

Kanshou (<u>kahn</u>-show) Peacekeeping officer or officers, either an Amah, a Femmedarme, or a Vigilante, depending upon the trisatrapy in which she serves. A guardian or watcher.

Kitchen Table Little Blue's global tribunal of nine Sifters (justices). The highest level of the planet's Judicial branch of government.

learntogether A companion in study or experience, often the term applied to a life partner.

lonth The lower body's balance-and-sustain point, between the second and third chakras, which with practice can be used to maintain any psychic or physical state. A kind of "automatic pilot" for spoons or gerts during long flights.

lovetogether Any two people who share intimate erotic or spiritual experiences of lovemaking.

lume Any source of light used to dispel darkness or to accent texts or drawings. An electronic pointer, as in a lumerod, lumestick, screenlume, or lumepoints.

magnopad Electronic writing tablet for memoranda or brief expendable messages. The pad's magnetic field can be programmed to save data or messages for short time periods.

Mother Right Feminist ideology built upon the primacy of the female, essential female values and sensibilities, the necessity of women's self-determination apart from men or patriarchal structures or processes, and the inalienable principle of a woman's authority over her own children and those of her species, exclusive of any male influence.

paque By a holo-imagery system, the simulation of walls, rooms, and 3-D projections of distant views in areas otherwise transparent or without walls. Whole environments can be paqued, depaqued, and repaqued quickly.

plastiped A soft, durable, and flexible polymeric compound that "breathes." Used universally as the substitute for leather, particularly in the manufacture of footwear as in a Kanshou's mid-calf boots.

Plenary Constitution Little Blue's globally negotiated constitution, ratified in 2057, delineating the responsibilities of Little Blue's Legislative, Judicial, and Implemental branches of government and the interrelationships of the planet's geo-political territories (e.g., satrapies, tri-satrapies). Further, the document sets out the values attendant upon the Earthkeep Consciousness and names those values as the spirit from which all legal statutes will thenceforth derive. Certain caveats attach to the Plenary Constitution, pertaining to specific indigenous cultures and sovereign communities.

Pr-24 The Kanshou nightstick, modelled on the traditional Monadnock Pr-24 Police Baton. Its hard plastic is featherweight and its flexible design offers two working ends. It is, however, used primarily for restraint rather than for striking.

protofobe An opponent of Little Blue's emerging proposals for Anti-Violence Protocols and Habitante Testing.

protofile A supporter of the Protocols and Testing.

Rainbow Sunday April 14, 2041, the day of the appearance of a double rainbow in the western sky, first sighted at Amsterdam, then globally for twenty-four hours thereafter, a phenomenon interpreted as a promise of the Animals' Return because of its near coinciding with the twenty-year anniversary of their Exodus, but also understood as a symbol of peace and diversity.

rhyndon The material of the Kanshou's comfortsuit, automatically controlling the temperature range selected by its wearer.

rolling beltways Part of the public transportation system in many large cities, powered by hydrogen-enhanced photovoltaics and consisting of both fast and slow lanes for pedestrian travel. Ordinarily coordinated with "swings," individual hanging cables that swing from rooftop to rooftop. Swings are accessed by elevators or moving stairways.

Rwanda Accords Internationally endorsed compact (2028 C.E.) delineating a prisoner's rights and the limits of a detaining institution's use of force.

satrapy (say-trap-ee) Any one of nine geo-political territories, roughly the equivalents of the traditionally named "continents:"

Africa, Europe, the Mideast, Asia, China, the Pacific Islands, South America, Central America, North America. A "tri-satrapy" is made up of three satrapies.

Shrieve Any Kanshou.

Sifter One of the nine "justices" to sit at the Kitchen Table global judicial body. Members of lower tables are also called "sifters."

sleepwork The field of psychic training that enhances one's capacities in the state of sleep. On Little Blue, sleepwork is the particular passion of women who wish to acquire the language or dialect of another culture, and they pursue the most immediate, thorough, and enduring acquisition of such material by sleeping with a native speaker of that language or dialect. Where both sleepers are equally trained and skilled, the language or dialect transfer can take place in a single night.

softself The spiritual echo of the physical body which may at the will of a trained practitioner of psychic skills leave the "hardself" and move independently in physical space. It may occupy the body of another (willing) person and thus experience what that body experiences. Not to be confused with a person's "soul."

spoon To fly together. Or a pair of women capable of flying together because of their present or past relationship as lovers, so named for the position their two bodies often occupy in sleep. A spoon is capable of carrying in flight almost double its own weight.

subvention belt A black belt of plastiped that is worn at the Kanshou's waist. It provides compartments or slings for weaponry, the folded tekla cape, magnopad, force-field nodes, stunner, and comunit.

tabard A Kanshou's sleeveless shirt or tunic of heavy cotton that is lightly fitted to the torso. Its mandarin collar bears rank and/or division pips. Its color is that of the Amah (cardinal red), the Femmedarme (shamrock green), or the Vigilante (cobalt blue).

tanglestick Restraint device used by Kanshou that is made of net-ted strands of a loose nylon. The strands can be cast upon groups of violent offenders, temporarily immobilizing them by impairing muscle function.

tekla A mysterious material that is light, flexible, and apparently indestructible, whose chemical composition has not yet been determined. It was discovered simultaneously in southwestern Nueva Tierra Norte (old United States), central Australia, and the southern edges of the Sahara Desert in the third decade of the 21st century by three unrelated women, each on her personal Visionquest, and turned over to the newly developing Kanshoubu. The Kanshoubu has had exclusive ownership of all tekla resources on the planet ever since that time, constantly recy-cling it for use in Kanshou lariats, capes, cloaks, and cowls. Tekla "breaks" apart with ease and can be reconstituted as a seamless mass or sheet; it can be flattened into fabric or molded into a rope. Fire- and water-proof, it can nevertheless be dyed different colors. Also known as "zennatekla."

tote, mindtote To carry or sustain an object in midair without physical support. Preliminary exercise for training in telekinesis or the mental initiation of an object's propulsion in space from one place to another (as if it were being thrown).

transmog Referring to "transmogrifier," that replicative technol-ogy which allows the manufacture of any small artifact from nat-ural products or from the material of other artifacts by reconfiguring existing elements into new molecular compounds. Transmogrifier technology thus makes possible the filling of basic physical needs (such as food, clothing, tools) and the ownership of small items of personal property that have historically been available only within a system of currency or barter or which have been acquired as the plunder of war or theft.

Over the past two decades, all nine satrapy governments have provided their citizens with the intaglios or templates necessary for any individual's manufacture of "a thing or a substance," and the transmogrifiers themselves are universally available except in techless enclaves that have themselves rejected the use of such technology. With the exception of controlled substances or weapons whose intaglios are proscribed, any person can "own" anything she wants, and "personal property" has thus acquired a new meaning. Anything beyond or different from the capacity of the transmog to produce must be paid for with the appropriate credits.

Transmogrifiers are the critical element in Little Blue's recycling program. Though sewage is treated by separate processes, over 90% of the world's remaining wastes are transmogrified. Transmogrifier technology has altered the entire planet's economy.

vaporose A soporific mist developed for crowd control which when inhaled, induces sleep or deep relaxation.

Webster A member of the Central Web, the global legislative body. Members of lower webs are also called "websters."

work credits Value vouchers earned by one's labor or skill and deposited by employers to the accounts of workers. Transmogrifiers guarantee the free distribution of any of life's basic needs to Little Blue's citizens, but if an individual wishes to own or use something beyond or different from the capacities of the transmog, then she must sell her labor or her skills in order to buy those materials or items.

ziprocket A long distance air vehicle, powered by fusion thrusters and typically used as public transportation between Little Blue's large cities. "Lowrockets," more lightly powered, can make shorter jumps between rocketports, but do not boast the ziprocket's speed.

257

GEO-POLITICAL TERRITORIES OF LITTLE BLUE

Little Blue is divided into three geo-political areas called tri-satrapies, and each of these is further composed of three satrapies (<u>say</u>-trap-eez). The civic affairs of each satrapy (<u>say</u>-trap-ee) are under the directorship of a Kanshou (<u>kahn</u>-show) Vice-Magister. The civic affairs of the tri-satrapy as a whole are under the directorship of the Kanshou Magister of the tri-satrapy.

The *Asia-China-Insula Tri-Satrapy*, made up of the areas traditionally called Asia, China, and the Pacific Islands (including Australia) is currently administered by Kanshou *Magister Lin-ci Win.*

The *Africa-Europe-Mideast Tri-Satrapy*, made up of the areas traditionally called Africa, Europe, and the Middle East, is currently administered by Kanshou *Magister Flossie Yotoma Lutu.*

The *Nueva Tierra Tri-Satrapy,* made up of the areas traditionally called South America (including Antarctica), Central America, and North America, and now called Nueva Tierra Sur, Nueva Tierra Central, and Nueva Tierra Norte, is currently administered by Kanshou *Magister Zella Terremoto Adverb (Zude).*

Each satrapy is further divided geographically and demographically into local areas, usually called half-traps, quarter-traps, and demesnes (duh-<u>manes</u>). Except for the global laws articulated by the Plenary Constitution and the Central Web, a local area typically lives by its own laws, traditions, and values, though it has a financial obligation to the satrapy-as-a-whole and is responsible for providing candidates to the Central Web Pool of Qualified Websters and Sifters (justices) to the Kitchen Table Pool of Qualified Sifters.

BRANCHES OF GOVERNMENT

Legislative

The Central Web

Little Blue's global legislative body, composed of 15 Central Websters, five from each tri-satrapy, chosen by lot from the Pool of Qualified Websters whose members have been elected by each satrapy. This body formulates global law in accordance with Little Blue's Plenary Constitution.

The Lower Webs

Legislative bodies in satrapies, half-traps, quarter-traps, and demesnes which support the structure, processes, and responsibilities of the Central Web.

The Boards of Use

On the satrapy level and below, Boards Of Use are elected to govern the use of land, water, and airspace within their area of jurisdiction.

Judicial

The Kitchen Table

Little Blue's global judicial body, composed of nine Sifters (or justices), one from each satrapy, chosen by lot from the Pool of Qualified Sifters. This pool is composed of citizens trained and/or experienced in arbitration, mediation, and the study of constitutional law. Its duties are to interpret the meaning and the spirit of Little Blue's Plenary Constitution and to determine the justice of claims that come to its hearing on appeal from lower tables where interpretation of the Plenary Constitution is involved.

The Lower Tables

Judiciary bodies in satrapies, half-traps, quarter-traps, and demesnes which support the structure and processes of the Kitchen Table. Their responsibilities include the settlement of disputes that are appealed from Boards of Arbitration and Mediation, particularly those which may potentially be appealed to the Kitchen Table.

The Boards of Arbitration and Mediation

Bodies on satrapy, half-trap, quarter-trap, and demesne levels, composed of citizens trained and/or experienced in conflict resolution and mediation. The majority of disputes between or among citizens are settled by such boards.

Implemental

Civic Bureaus

Little Blue's global, tri-satrapy, satrapy, and lower level governmental organizations handle the needs of citizens in accordance with the priorities set forth in the Plenary Constitution. The planet's mixed economy requires cooperation between government agencies and the free enterprise system. The Civic Bureaus thus complement and support the free enterprise elements of the economy in their mutual effort to meet the needs and desires of individuals and groups of citizens. Their responsibilities are largely regulatory in nature and include Bureaus of:

Size Control (of Population and Enterprise)
Air-Land-Water Use
Health/Sanitation
Recycling/Transmogrifying
Employment
Art-Culture-Language
Science-Technology
Industry
Transportation
Communication
Education
Citizen Opinion
Public Media
Value Exchange
Weather

The Kanshoubu (kahn-show-<u>boo</u>)

The Kanshoubu implements the legal statutes and decisions made by the Legislative and Judicial branches of the government. In the absence of national military forces, peacekeeping and public safety services have developed into a quasi-military global responsibility that is the purview of the Kanshoubu.

Earthkeep *PEACEKEEPING*

ORGANIZATION OF THE KANSHOUBU

<u>Geographical Orders</u>, each under a Magister chosen by her tri-satrapy's Kanshou (<u>kahn</u>-show) and ratified by The Heart Of All Kanshou.

The Amahrery, training Amahs and serving the Asia-China-Insula Tri-Satrapy, bearing the color of cardinal red.

The Femmedarmery, training Femmedarmes and serving the Africa-Europe-Mideast Tri-Satrapy, bearing the color of shamrock green.

The Vigilancia, training Vigilantes and serving Nueva Tierra Sur-Central-Norte Tri-Satrapy, bearing the color of cobalt blue.

<u>Branches (within all orders)</u>

The Ground Shrievalty, composed of Kanshou officers known as Foot-Shrieves or Flex-Car Shrieves and holding one of the following ranks:

Brigadier	(A Femmedarme Hedwoman)
Marshal	
Matrix Major	
Adjutant Major	
Captain	(A Femmedarme Aga)
First Lieutenant	(A Femmedarme Sub-Aga)
Second Lieutenant	(An Amah Jing-Cha)

The Sea Shrievalty, composed of Kanshou officers known as Sea-Shrieves, sailing the high seas, coastal waters, large inland lakes or waterways and holding one of the following ranks:

Sea Admiral
Sea Captain
Sea Commander
Sea Lieutenant Commander
Mariner First Class
Mariner Second Class
Sea Ensign

The Sky Shrievalty, composed of Kanshou officers known as Sky-Shrieves, piloting rockets or cushcars and holding one of the following ranks:

Sky Admiral
Sky Captain
Sky Commander
Sky Lieutenant Commander
Flyer First Class
Flyer Second Class
Sky Ensign

Note: Although usually associated with the Sky Shrievalty, Flying Daggers (Kanshou who fly in gerts) serve in all three branches of the Kanshoubu.

Kanshou Cadet Academies
The Amah Academy, Hong Kong, graduating Amahs
into the Amahrery
The Femmedarme Academy, Tripoli, graduating

Femmedarmes into the Femmedarmery
The Vigilante Academy, Los Angeles, graduating
Vigilantes into the Vigilancia

Each Academy trains cadets in every branch of service
(Ground, Sea, and Sky), and the core curriculum of each
Academy is standardized to include intense physical fit-
ness and combat training; the study of science, technology, law, government, commerce, ethics, computation,
and communication; the study of the humanities (litera-
ture, history, language, philosophy, the arts).

The Bailiwicks

Offenders against society are remanded to containment
areas called *bailiwicks*. As *habitantes* (those contained in
bailiwicks), they lose their status as citizens. The maxi-
mum sentence they can receive is thirty years, and the
credits they earn working in the bailiwicks are sent to
designated family members or friends or are held for
them until they are released. When they are released,
habitantes resume their status as citizens. Bailiwicks vary
widely in their rehabilitation programs, their job training
or educational opportunites for habitantes, the privileges
accorded to habitante trusties, and the work that is available to habitantes during their confinement.

Of Little Blue's 1,240,000,000 people, about 1,000,000
(or .08 % of the population) are habitantes living in bailiwicks. Worldwide, there are 780 bailiwicks, each holding
from 500 to 4,000 habitantes. In addition, approximately 120,000 citizens choose to live near or (in the

rarer cases of habitantes who are trusties) with habitantes in bailiwicks.

The management and regulation of the bailiwicks are the express responsibility of the Kanshoubu. Of the 600,000 Kanshou on Little Blue, some 375,000 are detailed to bailiwick duty.

GOVERNANCE OF THE KANSHOUBU

The Heart of All Kanshou

Eighteen retired Kanshou of all ranks and branches, two elected by the Kanshou of each of the nine satrapies, whose responsibilities are:

❏ to determine the policies of the Kanshoubu,

❏ to choose, review, and retain or dismiss its three Magisters;

❏ to approve or deny the Magisters' appointments of Vice-Magisters,

❏ to serve as the highest appellate body in disputes within the ranks of the Amahrery, the Femmedarmery, or the Vigilancia.

The Amah's Ear, The Femmedarme's Ear, The Vigilante's Ear

Courts martial, or boards of arbitration elected by Kanshou from within each satrapy, operative as-needed on varying levels or at various locations, whose responsibility is to hear and resolve internal disputes or grievances.

The Congress of Active Kanshou

Ninety active Service Shrieves representing Little Blue's 600,000 Kanshou, thirty of them elected by Amahs, thirty by Femmedarmes, and thirty by Vigilantes (ten from each satrapy) whose responsibility is to advise The Heart of All Kanshou on matters of concern to all active Kanshou. Though technically this body has no legislative power within the Kanshoubu, its influence is great and its opinion is actively sought by The Heart on every matter of consequence.

THE KANSHOU CODE

The Kanshou are pledged to implementing the statutes enacted by Little Blue's legislative bodies. Kanshou of whatever rank or branch of service are ultimately commanded by the Magister of the tri-satrapy in which they serve, and they honor the culture-specific traditions of that geographical area.

The Kanshou keep the peace and secure the physical safety of Little Blue's citizens, most frequently by restraining individual violent offenders. First and foremost, they are warriors, champions who choose, if necessary, to forfeit their own lives for those who depend upon them for their safety. Further, Kanshou administer the bailiwicks and protect the habitantes. They take into custody those who trespass against "commonweal statutes," laws that have been enacted to prevent harm to others or to the Earth, such as the global moratoria on cloning and genetic engineering or the statutes that outlaw the distribution of controlled substances or weaponry. Kanshou constitute frontline emergency forces in the case of flood, fire, hurricane, earthquake or other natural disasters.

The Labrys Manual, sacred to every peacekeeper, reflects the values and practices of each Kanshou and Kanshou cadet, including her priorities:

"As Kanshou, I am Earthkeeper before all things, for the Earth and Her biosphere are essential to the existence of all life. I protect and honor Her above all that is simply important or desirable. She is my highest priority.

"As Kanshou, I am guardian of each individual person's physical safety, for an individual's safety or assurance of continued existence is the most important element in one's life and, ultimately, in the life of our species. I protect the safety of our planet's people above anything that is simply desirable. This is my second-hightest priority.

"As Kanshou, I am protector and preserver of diversity, for diversity is the most *desirable* quality of human existence. I hold in my heart the vision of the return of one of the Earth's most extraordinary ranges of diverse beings, Her non-human Animals. Until their return, my desire for diversity includes the Natural World and is centered especially in the variety of human phenomena—our genders, our cultures, our myriad physical forms/colors/textures, our abilities, our ideas, our beliefs, our emotional expressions, our communications, our creations, and our delights. The protection and preservation of these things is my third-highest priority."

S ally Miller Gearhart grew up in Virginia and found her first love at a women's college. After inhabiting a dark closet for twenty years, she burst onto the political scene of the San Francisco Bay Area in 1970. San Francisco State University hired her as an open lesbian and tenured her in 1974. She taught there for two decades, helping to found its radical Women's Studies Program and publishing three books. Scores of her articles and stories have been anthologized in feminist publications.

Sally is well known for her leadership, along with Supervisor Harvey Milk, in defeating the 1978 "Briggs Initiative" in California which was designed to bar homosexuality and homosexuals from schools. This decisive victory helped turn the tide for lesbian and gay civil rights across the country. In 1984 Sally appeared in "The Times of Harvey Milk", the Academy-Award-winning documentary that chronicled that political era. She has also been an activist for animal rights and Earth First!, and now lives on a mountain of contradictions with many cats and a bluetick coon hound in a Mendocino County women's community.

Other Titles Available from Spinsters Ink Books

The Magister, Sally Miller Gearhart $14.00
Martha Moody, Susan Stinson $10.95
Modern Daughters and the Outlaw West, Melissa Kwasny . $9.95
Mother Journeys: Feminists Write About Mothering,
Sheldon, Reddy, Roth $15.95
Night Diving, Michelene Esposito $14.00
Nin, Cass Dalglish $12.00
No Matter What, Mary Saracino $9.95
Ordinary Justice, Trudy Labovitz $12.00
The Other Side of Silence, Joan M. Drury $9.95
The Racket, Anita Mason $12.95
Ransacking the Closet, Yvonne Zipter $9.95
Report for Murder, V. L. McDermid $10.95
Roberts' Rules of Lesbian Break-ups, Shelly Roberts $5.95
Roberts' Rules of Lesbian Dating, Shelly Roberts $5.95
Roberts' Rules of Lesbian Living, Shelly Roberts $5.95
Silent Words, Joan M. Drury $10.95
The Solitary Twist, Elizabeth Pincus $9.95
Sugar Land, Joni Rogers $12.00
They Wrote the Book: Thirteen Women Mystery Writers Tell All,
edited by Helen Windrath $12.00
Those Jordan Girls, Joan M. Drury $12.00
Trees Call for What They Need, Melissa Kwasny $9.95
Turnip Blues, Helen Campbell $10.95
The Two-Bit Tango, Elizabeth Pincus $9.95
Vital Ties, Karen Kringle. $10.95
Voices of the Soft-bellied Warrior, Mary Saracino $14.00
Wanderground, Sally Miller Gearhart $12.95
The Well-Heeled Murders, Cherry Hartman $10.95
Why Can't Sharon Kowalski Come Home?
Thompson & Andrzejewski $12.95
A Woman Determined, Jean Swallow $10.95
The Yellow Cathedral, Anita Mason $14.00

Spinsters titles are available at your local booksellers or by mail order through Spinsters Ink Books. Call 1-800-301-6860 to place an order today. A free catalog is available upon request. See also www.spinsters-ink.com. Please include $2.00 for the first title ordered and 50¢ for every title thereafter. All credit cards accepted.

Spinsters Ink Books

Spinsters Ink Books is one of the oldest feminist publishing houses in the world. It was founded in upstate New York in 1978, and today is an imprint of Hovis Publishing Company, Inc. in Denver, Colorado.

The noun "spinster" means a woman who spins. The definition of the verb "spin" is to whirl and twirl, to revert, to spin on one's heels, to turn everything upside down. Spinsters Ink books do just that—take women's "yarns" (stories, tales) and enable readers to see the world through the other end of the telescope. Spinsters Ink authors move readers off their comfort zones just a bit, pushing the camel through the eye of the needle. These are thinking books for thinking readers.

Spinsters Ink fiction and non-fiction titles deal with significant issues in women's lives from a feminist perspective. They not only name these crucial issues but—more importantly—encourage change and growth. We are committed to publishing works by women writing from the periphery: fat women, Jewish women, lesbians, old women, immigrant women, poor women, rural women, women examining classism, women of color, women with disabilities, women who are writing books that help make the best in our lives more possible.

Spinsters Ink Books
P. O. Box 22005
Denver, CO 80222
USA

Phone: 303-761-5552   Fax: 303-761-5284

E-mail: spinster@spinsters-ink.com
Web site: http://www.spinsters-ink.com